THE DESPERATES

THE DESPERATES

A NOVEL BY

GREG KEARNEY

Cormorant Books

The publisher gratefully acknowledges the support of the Canada Council
for the Arts and the Ontario Arts Council for its publishing program.
We acknowledge the financial support of the Government of Canada through the
Canada Book Fund (CBF) for our publishing activities, and the Government of
Ontario through the Ontario Media Development Corporation, an agency of the
Ontario Ministry of Culture, and the Ontario Book Publishing Tax Credit Program.

LIBRARY AND ARCHIVES CANADA CATALOGUING IN PUBLICATION

Kearney, Greg, author
The desperates / Greg Kearney.

Issued in print and electronic formats.
ISBN 978-1-77086-302-6 (pbk.).— ISBN 978-1-77086-304-0 (mobi).—
ISBN 978-1-77086-303-3 (epub)

1. Title.

PS8621.E23D48 2013   C813'.6   C2013-903668-7
C2013-903669-5

Cover photo and design: Angel Guerra/Archetype
Interior text design: Tannice Goddard, Soul Oasis Networking
Printer: Friesens

Printed and bound in Canada.

The interior of this book is printed on 100% post-consumer waste recycled paper.

CORMORANT BOOKS INC.
10 ST. MARY STREET, SUITE 615, TORONTO, ONTARIO, M4Y 1P9
www.cormorantbooks.com

For Dick, Arlene, and Cindy Lee.

"There was, in the way he stood, in the way he ate the peach, in the way he moved his mouth, the way he chewed, and in how his body weight shifted in the lowering evening light, a lewd perfection. It made me want to follow him wherever he would go, and though I'm not sure of this, I think he saw me, think he knew I was devouring him. For an instant, he seemed to look at me, too."

CHRISTOPHER COE, "SUCH TIMES"

1

THIS NEW PHONE SEX JOB is a fresh start, as fresh a start as tree-planting or massage therapy training at George Brown, or canvassing for Greenpeace, or any of the other job opportunities listed in the back of *NOW*. Who knows where it might lead, the phone sex? Maybe voice work. The half-day stint as janitor at St. Marc Spa last week didn't lead to anything except him running from the building after having to clean up a mound of feces someone left on a towel beside the whirlpool. But that was a bathhouse. This is phone sex.

Joel stands before his bathroom mirror and parts his hair down the middle; it seems a hopeful way of parting one's hair. It's an unflattering look for Joel, bisecting his long, lippy face into two gawky lobes, but the important thing, this first day on the job, is not his face but the intention of his face. A man with a middle part is a man who wants to work, pay back the student loan he blew through in four months, stop hitting up his mother for money every few days, and beat back the great, sucking fear that he is destined only to step barefoot on a thumbtack and die of septic shock.

The phone sex office is in Scarborough, thirty minutes by transit. The travel time gives Joel the chance to read or, more likely, fantasize about men with enormous hands that cup and warm him, small as a robin's egg, and then set him gently on a silk pillow made especially for his small self.

The manager is a woman named Brenda, who smells of fabric softener and wears her lank grey hair pinned tightly behind her ears. She constantly adjusts a pewter rose brooch that droops from the thin linen lapel of her black blazer. She says she's thrilled to have Joel join the team, although, in their walled-off carrels spread out in a huge room, there is nothing team-like about the team. She has Joel sit beside Bernie, a middle-aged, sunburned guy who Brenda introduces breathlessly as "phone sex royalty." Joel is to listen in on a few of his model calls.

"Straight in, you've got to give 'em permission to be sexy," Bernie tells Joel, setting aside his paperback copy of *The Stand*. "Otherwise, you'll be talking about the fucking weather for ten minutes. I mean, you want to keep 'em on the phone as long as possible, obviously, but you also have to keep things on topic. I pretend they've happened to call just as I've started beating off. 'Oh, hey, buddy, it's fucked up that you called in when you did, because I just started beating off!' That kind of thing. And then you do lots of *masturbreathing*."

"Masturbreathing?" Joel asks indulgently, even though he already knows what's meant.

"Yeah, like this," he says, emitting several short, punchy breaths. "So it sounds like you're pounding your meat. Dudes love that shit, always does the trick. I've been doing this for a year and a bit, and I've got lots of regulars, and I've never been with a guy in my life. My ex-wife got shot in the pelvis last month — we were still fooling around occasionally, but I guess she'll be out of commission that way for a while."

Bernie takes a call. He describes himself as having "super long hair" and a "nice dick, not big and scary at all." Immediately Joel knows that Bernie did not lie when he said that he'd never been with a guy in his life. He repeatedly asks the caller if he's getting close to coming, and when the caller confirms that he is about to come, Bernie, not looking up from *The Stand*, grunts "me fucking too," and lets loose a series of diminishing moans. At the end of the call Bernie tells the caller to have a good one.

"See? Nothing to it," Bernie says. "Only thing you gotta watch out for — don't talk about, like, feelings and all that, like you would have to do with a chick before she'd let you go for it. I made that mistake early on with dudes on the phone — 'oh, hey buddy, glad you called, I think I'm falling in love with you, I'm so lonely' — and they'd fucking hang up."

"No feelings. Got it."

Brenda leads Joel to a nearby cubicle. He is anxious; he has never done dirty talk. The few encounters he has had with men since arriving here in the fall have all been mute, glancing, furtive, sad affairs: some mutual masturbation, a bit of frottage — oh, and that older guy in the porno video booth who knelt to blow him but then made a stink-face and waved him off ... Why?

Were his balls musty? Was it a foreskin thing? Still, he knows himself to be a passionate person, boundlessly so, so surely a little dirty talk should be easy.

The first call is breathing and a hang-up. The second one asks if Joel is Chinese; Joel decides to say that he is Chinese to keep things going, but the guy says that Joel doesn't sound Chinese and hangs up.

The third call is a very cordial gentleman who greets Joel with "Hello, how are you?" Sounds like he has a slight accent that could be English, lockjaw or exhaustion.

"I like your voice," the man says.

"Really? That's so nice of you. I hate my voice. Shit, that was an emotion! I should say, I have no feelings about my voice one way or another. I have thought about maybe trying to get voice work. I always thought my voice had an annoying sort of twang to it though. Not that I care, at all."

"I disagree. You evoke Mandy Patinkin. Do you know who that is? He's in musical theatre. A high tenor. He also featured as the romantic lead in *Yentl*."

"Oh, yeah! I remember him. My mom loves that movie. He was really hot in that. But Barbra couldn't settle for only 'A Piece of Sky.' So wow — you think I sound like him?"

"Yes. You have the same singsong, slightly nasal quality to your voice. It's very rousing, very 'strike up the band.'"

"You're so nice. So warm. I've found Toronto to be a pretty chilly city, socially."

"It can be, yes, definitely. We're a pretty cautious lot."

"Yeah. I've been really lonely — Shit! No, I haven't."

Joel looks up worriedly at Brenda. Brenda looks down worriedly at Joel.

"You sound a little conflicted."

"Me? No, not at all. I have no feelings."

"What's your name?"

"My name is Joel —"

Brenda shakes her head violently: no real names!

"— but everybody calls me, like, Rocky. Or Chad. Yeah, Chad."

"Well, hello to all of you. Edmund here."

"Hi, Edmund. Nice to meet you."

Joel shrugs his shoulders at Brenda; he can't not acknowledge someone who has just introduced himself, and Joel is starved for human contact, and this man is attentive and sympathetic.

"Anyway," Joel interjects, "It's so funny that you called when you did because I just started masturbating. Beating off, I should say. I have super short hair and a gigantic cock."

"That's great. Are we going to talk about sex now?"

"Ooh, yes. Sex is great."

Mollified, Brenda goes to answer the ringing phone at her own desk.

"We don't have to talk about sex, you know. I don't necessarily need to get off. I'm bored. The house is so quiet. I'm looking for a friendly voice, more than anything."

Joel squeaks with delight. "I'm looking for a friendly voice more than anything, too! It's my first day here. I'm supposed to pretend that your phone call interrupted me while I was masturbating, but I think that's so forced, don't you?"

"I do. That approach may hold some appeal for people with a tight schedule, but happily — ha ha — I don't have a tight schedule."

"What do you do? Are you a psychiatrist?"

"No. Why do you ask that?"

"Your tone is so even and calm."

"Ah. No. I don't do anything anymore. I had some business interests there for a while, but that was some time ago. I'm in — transition, I guess."

Brenda approaches.

"It's my supervisor again. I'll have to say sexy things. Isn't that hot? Wow. Hot."

"Why don't you call me sometime?"

A nice older man is asking Joel to call him. He starts to shake. Must be subtle, with Brenda right beside him.

"I'd love to," he says, scribbling Edmund's phone number on his left hand. "That is so hot. You're coming? Me fucking too! Talk to you soon. Take care."

Brenda starts to say something but Joel immediately gets another call.

"I need some major CBT," a breathy guy says.

"CBT? Cognitive Behavioural Therapy? I don't know if this is the right line to be calling for that, although I did that for a few months in grade eight. Didn't really do much for me, but I didn't really give over to the process, so ..."

"What are you talking about? I need some major CBT. Cock and ball torture."

"Ohhhh ... sorry. Right. No problem. Sure. CBT is so hot."

"Fuck yeah. Fuckin' hammer a big fuckin' nail through my dick. And my balls — just fuckin' crack 'em. Stomp on 'em."

"Okay. How do I — okay. Crack, crack. Stomp, stomp."

"Fuck yeah. Fuckin' stomp on 'em 'til they're just fuckin' slush, man. Then fuckin' slit my bag and fuckin' drain that fuckin' ball slush and pour it into a fuckin' mug and fuckin' make me drink it!"

Joel gasps a little. Is this a prank call? But who would pay $3.99 a minute to make a prank phone call? Must be the real thing. But who would get aroused by drinking liquefied testicles? Joel is worldly, but ... Well, actually, he is not worldly.

"I'm sorry, I think I might have a boundary issue around this. I know that you can't legislate desire and everything, but violent castration? And the ingestion of liquefied ... I can't engage that. Sorry."

"I want to speak to your supervisor."

Joel motions at Brenda, hands off the phone to her.

"Man Handlers, this is Brenda speaking, how may I help you?"

Joel wanders off. He wasn't told that he'd be expected to handle extreme kink, straight out of the box. And the previous call had been so romantic. He isn't sure he can handle such whiplash.

2

EDMUND LOOKS AROUND HIS DINING room, checking the newly repainted, sunburst yellow ceiling for erratic brush or roller strokes. Miguel is normally reliable, but this year he slipped up. He was about to paint *around* the dining room chest of drawers, until Edmund said something. He was quite dour, he didn't hum to himself as he worked. "The dead have risen," is what he said when Edmund met him at the door, and although he was smiling he sounded almost annoyed by Edmund's return to health. As though Edmund had done something unseemly by surviving, as though he should've refused the new anti-virals and meekly followed his lover into death. Edmund apologized in response: "Yes, still here. Sorry." He said it breezily but not entirely without real remorse. Maybe it might be time to start looking for a new house painter. Even the sturdiest relationships can suddenly rupture for no reason.

Eighteen months, it's been. Eighteen months ago he was bed-bound, skeletal, a mouth full of thrush. Not quite yet a

Casey House candidate, although Lila had been more nurse than personal assistant for some time. He'd been quietly, even contentedly, dying for more than a year, shuffling through his cold, bare house, holding up crosswalks and grocery lines unapologetically when he ventured out.

Then came the cocktail. Within a few weeks he was free of fever, full of vim, and endlessly hungry for bread, vinegar-drenched vegetables, bag after big bag of marshmallows. At first he threw it all up, but soon enough it stayed down and moved through him leisurely; his first solid bowel movement in three years had him laughing to himself in disbelief.

Disbelief. That has been his prevailing state, this past year and a half. He wanders through his spacious days, still braced for the violence of illness, only to find himself dazed, worn down by a gusty sense of emptiness, at the end of each healthful day. For so long he took baroque sickness in stride — black and bloody diarrhea, hands and feet sizzling with pain — and now there's maybe the odd bit of tummy upset, easily tamed with milk and gingersnaps while watching *Antiques Roadshow*. This relative wellness is nice. It also makes him anxious.

Initially he filled his time with urgent errands — power walking to the post office, the bank, Holt Renfrew. Then he ran out of errands.

He tried to reconnect with loved ones, but with Dean and all of his closest friends long dead, he found he had run out of loved ones. (He still has his mother, of course, although her vain, silly, insular, long distance presence has never counted for much. *I DO know the depth of loss you've experienced, thank you very much,* she wrote back, years ago. *I've been reduced to having my hair done by a WOMAN, and a woman hairdresser is only a saboteur when cutting another woman's hair. I would honestly rather be bald.*)

His remaining friends have mainly gone bilious or druggy from fear and grief. Incapable of introspection, they talk about celebrities, or they nod and murmur over shared memories of incompetent drag acts or falling down the stairs at Chaps. The few times that Edmund has brought up the subject, no matter how elliptically — *Remember those brother bartenders at The Barn? Tino and Sly? Did Tino die first, or did Sly?* — these equally empty men look at him like he's psychotic and then make a diversionary, huffy fuss about lighting a cigarette. And so he has stopped asking questions. He has stopped having friends.

Well, he *does* do one thing, all day, every day: he listens to the house. He stands motionless and strains to hear spirit voices; not necessarily Dean's, but any spirit voice, faintly saying something, anything, one little thing. *Hi. Here. Me. Us. You.* He was always openly scornful of other people's plunges into magic when things got bleak, and he still doesn't consider this listening of his to be some psychic endeavour. It's ... what one does, after a loss, in a lonely, old house.

He has also been calling phone sex lines, looking for a pleasant, sprightly living voice. Apart from this boy just now, Joel/Rocky/Chad, they've all been disappointing. Through the clack of knitting needles, the tubular scrape of Pringles in their can, and the din of other bored, boxed voices, they've all been robotic, terrible listeners. It's unrealistic to expect good listening skills from a phone sex guy, of course, but who else is he going to call? He can't ring a crisis line just to gab.

He hears Lila let herself in the front door. Dear, doting Lila. Still drops in once a day on her lunch break, even though there's less and less to do. Edmund wants to pay her still, but she won't hear of it. When he was sick she was indispensable, but now ... Dean was the one who needed an assistant: he was hopeless with all things clerical, all things practical. They came to love Lila as family. A lesbian fag hag, she thrilled to the minutiae of urban gay male culture, but was so shy around other women. She sometimes wept with worry that she'd never find a lover. But she did, a year ago. Marci. Very strong, protective of Lila, which is what Lila needs.

She has his dry cleaning. She looks like she has a slight sunburn; she may just be flushed.

"Edmund White?"

"Not quite." Ha ha. It was almost funny ten years ago. It's hard to let go of shtick once it's set in. Dear, indulgent Lila. She's never read Edmund White, only knows the name. He gave her *The Burning Library*, a collection of his essays, but it reminded her of so many lost friends that she had to stop reading it.

"What's up for today, Mister Ed?"

"You know me. I'm a dervish. I may cross my legs or cough at some point. Go, go, go."

Lila strokes Edmund's sparse black hair. She started in with this maternal affection when he was sick. Edmund savours her touch and leans into her palm like a cat. She plops down beside him. They watch *The Young and the Restless* for a bit.

Lila will be thirty-seven soon. Last few months, she's also been working as a nanny for a wealthy, hapless couple who call her in the middle of the night because their daughter's had a nightmare and they don't know what to say to soothe her; annoyed by the parents and, for that matter, the haughty daughter, she gave her resignation a few days ago. She is a tender yet prudent caregiver; she can't blindly dote on people she doesn't enjoy.

Lila is Edmund's only real friend, and he sees himself going to seed without her: talon toenails, KFC buckets strewn about, an ever-dissolving comprehension of conversational English. He's open to getting to know Marci better; if Lila loves her, there must be more to her than her somewhat twitchy officiousness, brittle phone manner, surgically geometric black bangs, Nana Mouskouri glasses, and taught-tendon neck. Lila says Marci is the most charismatic woman she's ever known, but charisma gets old when you're folding its laundry and watching it chew. There must be more to Marci.

"So," Lila says reluctantly. "A bit of news." Edmund's stomach sinks. How many times has he heard that awful preface, from friends, from doctors, from Dean. He braces himself for the worst.

"I'm preggo!" she says, pushing at him playfully with her knuckles. "Molto preggo! Preggo, preggo, preggo!"

"Congratulations! How far along are you?"

"Thirteen weeks."

"Wow. So you've been pregnant for three months and you're only telling me now."

"I know. I'm sorry," she says, biting a knuckle. "I was so scared I'd miscarry. And I was worried you wouldn't ask me to run errands for you for fear that you'd cause me to miscarry."

He puts his arm around her. How Lila of her to fear for his fear. He's happy for Lila. A girlfriend and a baby is all she has ever wanted. This will be one lucky baby. She goes on to explain that Marci has been promoted at her film production company, freeing Lila to experience the pregnancy process in an uninterrupted, meditative way.

"So that means ..." Lila wells up and breathes deeply. "Marci is adamant that I take time for myself. I probably might be a little hard to reach for the next little while."

Of course. The baby will consume her and he will probably never see her again. She was there for Dean's illness, all of it; she portioned out pills, cleaned him up, kept him out of Casey House, and mostly out of the hospital, until the last three days. She was at the hospital with Edmund those last three days, nestled against the right side of Dean, Edmund on the left.

"I am so, so happy for you. I really am. And I will be absolutely okay without you. I've never felt better. I'm seriously considering ... big things. I love you."

They hug. Lila sobs. Edmund leaks a tear or two. Also he stares at the Roy Lichtenstein print on the wall, a blond girl sobbing like the one in his arms. Dean insisted on that print; Edmund found it gaudy. Now it's the only hint of humanity in the room. When Lila leaves, Edmund will go and stand beside it, as if warming himself.

3

TERESA FINDS TWO LETTERS, ONE to Joel and one to Dallas, going through her husband's pockets in the laundry room. The one to Dallas is all chatty and breezy — *How've you been keeping? Any interesting crime scenes lately? Anyway, your mom's a bit under the weather these days. Give us a dingle when you get the chance.* — completely undercutting the severity of the situation. The one to Joel — *The lungs are full of cancer. It's in the liver and a little bit in the brain.* — is much too hysterical, almost cruel. This isn't what they'd agreed on; they were going to say it was serious but not horribly serious, a female problem, vague and uninteresting like that. Since when does Hugh write letters to the boys? She may be full of cancer, but she still writes the letters in this family, is still the one who organizes such proceedings, lets each family member know which bit of information they should know and how they're supposed to feel about said information. She is still very much at the helm of this family — even sick she is the only one who has a true sense of what is best for everyone.

Hugh doesn't know what's best for himself, does he? Left to his own devices, he'd have a beard down to the floor, he'd forget how to speak, all of his whites would be grey. Dallas, her firstborn, he's a great kid, but there's not a lot of depth going on there apart from his basic, unstinting stamina — he can be OPP and do extreme sports on his days off and keep his spindly girlfriend off his back with his goofy swagger and simple, simply stated needs. There's no reason to send him a follow-up letter to his father's letter. *Give us a dingle* will do for Dallas.

Joel will need a follow-up letter. Jolie is so tender, so fretful as it is, so lost despite her constant, harsh criticism and instruction. Hugh's letter will terrify him, God knows what stupid thing he'll do to cope with the news, and he'll feel betrayed that she didn't confide everything straight away, as she has with everything else.

So she'll put together a nice, thorough letter for him, along with a box of those sugared jelly slice candies he likes. Good, something to occupy her, keep her from thinking about her situation, keep her from tearing off into the night, screaming the awful vowels that already swarm her head all day long. *Ooooooooh Aaaaaay Uuuuuuuh.* A nice letter and some candy. Good.

Something else, first time ever in all her years of doing Hugh's laundry: a skid mark in his underwear. He's always been so fastidious about that kind of thing, almost annoyingly so — he'd bound out of bed right after sex to shower himself off. It's plain that he is already falling apart. Something else to worry about. Good.

4

BRENDA IS BACK AT HER DESK, still dealing with the angry, thwarted castrato. They spoke for several minutes at Joel's station until the guy realized he was still incurring charges while complaining. She keeps looking up at Joel, only now with a weary warmth. He has always got along with middle aged women. They trust him with their anxieties, their immobilizing upset over uppity convenience store cashiers, their dismay at having to love men. He listens to them, playfully pushes them to be pushier versions of themselves. Truth be told, he's only known one or two middle-aged women well enough to counsel. His mother, mainly. Who is already pretty pushy.

Oh, but then there was Joel's favourite childhood babysitter, back in Kenora. Sveta! Sveta was fifty-something. When she first started she had him spellbound with stories of her spooky childhood in Czechoslovakia: the clay figurines in her living room that came to life to forecast who would be the next to die in the village; her grandmother's wooden teeth and empty eye socket; her first boyfriend, a huge mute who would roughly grab her by way of communication, and throw her hurtling through the air when he was in a really good mood. Joel loved Sveta. He told her she was pretty enough to be a movie star, although she was not pretty, was really almost startlingly ugly with her crazy grey eyebrows and broken nose. Sveta cackled at the thought of herself as a movie star, laughed until she cried. Sveta liked Joel. She taught him conversational Czech.

One afternoon, Sveta asked Joel what he wanted to be when he grew up. He said he wanted to be a Barbie doll. Sveta said it wasn't possible for a person to be a doll. "Farrah Fawcett, then," he replied. Sveta didn't understand; she thought "Farrah Fawcett" might have something to do with plumbing.

To clarify, five-year-old Joel enacted Farrah Fawcett, as he understood her. He hummed the theme from *Charlie's Angels*, which he had only seen in reruns; he flounced his imaginary, feathered hair while skateboarding away from the bad guys, focused but flirty, smiling with both rows of teeth, just like Farrah. He lost himself in the impersonation. It went on for a good ten minutes.

Joel gathered himself and asked Sveta if she now knew who he was referring to. Sveta, suddenly stony, spoke, lapsing into Czech. "Fear the — sílený sodomita! (Fear the insane sodomite!) "Se smíchem démon s noži pro zuby!" (The laughing demon with knives for teeth!)

She was otherwise silent until Joel's mother came home. Then she ran out of the house, never to be heard from again. When Joel's mother called, she hung up. Not long after, she choked to death on a hot dog while walking down Matheson Street.

That was years ago. It is June 1998, and Joel is nearly twenty. He's finding his way quite nicely without the approbation of his childhood babysitter. University wasn't his bag — it was so thinky, so listeny — so he dropped out after three weeks. He thinks he may be a performance artist, but that is only a hunch. He knows he wants be deranged with love, and to have holy sexual experiences in which both he and the other guy weep throughout from the intensity of the intimacy. How could he possibly cultivate such relationships whilst stomping balls and slitting scrotums professionally? He couldn't. He feels bad about what he has to tell Brenda when she gets off the phone.

"Wowee, he was a handful," she says as she hangs up. "Clients like him, special needs clients I call them, you want to basically let them do their thing and egg them along vaguely. That was a challenging call. You did pretty good considering."

"That means so much, thank you. Unfortunately, I can't do this job. It's already eating me alive. Sorry."

"You've only had three calls! You're just finding your rhythm."

"I'll never find my rhythm doing this. I'm not prepared to contend with so much human pain. It's one thing if they're like, 'Hey, I'm in pain. Please help me.' That I could deal with. But when it manifests as, like, cock and ball torture, I'm — yeah. No."

"You're taking it too seriously. It's all in good fun. These guys don't even know what they like. They think they want to have their balls crushed or what have you, but they don't. They're just like you and me — they go to work, come home, eat a pizza, watch

Friends, have some pie and ice cream, some popcorn, and a bag of Cheetos, and call it a night."

Is Brenda trying to play on his pity with this portrait of a lonely binge eater? He can't waver. She sighs. The mouth of her huge carpetbag purse is agape beside her desk. Joel sees a small bottle of mouthwash. A big pack of Benson & Hedges menthols. A hairy hairbrush. "I like you," she says. "I pride myself on our relatively low turnover rate. Why don't you go home, think on things, then give it another go tomorrow? How about that?"

"I don't know. I can't see myself feeling any different come tomorrow. But I like you, too, and I'm grateful for the opportunity, so ... Yeah. I'll give it another go tomorrow."

Brenda throws her fists in the air triumphantly, like she's just won Wimbledon. Why does she care so much? Is she this invested in every employee? Must be. That's what must make her a good supervisor. Joel suddenly feels terrible for whatever distress he may have caused her. Will she go home and eat something dangerous as a result? Something with glass in it? She's so fragile. He pats her on the arm and she shivers and smiles. Maybe he should give it another go tomorrow.

HOME NOW, AFTER his half-hour of transit, Joel paces his small room in the big house he shares with five mean gay men in their thirties. The men in his house all work in retail; they all eat takeout or TV dinners with plastic cutlery; they all, at least once each, have awoken from nightmares screaming, waking the other men, who may get up and press their ear to the door to listen for further screaming, but never actually check in on the person. They all have big problems, from the looks of their stricken faces in the common kitchen or on the front porch where they all smoke, ignoring each other. He would love to go over the day's events with one of them, but he knows better than to make conversation.

As a child he had two girlfriends, Cheryl and Shannon. Cheryl and Shannon were both fat, freckled redheads. They hated each other on sight, so Joel could only hang out with one or the other. Their play consisted of gruff, cruel improvisation: I Have Something Wrong with Both My Arms and Both My Legs; The Five Seconds Before I Get Hit by a Bus; Fatal Figure Skating Wipeouts. Joel loved these mean scenarios. They made him giddy, but they left the girls fretful — especially Shannon, whose father was a policeman and a born-again Christian. At the first hint of puberty, both Cheryl and Shannon forsook their imaginations to focus exclusively on the daunting task of Being Pretty for a Fat Girl and Totally Not Stuck-Up. Joel wishes he could find a new Cheryl or Shannon. He likely would've made new girlfriends if he'd stayed in school. That's no reason to stay in school though. Or is it? He wasn't going to call nice Edmund from the phone line until tomorrow but he can't wait. He doesn't care if he comes across as desperate. Why wait when love looms? He practises saying "hello" for a few minutes first.

"Hell-oh!" he says, too brightly, when Edmund answers. "Whatcha doin'?"

"I'm — I'm sorry, who is this?"

"Ack. I'm so dim. Sorry. It's Joel from the phone line? You gave me your number?"

"Oh, yes, of course. How great that you've called. How are you?"

"Great. Awful, but great. It's hard being in the adult industry. I just hope I don't have to do, like, drugs, to cope."

"I'm not worried about you. You sound far too evolved to get hung up on addiction."

"Really? That is so nice of you. What, like, specifically, is it about my sound that sounds evolved?"

"Just your general … I'd really need to experience you at length."

"That would be great. What are you doing right now?"

"Right now I'm sitting. You want to come over? The house is a mess."

"That's okay. I totally don't care about stuff like that."

"Well … and I should also warn you that I have erectile issues, so even if the mind is willing …"

"I don't care about that either. I'm all about intimacy that is, like, harrowing."

"That sounds — quite gruelling. I'm forty-one, you know. I don't normally do things that are harrowing."

"Please? I can't tell you how much it would mean to me."

"I'd be a monster to refuse, wouldn't I? Come over."

JOEL TAKES DOWN Edmund's address and transit directions. One of the directions is "turn left at the little statue of Aphrodite": obviously he lives in a fancy area. Hopefully Edmund will ask him to sleep over. Edmund will ask him to sleep over, and then watch Joel as he sleeps, and fall in love with him and ask him to move in with him and hold him in his gigantic hands.

5

A BOY IS COMING OVER. When did that last happen, not counting
nurses? Years. The last three-way he and Dean had was Christmas 1990. Some small part of him is slightly excited. Even if
the kid is homely, it's companionship. And Edmund is only
fully himself when he has someone to love and champion; only
then is he not a dim spectre. Even Dean was an urchin at first.
His native verve and his low-level, undulating rage could've
easily flamed out in needle drugs and bar fights if Edmund
hadn't helped him along. Edmund happily placed his own
hopes in abeyance (and what hopes were they, really — silly,
hashish visions of solar panels, luscious plates of fruit, maybe
a baby) and focused solely on Dean's high-profile edification.
Dean liked to make women look pretty and particular, and so
Edmund founded Molto Cosmetics for him. ("I want it to be
very, very — everything," Dean said when they were brain-
storming for a name. Dean was very, very into the word "very."
And so, "Molto.") Success came fast. Now Dean is dead;

although Edmund has divested himself of the business it will not go away: from billboards and magazine inserts it bellows *Molto! Molto!*, like a crazed Italian beggar woman whose voice seeps into his house despite closed windows, drawn blinds and all kinds of white noise.

Life with Dean: *molto* sweet, *molto* eventful, *molto* photographic, *molto* idyllic, *molto* enviable, *molto*.

So this kid will come over. He will be homely and needy, a diversion, and because Edmund has nothing of himself to offer, he can pretend to give of himself completely. He will introduce the kid to Thai takeout, and listen as the kid goes on and on about whatever it is he wants to be, and his young ideas of harrowing love. Maybe Edmund will take an honest interest, bask in the boy's enthusiasm for a while. At the very least he'll give the kid ample cab fare.

He takes off his bathrobe, puts on a big, black linen shirt and matching drawstring pants. He looks at his bare feet and their crumbled, fungal toenails, an afterthought infection when he was sick but one that is annoyingly persistent now that he's well. He steps into a pair of black leather slippers. No need to expose the kid to all the horror right off the bat.

6

IT'S THE NICEST HOUSE JOEL has ever seen. Much nicer than the Wallis's big house in Kenora; their house looked a little bit like a truck stop. This house, Edmund's house, is an old mansion mostly hidden by huge trees. The doorbell makes a stately sound that seems to come from the top of the building. Could there be a bell tower? Are there bell towers in Toronto?

Edmund has big, dazed eyes, grey skin, a small chin. His shirt is partly unbuttoned, revealing a hairless chest. He appears to be a thin man with a slight paunch, but it's hard to tell with the billowy black shirt and soft lighting. He welcomes Joel inside with a kind, narcotic voice.

Joel compliments Edmund on his lovely home. Edmund looks around like he has never seen the place before. He apologizes for Miguel's sloppy paint job. Joel smiles. He doesn't know what Edmund is talking about but he speaks so gently about everything that Joel can't help but be wooed.

"I'd show you the rest of the house," Edmund says, "but the

rest of the house is being renovated. Or it will be, soon. Really I just don't want to do all that walking, and showing. Do you want a drink? I'm a recovering alcoholic but I keep a full bar. Which probably isn't shrewd, I know."

"I don't know very much about mixed drinks. Umm. What did you drink, when you were drinking?"

"That's not a good question to ask an alcoholic who's about to pour a drink."

"Really? Oh my God, I'm so sorry. I'm such a fucking idiot."

"I was kidding. How about a Stella?"

Joel nods.

Edmund pries the cap off, hands Joel the beer. They move into the living room.

"What do you do when you're not indulging horrible men like me on the phone?"

"I —" Joel stops. "Wait. Can I put my hand on, like, your shoulder?"

"Do you feel unsteady?"

"No. I just wanted to make contact to, like, get that out of the way. Is that dumb?"

"Not at all. That's very charming. Why don't you put your hand on my shoulder, and I'll put my hand on your shoulder?"

"Really? That would be great."

Edmund puts his right hand on Joel's left shoulder; Joel puts his right hand on Edmund's left shoulder.

"This feels slightly like a Girl Guide ritual," Edmund says.

"I know. Well, I don't *know*; I wasn't in Girl Guides. But I wanted to be. This is still really nice. I haven't done a lot with men. Or women. I actually haven't even gone all the way with someone yet. Does that make me a virgin?"

"Do you feel like a virgin?"

"Um. Which is the sexier answer?"

"The honest one."

"Right. Yeah, I guess I do feel like a virgin. It's so hard not to sing the whole song when I say 'like a virgin'!"

Edmund chuckles. Joel wishes his taste in music wasn't so mainstream. He should've made a joke about Leonard Cohen or someone like that.

"My arm is getting kind of tired," Edmund says. "Let's sit on the sofa."

They sit. Opposite the sofa is a painting of a younger-looking Edmund sitting on a log on a beach beside another guy, blond with big teeth. They look very happy. Joel sinks.

"Is that your life partner? He's very good-looking."

"Dean? Yes, my life partner. He's been gone for many years now, unfortunately."

"Oh. I'm sorry. Can I — Did he pass away from, like, HIV/AIDS?"

"Just AIDS will suffice. Yes, he did. I very nearly did, myself."

Edmund is an AIDS survivor! He hasn't met one before. The devastation he must have experienced ... incalculable loss ... Joel senses the ghost of his beautiful, brave, fallen forefather, Don. Dean.

"Sorry," Edmund says in the silence. "Does that make you uncomfortable?"

"What? No! Not at all! I'm just so blown away and moved by what you've been through. I can't imagine. It was such a devastating chapter of gay history."

"Hmm. You sound like a tour guide! Progress has been made, definitely, but AIDS isn't over."

"No! Yes, I totally agree. I just don't have much first-hand knowledge. We rented *Longtime Companion* and I totally cried. My mom was like, 'You must not get AIDS, that is not an option, if you do I will be super pissed, do you understand?' And I was like, 'Message totally delivered!' But I'd love to hear your narrative from start to finish, if you feel like sharing."

Edmunds puts a hand on Joel's head. "That's sweet. It's very difficult to talk about with someone who wasn't there. At some point, in the future. Maybe."

"I love that you think we might have a future in some way. And I love your hand on my head."

Edmund strokes Joel's thick, greasy hair. Why didn't he wash his hair before he came over? Maybe Edmund will perceive the greasiness as silkiness.

"Sometimes," Joel says with heavy eyelids, "I think I'd be happy just being a housewife."

Edmund's hand goes still. Joel regrets the housewife comment. He doesn't want Edmund to think that he is unambitious, or that he is proposing marriage after ten minutes. "When I say 'housewife,'" he qualifies, "I mean that I have a lot of domestic energy. I could see myself having, like, a house-cleaning business."

Edmund nods, still displeased. "You're awfully young to

resign yourself to being a scrubwoman. What is your dream for yourself?"

"I don't know. Fame? Or acclaim of some sort? We can, like, lie down together if you want."

Edmund laughs. "Your ardour is moving. It's not necessary, though. I'm enjoying just sitting here chatting with you."

"Is it me? I know I'm hideous. My hair isn't silky, it's really greasy."

The hand falls from Joel's head.

"I'm sorry. I'm so gross. I'm getting better about hygiene. I'm sorry."

"Is it important to you that we lie down together?"

"No! Yes. Kind of. I'm sorry I'm so needy."

"Please stop apologizing. If anything is hideous, it's the constant apologizing, not you." Clearly Edmund has no interest in intimacy with Joel, but he's too tactful to kick him out. Or too tired, possibly. Joel should graciously remove himself. He puts his hand on Edmund's knee instead. Edmund takes hold of Joel's right index finger and stands.

"Let's go lie down then, dirty boy."

They climb the red-carpeted stairs. There is an onyx sculpture on a table at the top of the stairs, a seated woman with her severed head in her lap.

The bedroom features more gorgeous furniture, big pieces the likes of which Joel has only seen in those Barbara Walters specials where she goes to famous people's houses and makes them cry. Joel feels like a coarse intruder, the maid who sprays herself with fancy perfumes while the rich people are away on vacation. Edmund hoists himself onto his king-sized bed. He pats the spot beside him. Joel hesitates.

"You've probably had a lot of lovers, I guess."

"A few."

"So you're probably, like, a real student of male beauty."

"Ha. A student of male beauty. I suppose. Aren't we all?"

Joel smiles, not listening. "Where would you say I rank on your list?"

"There is no list. You're a very attractive boy."

"Thanks. I just haven't had very much affirmation. Would you ... would you say that I'm attractive enough to be, like, a prostitute?"

Edmund is visibly tiring. Joel is even annoying himself, but he can't stop. "Joe — Joel," Edmund sighs. "First of all, beauty and prostitution do not invariably go hand-in-hand. There are some stunningly ugly hustlers out there, making a good living, too. And — you've really got to ease up on yourself. Life is too short ... but it can also be too long. Either way, you've got to ... come on up on this bed now."

Joel draws breath to speak but stops. He shuffles toward the bed.

"Let's take our clothes off," Edmund says, undoing his shirt. Joel steps out of his pants, hesitates with his shirt, pulls it off slowly. He scales the bed in socks and boxers.

"All the way," Edmund says, now naked. Joel quickly pulls off his underwear. Edmund points at Joel's socks. Joel takes them off, cringing at the sight of his unkempt toenails. He throws himself on the bed. Edmund runs his hand up and down

Joel's torso, hovering just shy of contact, as though his hand were a metal detector. "See," he says, "isn't this nice?"

"I'm so nervous. My face is numb. Have you ever had such good sex that you both start weeping?"

"Not really. Good sex doesn't tend to end in tears. Gay sex, anyway. I think you need to stop listening to Roberta Flack's greatest hits."

"I don't have Roberta Flack's — oh! Ha ha! I have so much admiration for the really gritty humour of the longterm survivor. It's so great."

Edmund puts his hand over Joel's mouth. "Stroke your dick," he says. This command is startling but not unsexy. Joel strokes his cock, which slowly hardens as he grows more turned on.

"There we go," says Edmund admiringly. "What a nice cock. How does that feel?"

"Familiar. Nice. Can I touch your cock?"

"You don't have to, but yes."

Joel wraps his other hand around Edmund's flaccid-but-massive cock. He pumps it feverishly. Edmund's face doesn't change. Nor does his cock. "That old thing!" Edmund laughs, waving at his dick dismissively.

"It's gigantic, Edmund. It's so, so big. It's like a dream, it's dreamy. You must have so many guys clamouring for it."

"Not really. Not now, anyway. It's more like an *objet* now. I've never been really connected to it. Let's take a gander at your rosebud." Edmund scooches down; only when his face is right in front of Joel's ass does Joel realize what a rosebud is.

"I don't know if I can deal. I've never looked at my anus. It might be really unsightly."

"Impossible. I love ass. It's my favourite thing. Spread for me, baby."

Joel splays his legs apart, and parts his lumpy buttocks warily.

"I apologize for any residual feces you may encounter."

Edmund's mouth falls open. He snorts with laughter. "You *must* be joking. You do *not* talk about feces when a guy is about to rim you."

"Right. I'm sorry. It's just that you may encounter feces."

"You may also encounter vomit during a kiss, but it's not something you announce. Not sexy."

"You're so right. I'm sorry." Why can't he relax into inchoate sensuality? Here is a smart, kind man with an enormous penis, about to give him his first rim job, and he's prattling on about dried shit! Shut up! Edmund's tongue touches Joel's hole. Joel gasps. Nice. Yes. Nice.

"Oh my God you're totally rimming me. It's so great. Oh wow. Thank you so much."

His tongue goes deeper. Joel opens to him. Edmund starts sighing, all sexy.

"Stroke your dick, boy," he hisses into Joel's ass. Joel obeys. Suddenly there's not so much to say.

When he comes his body seizes and releases — this is it! Here it is! This! — again and again, and his arms and legs start shaking like that lady with Parkinson's who owns the thrift store in Kenora. Edmund comes up to kiss him. Joel puts a shaking hand to Edmund's face.

"That was, like, astonishing."

"I enjoyed it."

"You're so nice. I'm so happy."

"I'm glad."

"Can I sleep over?"

Edmund hesitates. Joel wants to die. He has shown his hand, and it's obviously a grasping hand. He braces for rejection.

"I don't know," Edmund says finally. "Will there be feces in the night?"

Joel needs a second to discern Edmund's irony. These adult men with their intricate patter and subtly shaded emotions! Their ease of being, right in the middle of their long, *lived* lives!

"I absolutely promise, there will be no feces in the night."

His shakes slowly subside. He sleeps in a man's arms.

JOEL IS AWAKENED by high morning light; the heavy bedroom drapes have been thrown open. Edmund is not in the room. Joel feels rested, sprightly. He pads around the top floor, looking for Edmund. He happens upon a room filled with armour and multicoloured marabou. It's a delightful sight, a waking dream, and Joel wonders if the rest of his life will now be similarly delightful. He heads downstairs.

Edmund is sitting on a small wooden stool in the living room. It looks uncomfortable; it's something a folksinger would sit on to sing in a coffee house. Comfy couches everywhere, and he chooses to sit on this little stool?

"I slept so soundly," Joel says. "I feel great. How did you sleep?"

"I didn't, really. After you fell asleep I came down and

watched TV. There was a *Kate and Allie* marathon. I love Jane Curtin. Then I ate a whole package of raw wieners. They were kind of disgusting, but I couldn't stop myself."

Joel tilts his head adoringly. Someone else who sometimes binges on weird food! His head whirls with visions of shared fun.

"Are we going to hang out today? What do you feel like doing?"

"I can't hang out today. No. I have errands to run."

"Cool. We can run them together?"

"No. They're personal. I need to fill prescriptions."

"Okay. No problem. Maybe tonight, then?"

"Possible, but unlikely. I'm pretty ragged today."

Joel decides not to feel rebuffed. Adults have obligations, they get ragged when they don't sleep well. It can't all be armour and marabou. Speaking of which —

"Hey, I went into a room upstairs that had all sorts of armour and marabou in it. What's that all about?"

"You went into the armour room. Please do not go snooping in my house."

"I wasn't snooping, honestly. I was just looking for the bathroom."

"End of the hall. It's the red door at the end of the hall."

"Got it. Won't happen again."

They are both silent. What can Joel say? There are no inroads to be made; they barely know each other. He can only apologize profusely and hope that Edmund will forgive him in the name of romantic love.

"I'm sorry," Edmund offers at last. "That room is full of

Dean's stuff. My lover. He had obsessions. It was very cute. The attic is full of dollhouses. It's all so beautiful. I'm not sure what to do with it."

"It must be impossibly difficult to sort through a loved one's possessions after they've passed away. You know, I'm impartial and have been told I have a good eye — maybe we could sort through his stuff together?"

Edmund wistfully scans Joel from left to right, as though he was a passing landscape seen from a car. "Thank you for the offer. I really do need to start my day now. Do you have all your belongings?

"I just need to get dressed."

"So let's do that, and we'll both be on our way."

Edmund starts toward the staircase to indicate forward motion, no time to waste. Joel takes the hint and runs upstairs. How can Edmund be so brusque all of a sudden? He stands and shadows Joel as he gathers his clothes and shoes. Joel tries a final time to make conversation.

"That lamp by the window — where did you get it?"

"I don't know."

"Why do you hate me suddenly?"

"I didn't say I hated you. We had a nice time, and now I have to start my day. I hope to see you again at some point."

At the door he gives Joel a bristly peck on the cheek, presses a twenty into his hand for a taxi, and holds a phantom phone to his ear.

"I will! I'll call you tonight!" Joel says as the door closes in his face.

A thrilling, transformative evening. Last night was the demarcation; there is only Before Last Night and After. He doesn't want to get his hopes up, but — his hopes are up. Good gay sex is no longer some damp, unknowable Atlantis. He's living for good gay sex now. He's living for the mercurial man who just shooed him out of his house.

The first pay phone he passes he calls Brenda at work. He gets her voicemail.

"Hi, Brenda, it's Joel. I won't be coming in today. My circumstances have changed, and now the job is no longer compatible with my lifestyle. I can no longer perform sexy, now that real sexy is really real to me. Sorry for all the trouble. You're a really nice woman. You need to stop relying on food for comfort and really strive for connection with people. If I can do it, you can do it! All the best. Thanks so much."

Joel gets home to find two letters slipped under his bedroom door (one of the roommates distributes the mail this way; Joel finds the practice slightly invasive, but he'd never say anything). One is from his mother: not unusual, she's always mailing little notes and clippings from magazines. The other letter is from his father. He has not received a letter from his father before. The handwriting is unfamiliar; he doesn't know his own father's cursive.

Joel,

I'm writing to you because if I call, your mom will hear me and get upset. She's not doing too good. She was coughing bad, bringing up blood, had a lot of pain, got really skinny.

This was after Christmas. We got back from the oncologist in Winnipeg this morning. The lungs are full of cancer. It's in her liver and a little bit in the brain, too. She didn't want me to tell you. She said to tell you she just needed to get her female parts pulled out. But then what am I going to tell you when she really starts to go downhill?

They put her on morphine. That's really helped.

I wrote to your brother, too. Him and Shary are busy getting ready for the baby. Now is not the time, but I can't tell you how disappointed we both were that you dropped out of school. Your mom especially. I'm not blaming you for her sickness, but the timing of the two things does make you think. You should come home. I'll put money in your chequing account for a bus ticket.

If you call, call after eight pm or so. She nods off pretty easy on the morphine, and she's out like a light after eight.

Dad

He is dizzy. He opens the second letter, from his mother.

Dear Jolie Joel,

I just now came across your dad's letter to you, in the back pocket of his work pants. Don't tell him that I found it. Don't tell him that I'm telling you what he tells you in his letter, because I told him to tell you I'm going in for a hysterectomy. If he knows that I'm telling you the truth in this letter, he'll worry that I'm worrying about how you're going to react to the bad news instead of just lying around not thinking about anything, like he wants me to do.

So yes, my Jolie, I am full of cancer like your dad's letter says. It's not fun. There's no lung cancer in our family, so I don't know where this came from; I've always been more of a social smoker. I'm still a bit dazed about it. This fall/winter was shaping up to be a really nice time for me. I was thinking of opening my own jewellery business. All that's out the window now. It's funny, now that I look back — maybe I was so hesitant to get going again in the months after you first left because I intuitively knew that I was going to get lung cancer really soon? Maybe not.

What I can say with certainty is that your dad is full of shit when he suggests in his letter that you going away and then dropping out of school and doing God knows what with your time was somehow the cause of my cancer. That's just your dad being his usual bonehead self about emotional things, trying to rationalize our rough go right now. You did not cause my cancer. Don't get me wrong — I was shocked, furious, and bitterly disappointed by your recent failures. It's like the smart, talented son I brought up all these years — remember how smart you were in high school, with that big vocabulary of yours? — it's like he died and was replaced by a moron zombie. That cut me to the quick. What if you get some awful cancer all of a sudden? What are they going to say at your funeral? "He dropped out of school after a week because it was too thinky." How memorable. Please come home. Maybe the best thing for you is to take a step back from the godawful mess you've made of your life right now. Try and figure out what went wrong. I'd love to have the company. I'm lonely these days. All this time, your mother *thought she was a real lone wolf. I thought I didn't need friends, but that was because I had you to talk to. Now that you're gone I've got nobody. I love your dad, but he's as boring as he ever was. How much can you say about the taste of this year's moose meat versus last year's moose meat, or whether or not the lawn mower sounded a bit grindy the last time he ran it? I know you know what I mean.*

I'll tell you one thing. If you come home and you're on drugs, you are going to wish you'd never been born. I will throw you out of the house and never talk to you again. I will wipe you from my life, and you will never get another penny from me.

Enclosed please find a cheque. Your dad has sent you bus fare, so this will be for incidentals. Please do laundry. Please bathe. Need I remind you of the painful foreskin infections you had time and again in junior high school?

> *Lots of hugs and kisses*
> *Love from Mom*

The last time they spoke, just two days ago, she sounded totally fine. There was sometimes a little gasp in her voice; that gasp could've been pain, although it sounded almost exactly like her taking a drag off her cigarette. They're so close; why didn't she share this with him as soon as it happened? Why choose now to hold back, when she has always been so forthcoming with him over other issues that were often none of his business?

She really did sound fine on the phone two days ago. And, apart from delivering the bad news, she sounds fine in her letter. Maybe she's exaggerating the direness of her condition;

she does like to exaggerate. He'll call her. He's afraid to call her, in case she doesn't sound fine now. He'll call her later.

He puts a pillow to his face, so he won't disturb the other men in the house.

7

TERESA'S WIG, ON ITS STYROFOAM head, casts an oddly long shadow in the afternoon sun. The shadow looms over her bed like a mean nanny. Teresa slowly rises, pulls the curtains, switches on her red ceramic sleeping cat side lamp, slowly lays herself down again. If she is absolutely still, the nausea recedes slightly and she is able to get almost comfortable. A few months ago she was so toned and tanned that a young bagger at Safeway asked her if she'd ever been a fitness model. Now this.

And that wig. She doesn't know why she hasn't pitched the stupid thing. She wore it once, to the Valdy concert at the harbourfront; it itched like a bitch and she felt silly in it, like it was Halloween in June. She was almost certain that Valdy saw her and smiled sarcastically, during the first chorus of "Yes I Can."

Hugh paid a fortune for it, though. Human hair from Europe, custom-made to look like your old hair. When he presented her with it, though, she wondered how he had been perceiving her, all these years; the wig was red and curly, where Teresa's hair was only wavy and auburn. She looks like Little fucking Orphan Annie in it. And the way he gave the wig to her, all expectant, telling her that, with the beautiful wig, she'd be herself again — it was exactly the wrong thing to say to her, to any woman disfigured by illness. Hugh never was very intuitive about stuff like that. There are twenty-five years' worth of lamely inscribed birthday and anniversary cards in a box in the closet. *Happy 20th Anniversary. I think you know how I feel. From Hugh. Lordy, Lordy, look who's forty! Good stuff, from Hugh.* Oh well. He's a solid guy, ever dependable, a real comfort, with those long arms of his. She'll leave the wig where it is for now. Maybe she can take it to the girl she goes to at Heights of Fashion and she can shape it a bit, take out the curl, even dye it. That would be a lot of work. She'd have to get out of bed, dress. She'd have to click her seatbelt into place. Too much work.

"Maybe a year" is what the oncologist said when they pressed him. What a kick in the teeth. Her high school friends Vicki and Dina both licked cancer: a little surgery, a bit of radiation, no problem, back in the saddle in a few weeks. They both had breast, though. Everyone gets breast. Teresa would've killed for breast. Lung is a different plate of potatoes. How the hell does a forty-four-year-old woman come down with lung? And not simply lung: mesothelioma is what they called it. Caused by exposure to asbestos! Coal miners tend to get it, and she was certainly not a coal miner. Where could she possibly have inhaled asbestos? She's always liked girly things: she's had a subscription to the Mary Maxim craft catalogue since high school. Is she being punished simply for being vivacious? Because she liked having fun, a drink and a toke now and then, a little bit of the dirty business when the timing was right? She probably was. If she had married an accountant and taken in a First Nations fetal alcohol orphan like Vicki did, would she be free and clear? Probably, yes. Teresa loves life; she has a real zeal: even now she awakens with a sparky start in the morning, eager to taste coffee, smoke a first cigarette, listen to neighbours' cars pop along gravel driveways on the way to work. There will be mail to read or at the very least flyers and glossy junk, and there will be the radio, always the radio, with Nick Haddock in the morning and Cal Benoit in the afternoon and Ronnie Golding through the night. Teresa had fun with Nick a couple times in '87; she danced once with Cal at the legion hall when she was six months in with Joel, the spring of '78. Ronnie she's never met, but from all accounts he's a really nice guy, an avid snowshoer, reliable neighbour. He bought Mrs. Hensrud's old place on Redditt Road, and he's made many circular beds of marigolds in the shade of the bent and broken oaks, front yard and back. Mrs. Hensrud let the lawns go all to hell in her last years.

Hugh is hammering something in the living room. He's buggering something up, rendering furniture rickety for no reason. He fancies himself a handyman, but he isn't. He hacked up Teresa's cedar chest last year; he said he wanted to try something. That chest was one of the few nice pieces Teresa had. Now it's legless and won't close unless she slams it shut. She's glad he's getting his woodworking jollies — if only he'd try it on something ugly.

He's good at what he does at the paper mill, by all accounts, whatever it is that he does there. Thirty years he's been at it. Give Hugh an assignment requiring improvisation or spatial reasoning, though ... How many times did Dallas slide out of his crib before Hugh finally let Teresa get a store-bought one? Who builds a crib with no bars on the sides? She had to laugh.

With the pain contained by morphine, Teresa can get some of her own work done. She's not going to get all morbid and precious about it like her friend Marlene did when she was dying — *I need to see Fenelon Falls, one last time!* — nor is she going to make her kids feel like shit for not being at her bedside round the clock like her rancid grandmother did with her equally rancid yet at least borderline-literate mother when she was dying. Obviously the whole jewellery business dream is out the window at this point. Teresa just wants to do some shopping, see a few people, have a bit more fun.

She's going to start by getting up, pulling the hammer from Hugh's hand, and throwing it in the garbage. In a minute. In a few minutes.

8

JOEL IS NOT LEAVING THE city until he has given a performance of his work somewhere. This much he knows. He has to leave his scent on the city in some way. He has had good gay sex and found a love object. All that's left is a big-city artistic undertaking. Then he can leave, serene in the knowledge that a delightful, well-rounded life awaits him upon his return to Toronto.

He is going to perform a medley of his melodic, automatic poetry. It says, in *NOW* magazine, that there is a west end bar called Tandem starting up an open mic night on Wednesdays.

He flips through his notebook. Slim pickings, mainly juvenilia. He couldn't possibly perform "Remember Bright Mountain" or "Only Sveta Knows." He couldn't possibly perform any of them, now that he's sifted through all twenty-two pages. None of them evoke anything. None of them contain memorable images. His work is shit. What makes him think he's a performer? Because he drunkenly sang "Crying" at karaoke and some woozy woman approached him, crying, and said that he sounded, if not like Roy Orbison himself, at least like one of his relatives?

Joel exhales violently, a kung fu exhale meant to silence himself. It does not matter that his poetry has no merit or that his ability as a performer has not been validated. What matters is that he is passionate. Yes. He is almost certainly passionate about performance art. And if he isn't passionate specifically about performance art, he is certainly passionate in general.

He picks up a mustard-encrusted pen off the floor.

He said, "She has cancer,"

> *But I'm ensnared by an armour and marabou romancer,*
> *Don't take me back to my hometown*
> *Woo hoo, Bobby Brown.*

What more is there to say, really? He rips a page from his notebook and, in balloon letters, writes "Come and see me perform at Tandem, next Wednesday! Love, Joel." He takes it downstairs and pins it on the otherwise barren bulletin board in the kitchen.

When he goes downstairs again an hour later, the note is gone from the bulletin board. In its place is another note, this one in black block letters: "THIS IS A PRIVATE HOME, NOT A TELEPHONE POLE!"

9

BEHIND THE OREGANO IN THE spice rack Edmund finds a tiny vial of coke. Dean must've stashed it there ages ago; Edmund has never liked coke. He never enjoyed the feeling of euphoria, nor any arcing sensation that didn't ultimately result in a nap. Booze was his thing; for the longest time his biggest happiness — the face of God, even! — was the rollicking stupor that happened after six Jack and Cokes. Seven years, he's been sober. It seemed important seven years ago, sobriety. Now, though ... Maybe if he had got that clingy kid drugs he would've stopped talking and thrown himself into the sex. All this time he thought he wanted someone to talk to; with Joel all he wanted was to muzzle the kid and eat his ass. No, no — he *does* still want someone to talk to, someone who understands. What he doesn't want is to *explain*. It's too gruelling to be a tour guide through all those awful years. Joel is sweet, he has a nice face. Someone will gobble him right up. Besides, when Dean did coke he was an absolute motor-mouth. Coke is the last thing that kid needs.

He wonders: do party drugs go bad? If so, how will he know? If he sniffs a little of it, will he seize and die, or will it simply have no effect at all? He holds the vial tightly in his palm. How he railed against Dean's drug benders when Dean was first diagnosed! How his drug benders drove Edmund to booze benders! But now, in the silence of the chilly kitchen, with this little old vial, the image of Dean running up and down the stairs for no reason ... Edmund remembers the breeze of Dean, rushing past him through the house. He opens the vial and taps out a bit of powder onto the window sill.

"What do you think, Dean? Should I try some?" He listens. No word from Dean.

He takes a hesitant sniff.

Nothing. He feels no different. He pulls up a stool to the marble island. His growing gut has made sitting on a stool uncomfortable. If this is partying, then drug addicts must be addicted to tedium. He's had a better buzz off a glass of Pepsi. It must've gone bad, the stuff. He has another huff.

He stands around. Someone nearby is mowing their lawn. Should Edmund mow his own lawn right now? It suddenly seems urgent that he also mow his lawn. Edmund maybe sort of does feel kind of ... amplified. He looks at the stairs and considers running up and down them like Dean once did. He knows that he'll turn an ankle, so instead he pops Tracy Chapman's *Crossroads* into the cassette deck, and begins to dance around the house, his lurching dance, the dance he danced at Chaps and Boots and Komrads and The Barn, a dance that more than one dance floor partner has likened to a drunken woman looking for a place to puke.

After a few minutes Edmund finally concedes that Tracy Chapman isn't especially danceable. He stops the tape and sits. For once his loneliness does not strike him as quaint, some small household imperfection that can be easily sidestepped, like a gouge in a floorboard. He is punctured by his loneliness. He has learned all he can learn from austerity. It's officially Time for Fun. He could call the phone sex line, try to find new flesh to replace the gawky, fey flesh that just left, but who's to say that he won't encounter another mewling virgin who'll paw at him like a fucking orphaned infant chimp?

He's going out. Yes. On the town, to the village, to bar hop, to tilt a bottle of water against his breastbone and stand around, sway and bop a bit and stand around. Sure, these stand-around outings were only ever stultifying for Edmund, back in the day. But it's a new day, and he's on drugs.

As he manically swipes through his closet for a flattering shirt, delighting in the scraping sound of hangers moving on the metal rod, he tries to convince himself that times may very well have changed for the better since he last went out on the town. People may have become more playful; the epidemic may have worn away at gay men in a good way, rendering them more open, more empathetic, sweeter. Maybe? Possibly. Probably not. He picks out a black corduroy shirt that goes nearly to his knees. He can blouse it out around his belt, concealing his tummy.

In the bedroom half-bath he applies Molto styling pomade to his widow's peak, spiking it into a modest Mohawk. It's quite possible, he thinks as he studies himself in the mirror, that he can still look, with some effort … like a sad, pasty man making the most of the last of his hair. Still, "A" for effort, no? And he was never all that attractive, even when he had hair.

He locks up the house. Once outside he stands on the lawn and studies his lamp-lit rooms. How warm and inviting his home is, when he's not there.

10

THERE ARE FOUR PEOPLE SET to perform at the open mic. There is a thin, bearded man with an acoustic guitar. There is a young woman Joel's age with a ballerina bun and a long sweatshirt overtop a blue spandex bodysuit. There is a tense-looking woman in a long black raincoat, the left lapel smeared with what looks like old toothpaste. And Joel.

The host is an older guy in blue-and-white tie-dyed MC Hammer pants; he holds a martini glass and babbles on about what a dangerous, provocative evening he has in store for the audience of twelve people, more dangerous even than his great experiment at Theatre Passe Muraille, summer of '72. He seems to assume that the sparse audience knows exactly what his great experiment was.

Guitar guy goes first. Joel doesn't pay much attention to the song — he hears the words "eternal" and "sexy damsel." At the end of the song there is a smattering of oddly damp-sounding clapping, like the few people in attendance are all trying to burp babies. Guitar guy hoists his instrument in the air. You'd think he'd just closed the show at Farm Aid.

The lady in the raincoat is next. She holds a crumpled piece of paper, and before saying a word she looks around the room with exasperated contempt, as though she'd been locked in a closet, banging for hours to be let out, and they, the audience, have only now deigned to free her.

She glances at the crumpled paper, then resumes her hateful stare. "I remember the sex abuse!" she barks. "Zaydie! Zaydie! Which is Yiddish for 'Grandfather! Grandfather!' Why did you diaper me in such a lurid way when I was four months old? You didn't think I'd remember, but I do! Everyone always says to me, 'Oh, Shoshana, you've got the world at your feet, you're a shift supervisor at Bally Total Fitness,' but that is not the case, because I'm coping with trauma. It would be much more convenient for everyone concerned if I didn't remember the sex abuse, but I do! The memory of it popped open in my mind like a daffodil! Except that this daffodil wasn't all pretty and yellow and plucked from a garden. The petals of this daffodil were made from the tanned skins of exterminated Holocaust Jews! If that is an intense image, it's supposed to be! I have come upon the sex abuse Holocaust-Jew-skin daffodil, Zaydie/ Grandfather, and you know what I'm going to do? I'm going to pick it! Then I'm going to go to your grave and I'm going to picket it! I'm going to pick *it*, and then I'm going to pick-*et*! Incestuous pedophile scum! I hate you!" She bows. "Thank you so much."

The room is silent. Joel is reminded of when Sinéad

O'Connor tore up the picture of the Pope on *Saturday Night Live* and nobody clapped. By way of apology for his gender he bows his head and leans away from Shoshana as she walks past him back to her table, where a woman with long, black Cher hair awaits her, weeping.

The boozy host takes the stage again. "Wow, Shoshana," he says, "That piece was every bit as powerful and dangerous as when you read it last week. I think we maybe need to impose a new rule where returning performers only perform new work. Just to give us all a chance to gather ourselves in the wake of such a powerful piece as ... What is the name of that piece again, Shoshana?"

"'Forgiveness,'" Shoshana shouts.

"Right. Yes. Good stuff. Next up is another performance poet, Joel!"

Joel has suddenly lost all desire to perform. His work is idiotically slight compared to Shoshana's, and any attempt at a performative tour-de-force would only come off as a pale copy. She is actually applauding wildly for Joel, nodding and smiling. He briefly considers running out of the bar, but Shoshana is so encouraging, with her clapping and hooting, he's afraid she'll beat him up if he bolts.

He says "hello" into the mic. He holds his notebook with both hands. He studies his piece. It is very stupid. What a directionless mess his adulthood has turned out to be.

"He said 'she has cancer,'" he begins. "But I'm ensnared by a ..." Prickly heat migrates across his chest. "I'm sorry. This is too horrible. My piece, I mean. Not the evening as a whole.

Sorry. I'm going to — try some — free-association. Starting, like, now. Okay ... hair ... curly ... red ... hair ... hair ..."

"Hair-hair?" he hears someone in the front ask the person beside them.

"I'm sorry. My free-association isn't yielding anything interesting tonight. I'm not at my best. I'm kind of in crisis. Thank you."

He walks off. As he passes sex-abuse Shoshana she snatches at his sleeve — "Wait, I'm in crisis, too! Do you want to maybe hang out sometime?"

He smiles and pulls away.

Once outside he realizes he has forgotten the brown poncho he arrived in. Oh well. It's not like he's cold; he's dripping with sweat and his ears pulse. And he looked horrible in it, anyway.

11

EDMUND GOES TO COLBY'S. THERE are two other people there.
He stands at the edge of the empty dance floor and watches the
lights streak and retreat, in starburst and laser beam, white,
green and magenta. He still feels quite up, quite whippy, quite
swingy, quite backflippy even, and it takes all his reserve to not
bound onto the dance floor and do some antiquated sock hop
step sequence.

Two songs later a tiny woman with jagged front teeth and
a tinsel wig comes up to Edmund and asks him if he knows
where she can score rock. Edmund looks around himself,
swiping this way and that with his head, certain that there
is someone standing behind him, someone rough and obvious,
someone who knows where one can score rock. "I'm sorry,"
he says finally. "I can't hear a thing you're saying, with the
music."

"Sure you can hear me, honey," the woman says.

"I'm sorry, I really can't hear you."

"Don't be a bitch, honey. I'm so nice. Talk to me, honey. You can talk to me — I love that song."

Edmund squints. Sudden exchanges with the addicted or mentally ill happen to him all the time, for some reason. He remembers the time a huddled homeless man grabbed him by the pant leg as he passed by. Edmund fell face first into a pushup position, and the homeless man asked him how it felt, falling down. It felt bad, Edmund said to the man, turning his head from pushup position. Well, there you go, the man said. And then there was the nude lady on Gerrard Street who offered him a bite of her imaginary slice of pizza ...

Edmund puts a hand to his bladder to indicate that he has to pee and walks off. The woman says something, but this time Edmund really can't hear her. As he walks to the next bar — the newish, ugly one at the bottom of the street, all clapboard and yellow paneling — he can't help but feel slightly smug at the elegant way he enacts his own loneliness, unlike some people — like this crack woman and Joel the orphaned monkey — unlike most other people, for that matter. Other people tend to dump their need at your feet like dead game. He likes to think that he brings a little levity, some disarming music to his need. He isn't repulsive. He is still approachable. This could all be vain bunk, though. He is not above vain bunk, God knows. All of this, he now realizes, he is saying aloud.

The doorman at the ugly, clapboard bar laughingly asks Edmund for ID, then pats him on the back and lets him through.

This place is also almost empty. No light show here. A few

guys slumped at a bar that runs the length of one wall, and a bartender flipping through an old *Chatelaine*. This looks like a real drinker's bar, the sort of bar he'd use as an example of the rock bottom he was absolutely nowhere near, when he was still drinking. Edmund briefly considers sitting at the bar; alcoholics tend to make for great conversation, in his experience. It's as if their addiction, while most definitely ruining their lives, has also freed them up to make inspired inductive leaps while chatting. But a brightly lit room in the back of the bar gets his attention.

A scrawny boy is sitting sidesaddle on the lip of a pool table. He holds a pool cue against his chest like it's the neck of a cello. He does not have a drink. He is waiting for a pool partner. When he sees Edmund he looks at him with a weary scrutiny, as though Edmund is a second-hand sofa that he is sizing up after a long, fruitless day of secondhand sofa shopping.

Edmund thrills to the kid's face. It's a fist of a face, wind-burned and blunt, with small, spiteful grey eyes and a tight, angled mouth, like a hasty hem. Edmund is reminded of a book of photographs he has somewhere on the second or third floor, page after page of Russian immigrant children, tired and terrified at Ellis Island. This kid could be one of those kids, but for the bleached white hair and battered, black, oddly dandyish high-heeled boots.

A song comes on that the kid likes and he starts rolling his shoulders, tossing his head this way and that, wagging his finger at the cruel womanizer that the female singer confronts in the choruses. He is possessed, oblivious to his surroundings.

By the end of the song he is stalking up and down the length of the pool table in a terrifying war dance, arms arcing like startled wings, his reprimand now aimed not at one bad man but all of bad mankind. The song ends, and he instantly resumes his bored pose with the pool cue.

Edmund sidles up softly. "That was really intense."

"What was?"

"Your performance just now. It was wonderful. You completely inhabited the song."

"'It's Not Right, But It's Okay.' Diva Whitney, pop princess goes ghetto, she's going to make it anyway realness. Oh yes I am *riding in the car* with Diva Whitney, rumours of crack cocaine addiction realness."

Edmund doesn't understand any of this, nods anyway. "Wow. Are you a professional performer?"

"Yes, I am! Thank you very much!" he snaps imperiously, then folds slightly. "Well, no, I'm not at this present moment in time a professional performer, I should say. But that is a goal, definitely. My talents are ... many. I do it all. Have you seen *Paris is Burning*?"

"Is that the one about the drag balls? Yes, I think we did see that when it came out."

"Directed by Jennie Livingston, 1990 realness. I watch that movie over and over, when I have a vcr. I want to live in that movie so bad. I've been beaten and raped and stabbed and left for dead but I am a soul survivor, like Diva Tina, Wildest Dreams Tour presented by Hanes Pantyhose realness. So it is all good."

It is apparent that this person is either manic or high, or

both, but Edmund, himself amped up, decides that he likes this person's mania, and asks him his name.

"My real name is long and Russian — Ow! the way I like my meat! Ow! Catch me I'm falling! — but I go by Binny. And this one time, in the heat of the night, when it was feeling all right, someone called me Waterfall. So, the choice is yours."

"I'm Edmund. Can I buy you a drink, Waterfall? I'm sorry, I don't think I can call you Waterfall, Binny."

"Like I said, the choice is yours, kind sir. I'm only drinking Pepsi. I don't want to fuck with my buzz. I did a big bulbie before I came here."

"Oh. What is that? Is that crack?"

"'Is that crack,' she says! I'm not that ghetto. I'm only *riding in the car* with Diva Whitney, 'I Will Always Love You' video filmed sitting down because of pregnancy realness. I'm a T girl."

"Oh. T. Testosterone?"

Binny rolls his eyes. "'T' is for 'Tina.' And I don't mean Diva Tina, 'Master Blaster runs Bartertown two men enter one man leaves Thunderdome' realness."

"Right. So what do you mean? Sorry."

"Crystal! Speed! God. Where you been?"

"I haven't been out for years. I actually did some coke before I came here. I think it was coke, anyway. It might have only been seasoning."

Binny is manically scanning the bar. "Where's my Pepsi at?"

Edmund apologizes and goes to the bar. He waves a twenty. The bartender will not look up from his *Chatelaine*. Finally Edmund yells "bar order!" and the alkies all look at him like he's some over-caffeinated schoolmarm. "Bar order" does sound awkward and formal; Edmund hopes Binny hasn't over-heard him.

He hands Binny his drink. They clink glasses. "I've been bar hopping. At the other bar I came from there was … music. That's not very descriptive, is it? Actually, the other bar was pretty dreary. It was quite disheartening. I should've expected as much. What about you? Is this your big night out, too?"

"Every night is my big night out. You wanna get with me?"

It takes him a minute, but Edmund recognizes this as a proposition. "That would be very nice. Yes, I'm sure I'd like that."

"Yeah. I'm working though, okay?"

Again, Edmund needs to sit with that statement before he puts it together. "I see. I've never hired someone before. I'm certainly not averse to the concept."

Binny's face turns officious and he's about to start in with his hooker spiel when two young men approach the pool table.

"Hey," the shorter one says to Binny. "We're going to play, okay?"

"No, it is not okay," Binny says. "I've got the table right now."

"But you're just sitting there," the taller one says. "We just want to sneak a quick game in, okay?"

"Not okay, bitches. I've got the table. You can either win the table offa me, or fuck off."

The guys look at each other, stunned, as if Binny has just said he loves Hitler. They ripple back in the wake of his out-burst, then gather themselves and advance again.

"We are living in something called a democracy, y'know," the tall one says. "You don't own this bar. Do we need to get management involved?"

"Go right ahead. Be prepared to get your ugly fuckin' face smashed in when you step out onto the democratic sidewalk, though. I can go from zero to psycho in a heartbeat."

Edmund waves his arm like a windshield wiper. "Actually," he says, "my friend and I were just about to play. Weren't we?"

"We were! So beat it! Step off."

The boys huff off. Edmund is not put off by Binny's anger. He likes it. It's vigorous, snazzy. Dean was volatile. And in Dean's rage there was real threat; while they never came to blows, Edmund knew to tiptoe around Dean when he was angry — one wrong move and Dean would set a loveseat aflame, or flush Edmund's watch down the toilet. Binny's rage is showy, a righteous pantomime, but not outwardly dangerous: it's an ideal anger for this older, weaker, less durable Edmund. It'll make for some fun shadowboxing, heavy on the shadow. Binny has promise. His presence makes Edmund's dick get hard; when was the last time he had a hard-on that he didn't have to frantically pump into existence and then pinch off with a cock ring to preserve?

He leans into the kid. "I bet you're a real mean fucker sometimes," he whispers.

Binny looks hurt. "I am not mean. I always try to be nice. I am a soul survivor. I've had it hard. My mother got rid of me when I was two so she could have sex with her new boyfriend in the kitchen and living room. She had me, she had a good look at me, and decided I wasn't worth keeping. She kept my Down Syndrome sister though. How about that? Well, the winner takes it all, Diva Agnetha Fältskog, I dated my stalker realness."

"I didn't mean to offend you. You're obviously a very strong, sensitive person. I think you're doing amazingly well, given what you've been through."

"They say I have attention deficit whatever-it-is and one of them said I was autistic. What-evah! So. I do what I have to do. But I am not mean. I am a good person. I'm so good it's sick."

"I'm going to rack 'em up," Edmund announces, trapping the balls in the triangle. "This is going to be so much fun. I don't know why I've been afraid of pool, all these years."

Binny rolls his head around and around. "I think I'm gonna go."

"Why? We're just getting to know each other."

"I don't like that you think I'm mean."

"I don't think you're mean. I think you're beautiful and fascinating."

"Don't fuck with me, fuckface."

Edmund feels slapped. The voice of God demands that Binny be Edmund's lover. And the thought of standing alone with a pyramid of pool balls in the chill yellow light of this dingy room is too, too, too. It's Wednesday. Garbage day on his street is Thursday; the bins will already be out, both sides of the sidewalk. He'll probably be awake all night. Again he comes in close to Binny.

"I will never fuck with you. I'll give you three hundred dollars if you'll come home with me. We don't have to have sex. We can just watch TV or —"

"I don't know. Yeah, okay. No scat, no necro. And I don't want to hear about your ex-boyfriends. And I don't do *listening to your vacation memories* or *looking at and talking about your collectibles*, or any of that. And if you have a dog, you have to lock it in another room. I don't want no dog starting at me when I'm sucking cock."

"That's all fine, better than fine. Perfect. And I don't have a dog. Not anymore. Simba died year before —"

"Hey, what did I just say? I don't want to hear about your life things."

Happily chastened, Edmund stops talking about his life things. They gather their coats and head out.

"So, who are your divas?" Binny asks in the taxi.

Edmund thinks of the women in his life — Lila, his mother, Mrs. Sanchez at the corner store — before deciding that Binny only wants to hear about his favourite female singers.

"I've always liked Linda Ronstadt."

"Yes. Diva Linda, hypothyroidism, shot from the neck up in the 'Heartbeats Accelerating' video to hide weight gain realness. And?"

"Umm. When I was a teenager, I loved Olivia Newton-John."

"Yes. Diva Olivia, breast cancer and Koala Blue bankruptcy survivor realness. Nice."

Edmund laughs. "How on Earth do you know all this pop trivia?"

"I read all the magazines, every week. *Billboard*, *People*, *Us*,

Rolling Stone, *Hello*, *Spin*, *Q*, as well as all the tabloids. Always have, since I could first read. I keep up with my divas. Diva Whitney, Diva Tina, Diva Diana, Diva Patti, Diva Mary J, Diva Chaka, Diva Donna, Diva Janet, Diva Millie, Diva Gladys, Diva Dionne. They're my friends. I try to keep up with all the white divas, too. Even, like, the shitty divas, like Diva Gloria Loring or Diva Tiffany. It's my thing. Can I borrow your cell phone?"

"I don't have a cell phone."

"You don't have a cell phone! How come?"

"I'm home all the time. Also, most of my friends have passed away."

"No excuse! You have to have a cell phone. What if you have like an emergency or you need drugs or a pizza or something? Promise me you are going to get a cell phone."

"I promise," Edmund vows, solemn as a praying priest.

"Yay! Work! Take me to the river!"

EDMUND WATCHES BINNY ogling the interiors of Edmund's home. He reaches up to hold a glass dewdrop from the chandelier in his palm.

"You have the nicest house I've ever seen," Binny says, fixated on the dewdrop. Edmund smiles. He feels house-proud, which he hasn't felt since the dinner party days of the late eighties. Then he remembers the bedpan that he still sometimes uses out of habit, and the rooms filled with Dean's mouldering things, and the pride vanishes. He pours Binny a glass of flat RC Cola. They head upstairs, Binny yammering about his own dream house, its various dream features, what he might do differently were Edmund's home his own home. These stairs, for example: Binny thinks these stairs would be amazing if they were made of glass.

In the bedroom he is just about to show Binny the small Basquiat above the bed, but he catches himself before he accidentally talks about a collectible.

"I don't think I want to take my shirt off," Edmund says. "Is that okay?"

"I totally don't care. I guess you want me naked, though?"

"That would be very nice. Also, I must tell you that I'm positive."

"Girl, who isn't? I've had it since I was eleven."

"Oh my goodness."

"What do you mean, *oh my goodness*, like I should've known better or something?"

"Not at all. It's just … That's an awful lot for a child to cope with."

"I told you, I come up hard. Hard times. Rape. For real realness. Oh well. I like you. You're nice. At least we don't need to bother with rubbers."

Edmund hasn't had anal sex in eight years.

"What about reinfection with a more virulent strain?" Edmund asks.

"What?"

Edmund shrugs. Sex without a condom has never crossed his mind, all these years. It still seems like such a brutally anarchic, stupid thing to do, regardless of serostatus, regardless of the new drugs. Even with Dean he didn't fuck unprotected after they were both diagnosed. They stopped having sex instead. Edmund's decision, mostly. Why did he insist that they stop having sex? Their sex was always good, nasty *and* tender. Edmund was afraid his own virus would further weaken Dean somehow. But if he hadn't forsaken Dean sexually, if he'd adhered to his libido instead of getting all whipped up about viral etiquette, niceness, refashioning his lust into an antiseptic apology for past nastiness, would Dean have died faster with further viral onslaught from Edmund? Or would he have hung on longer, inspired by desire?

"I like it rough — nice 'n' rough like Diva Tina, file it under Foreign Affair realness," Binny says. "Majorly rough. I need to do a bump first though. Can I use your phone?"

Edmund points at the telephone by the bed. What constitutes "majorly rough"? He's coming down now; he's certain he doesn't have the oomph for "majorly rough," or even regular rough.

"It's B, it's your waterfall, I need some," Binny says into the phone. "I'm, like, at — hold on — Hey, Edmund, where are we?"

"I really don't want drug people knowing my address," Edmund whispers. Binny covers the mouthpiece.

"Just the main intersection," he says.

"Sackville and Dundas, roughly," Edmund offers.

Binny arranges to meet the drug person outside a Coffee Time a few streets over in twenty-five minutes. Apparently the drug person lives close by.

"We're going to have a killer time when I get back," Binny says as he puts his shoes back on.

"I hope I won't be too boring. I am fading a bit."

"We'll do a big bulbie when I get back and we'll both be rocking in the free world!"

"I know that reference! Diva Neil Young, right?"

Binny lets the laces of his left shoe fall from his fingers. He sits up, all solemn.

"Men cannot be divas. Not ever."

"Why not?"

"No. Not in my world. I roll old school. My divas all wear high heels. Even the chubby girls like Diva Linda, I hate all of my records except for the Mexican ones realness. And I don't necessarily mean that my divas have to actually wear high heels — it's more of a, like, a symbol. A metaphor? Yeah."

"I understand now."

"Wicked," he says, returning to his shoe. "I like you. I like your house. I feel all cozy. I never feel that way."

Edmund has never thought his house cozy, not even with Dean. But any safe shelter would seem cozy to a homeless person; what a cosseted dolt he is! Then again, he doesn't know for a fact that Binny is homeless; not all addict sex workers are destitute. How presumptuous and reductive.

Binny leaves the front door wide open and sprints down the street. Edmund stands on the porch, arms folded like a suburban mother waiting for her kid to come in for dinner. Then he remembers that Velvet Underground song, about Lou Reed waiting for his drug dealer, and how you always have to wait for your drug dealer, who's always late. So he goes back inside and closes the door. He leans against the door with his forehead. This is how he'll wait for Binny to come back.

12

WOULDN'T IT JUST FIGURE THAT Jocelyn Walsh, the mayor's wife, would be having her chemo at the same time as Teresa. Jocelyn, from what Teresa has heard, has — naturally! — breast cancer, but it was caught early: no lymph node involvement, tiny lumpectomy. Apparently she still insisted on reconstruction — God forbid fancy Jocelyn should have a slightly dented boob as she copes with the onset of menopause. Really, after a certain age, why bother with reconstruction, even if you are all hacked to pieces up top? Nobody wants to look at you anyway. It's not like her Digger has given her a second glance in decades. Granted, Jocelyn was once a real beauty; she is tall and willowy, still nice-looking if maybe a bit more coarse, more horsey than in her heyday. Teresa went to high school with Jocelyn. More accurately, they were in the same high school at the same time; Jocelyn was in the advanced stream, while Teresa was in the general stream, the one for future auto mechanics, mill workers, car dealership receptionists and miserable housewives. Jocelyn went on to obtain an English degree at the University of Manitoba. Teresa went on to get pregnant in grade eleven and drop out before she started to show. The "Business Fundamentals" course she took at Confederation College five years ago doesn't count.

Jocelyn hasn't lost her hair. The nurse, a tiny, beaming Chinese woman in teddy bear scrubs, is running her hand through it and exclaiming at how thick and lustrous it is. Jocelyn's secret, she says, is that she wears an ice cap every day for as long as she can stand it, and — touch wood, she says, touching the nurse's head — so far she hasn't lost a single strand. Teresa pretends to be engrossed by a *Reader's Digest* from 1983.

Thing is, Teresa once liked Jocelyn. Jocelyn owns and runs the bookstore downtown, and she always went out of her way to say hello to Teresa and ask after Hugh and the boys and, if the store wasn't busy, point out the newest murder mysteries she knew Teresa would enjoy. There was a time when Teresa — this was back when she had just started power walking and Joel told her that the sight of her flapping her arms down the road as he passed with his friends in the school bus was the most humiliating moment of his life; he was twelve so it would've been '90 — went back and forth on calling up Jocelyn and asking her if she'd like to walk with her sometime, or even just grab a coffee. Teresa has never had many female friends. It was uncharacteristic that she would want to reach out to another woman.

And there was the monthly country and western dance night that Jocelyn and her two sisters, Brynn and Suzanne, founded, called "Swing Yer Partner!," that coaxed elderly shut-ins to the legion hall, free transportation provided. Teresa's own mother went once. Of course, to hear Teresa's mother tell it, she was literally pulled, screaming, from her apartment by Brynn and Suzanne and hurled into a big van filled with other old, weeping people. But Teresa's mom is hysterical at the best of times and a world-class liar.

Teresa didn't mind Jocelyn at all, and she really liked Jocelyn's husband, Digger, a hulking, huggy man, recovered alcoholic, mayor since forever, who cleaned up the waterfront, laid down lush sod and put in a small amphitheatre, turning Kenora back into the tourist attraction it once was. They have four kids, three boys all close together in age, and a much younger daughter. Teresa remembers the daughter as shy and awkward; she was retarded and probably still in high school. The boys were all fidgety but polite, heavy into hockey. One Halloween they came to the door all dressed as the guy from *Nightmare on Elm Street*; "Trick or treat or DIE!" they all yelped. Teresa thought nothing of it at the time. In fact, she recalls finding it endearing. She recalls pretending to be scared for her life, and laughing.

Then came Joel's grade seven year. In his junior high homeroom that year was the Walshes' middle son, Craig. Halfway through September, Joel started weeping at the dinner table. Several boys, led by Craig, had taken to calling Joel a "fat faggot," a "bag of AIDS," a "fatass fag face," an "ugly faggy fag fat fag boy." They called him these awful names every day, all day, quite often within earshot of a teacher, and no one took action. Telling a teacher would only make it worse, Joel cried. And because Joel was big for his age, and Craig small, he'd look even more like a crybaby. Joel spoke of Craig's crazy, angry eyes, which never softened, even after all the other kids had gotten bored of the joke. Joel begged his parents to put him in St. Thomas Aquinas, the Catholic junior high school, even though they weren't Catholic.

Teresa was outraged. Hugh was no help; such torture was simply "par for the course" and "the sand that makes the pearl." After all, Hugh himself lost most of his teeth in high school fights, was tied to the back of Bud Koslowski's truck and dragged for half a mile in grade ten, and now he and Bud were good buds. Joel just needed to toughen up a little. Teresa had never been more dismayed by her husband's inadequacy as a father and husband as she was right then, but she filed that resentment away for the time being.

She met with Joel's homeroom teacher, a bearded, lipless twit named Carnegie Kitson, new in town from Vancouver. He dismissed her concerns with nonsense about the rituals of boyhood, how crucial such tussles are for the firmament of healthy manhood — the same crap Hugh spewed, fancied up. What if it were his kid being harassed, she asked. He said that he planned to marry and have children only when he was very old, so that he could sit at length with the child and counsel him, like Socrates and Plato. She rolled her eyes. Carnegie Kitson died of a heroin overdose three years ago — the first heroin overdose in the history of the town, to the best of Teresa's knowledge.

She tried to meet with the principal, Reg Cembal, but was repeatedly told by his secretary that he was experiencing a family crisis, and that he would not be available for conversation well into the foreseeable future. Turned out he was renovating his cottage.

Finally, Teresa called the Walshes. She calmly explained the situation to Jocelyn, who listened quietly, expressed her own concern, agreed that the situation was untenable, and then suggested they meet for coffee. Jocelyn proposed that they meet at the Husky on the edge of town. Now, no one ever meets for coffee at the Husky, unless you're meeting up with a drug dealer or an adulterous lover. The message was clear: Jocelyn, for all her public nicey-nice and despite her cordial phone manner, considered Teresa trash. Teresa was duly offended, and chastised herself for once contemplating Jocelyn as a possible friend. But she filed away her hurt, as she did with her annoyance with Hugh, for the sake of dealing with the crisis at hand.

Teresa got there early. The waitress, a very old woman who moved slowly and arduously as though struggling through deep mud, greeted Teresa by her name. Teresa squinted at the woman, still not recognizing her. "It's Mrs. Clemens," she said. "I babysat you when you were just a little thing." Teresa, finally seeing her beloved babysitter, jumped up and hugged her. She apologized for not catching on; she hadn't seen Mrs. Clemens for years.

"I didn't know you were working here."

"My husband died in debt and didn't tell me. I don't want to be working, believe me. I'm eighty-eight next month. Oh well. Next week they're starting in with an "olden days" theme here at the restaurant. So come Monday I'll have to wear a big sunbonnet that ties with a ribbon, and tap shoes. I say, 'but I'm eighty-eight, a bone came out of my nose last week.' They didn't care. It was 'tap dance or get lost.' Oh well. You make do. How is that mother of yours?"

"She's ... alive. Still mean and dumb. Just like you remember her, I'm sure."

"I try not to keep bad feelings for anyone, but that woman takes the cake, she really does. To think that I would — I can't even say it ..."

"Get naked to babysit me. I know. It's crazy. Crazy, crazy. I've tried to tell her, but she's so deluded. I'm so sorry."

Mrs. Clemens was visibly upset at the memory of it all. Customers came in, and she began to wade her way toward them, but not before giving Teresa's shoulder a little squeeze. Teresa smiled. What a lovely lady Mrs. Clemens is. What a psycho Teresa's mother is.

She'd had two cups of coffee by the time Jocelyn arrived, forty minutes late. Jocelyn was wearing a navy kerchief on her head. They nodded at each other. Jocelyn apologized for being late, then complimented Teresa on her perfume. Teresa tartly informed Jocelyn that she wasn't wearing perfume. Oh, well maybe it's coming from the kitchen, Jocelyn said.

"We have a real problem," Teresa began. "My boy is coming home in tears. He can't sleep. He's got terrible, well, diarrhea. Explosive. It sounds like a tuba lesson all through the house when he goes to the bathroom. He's having a breakdown is what it is. And it's because a lot of the kids at school are giving him a hard time. And your boy in particular is giving him a real hard time. I think you know what I am referring to."

"I do. I know exactly what you are referring to. Craig has told me all about it. About the inappropriate ..."

"Yes, the inappropriate name calling. The ridicule all day long. The bullying."

"Can I just stop you right there? Bullying is not what's going on in this situation. My son was defending himself against inappropriate leering and innuendo coming from your son. Very chilling stuff. Your son is a predator, at thirteen. That's my opinion. But I don't even like talking about it. In our family we like to have conversations that are optimistic, and goal-oriented, and that have, wherever possible, a foundation in scripture. So for Craig to raise such a horrible topic, you know that he has to be in great distress. I would go so far as to say that Craig has been violated. So yes, indeed, we do have a real problem. No child should be subjected to homosexual sexuality."

Teresa began to pant with anger. She didn't know what to say to such breathtaking idiocy. Joel was so shy around boys, so uncertain of his own mind and body, he couldn't even look his own father in the eye when he spoke. He was simply incapable of leering and innuendo, homosexual or otherwise.

"This is all what Craig told you?"

"Yes."

"And you believed him?"

"Of course. We don't lie to each other in the Walsh family. No one has ever lied to anyone in our family. I don't know how you go about things, in yours."

"You know how we go about things? If one of us is getting

picked on for no good goddamn reason, the rest of us step in. And I am telling you to tell your son to keep his fucking mouth shut and be respectful."

"And I am telling *you* to tell *your* son to stop trying to — indoctrinate my son. There is a reason why, past a certain point, the man should grab the reins in raising a boy into adulthood. If the woman doesn't give up the reins to the man, with boys, if the woman is pushy, well," Jocelyn said, gesturing at Teresa, "you see the end result. Joel is a case in point. Effeminacy and effeminate leering. A level of sexual maturity that is just frightening. You have a very sick child."

"My son is not sick."

"You've been warned."

"You have been warned, fuckface!"

Mrs. Clemens waded her way back to Teresa's table. By the time she got there Jocelyn had zipped up her parka and had purse in hand. Mrs. Clemens asked if she could be of any help. Jocelyn said she was leaving, and left. And Mrs. Clemens sat with Teresa for a few minutes, got her a third cup of coffee, and gave her the loveliest old lady hug when Teresa had steadied herself enough to stand.

In the years since this exchange they've had a few run-ins. They were both at the David Clayton-Thomas concert at the waterfront in '96. Jocelyn was several rows ahead of Teresa and Hugh; Teresa whipped a gummy bear at Jocelyn's head during "Spinning Wheel," but it hit the man beside her instead. When he looked back at Teresa she quickly looked at Hugh. And then there was the time Teresa went into the bookstore Jocelyn runs, Scott Books, to buy a murder mystery — *One for the Money*, by Janet Evanovich — and Jocelyn was behind the counter and offered a judgmental "huh" at the book, as if it were too trashy for her to ever consider reading, and Teresa wanted to choke Jocelyn to death but didn't.

And then there was the biggie, Joel's last year in high school, when Teresa was driving down Second Street and spotted Jocelyn power walking. Teresa drove up onto the sidewalk and spat in Jocelyn's hair. The cops were called over that one, and they came to the house, but in the end it was just Jocelyn's word against Teresa's.

Teresa had no way of protecting Joel. She had no support. As close as she was with her son, she remained vague on the extent of her machinations to get justice for him. Who would it serve for him to know that his mother went ape-shit on Jocelyn Walsh every time she saw her? Joel was gentle and reflective; he would've been ashamed of her — not just mortified like with the power walking but truly ashamed — and Teresa couldn't cope with deep, silent disapproval from her beloved kid and closest friend.

So she tried to home-school him. For three days, they went through the motions, with various textbooks open between them. She can't remember what they talked about, except for one exchange about an assigned book, *The Story of My Life*, by Helen Keller:

"As great and courageous as she was," Teresa said, "there must have been times where all she wanted was a fucking beer and a cigarette."

"I doubt it," Joel said. "Your life is not every woman's life."

True, that. Her life is not every woman's life. Smart kid. Anyway, after three days they ended up just watching the soaps. Eventually, Joel demanded that he go back to school. There was an easy out for Teresa, were she another kind of mother: with Joel insisting on an education, she could've said she'd tried her best, she was washing her hands of it, if that was his decision he'd have to live with the consequences with no further hand-holding from her. But she could never do that; she would always hold her son's hand.

Joel was never threatened with violence, so he toughed it out, grade by grade. He kept his head down and said nothing. Craig Walsh never grew past 5'2" and, demoralized by his lack of success with girls, his own band of buddies now all tall and tawny, he would only occasionally toss out an epithet in the hallway or by the buses. By grade twelve Craig was a pothead with a braided soul patch; he'd sometimes stare at Joel in the parking lot, almost wistfully, almost as though taunting Joel was a bright, innocent thing from back when Craig still had hope. That's how Joel described the latter-day Craig to his mother, at least. Teresa didn't want to hear it. In her experience people did not change their basic nature, no matter what profound experiences a person might have. Her mother weathered the deaths of her husband and son and, while there may be a slight hitch now in Hazel's speech before she launches into her trademark contempt and paranoia, she's as horrible at heart as she ever was. She didn't care that Craig had grown into a midget burnout with lost-looking eyes. Once a monster, always a monster.

Then Joel left for Toronto. She and Hugh saw him off at the Winnipeg airport. She hugged him hard, as though he was about to be executed. She was so fraught she accidentally told him she loved him in the third person: "She loves you!" "Yeah, yeah, yeah," Joel said back, with perfect timing. How did he get timing like that, like a comedian's? Was it because she let him watch *Saturday Night Live* when he was only nine?

And where did her boy's departure leave Teresa? Sure, she was proud as hell that her son was off to university; Dallas, her eldest, joined the OPP, also an achievement, but it wasn't university, it wasn't something that required intelligence — *intellect*, she should say. She made every attempt to get on with her life — new haircut, bowling, plans for the flower beds next year that involved something other than red and white petunias — but without Joel, as a cause and a culprit, Teresa still felt herself floundering. Now, with Joel gone, when Teresa saw Jocelyn Walsh across the street in town, she couldn't muster the same disgust anymore; at most, Jocelyn struck Teresa as simply some snooty lady who maybe once failed to hold the elevator door, who took the last parking spot. That middling level of disgust. Teresa lost her get-up-and-go.

There was one winter morning when Teresa, crazed from two pots of coffee, came upon the idea of starting up a Kenora chapter of Parents Whose Kids Turned Gay But That's Okay or whatever it's called; Joel had told her about it a while back. She knew for sure that Merle Dupuis's middle-aged daughter was a lesbian, at least until she fell headfirst working construction and went retarded, but that wouldn't affect your sexual tastes, she didn't think. And, of course, there was the museum curator, Donald Tait, with his greasy ponytail and haughty bearing — if his mom was still alive, it was only barely; Ena was in her nineties, still lucid, but not the sort you'd want on board for a support group, with her gruff talk of old-world self-reliance, living off a single cob of corn one bleak week in 1936. That wasn't the best pool of people to pick from. She went through all of Joel's yearbooks, scanning for girls who looked tough and practical, boys who looked fussy.

She'd been hacking and wheezing, but chalked it all up to the anxious chain smoking that helped her cope with empty nest syndrome. Same with the mild chest pain: what bereft woman wouldn't have a bit of chest pain? One morning in March, still in her nightgown, she was seized by a coughing fit in the kitchen; later, in the bathroom, she saw in the mirror that the front of her white nightie was blood-spattered. That was a real jolt. She called Hugh at work. She never called Hugh at work, so he came home within the hour. She met him at the door. She grabbed his wrist. "You got blood on your nightgown," he said casually, like she'd made a mess chopping the head off a chicken.

The doctor told her she was jaundiced. "How come you never told me I was jaundiced," she asked Hugh, smacking his arm. "I don't know," he said. "I don't look at ya every day."

Tests in Winnipeg revealed that Teresa had mesothelioma, "among the most frustrating cancers," the oncologist said, in such a way that Teresa almost felt compelled to apologize for having a frustrating cancer. It would figure, she said to her stunned husband as they left the hospital, I would have to come down with the shittiest cancer possible, just when I was going to start bowling again.

"Let's just wait and see," is what Hugh kept saying in a slowed-down voice.

"Wait and see what? See how fast I can die? There's nothing 'wait and see' about it."

Now, halfway through her sixth chemo treatment, here comes Jocelyn Walsh, coming up, pitty pat, in ballerina flats, to Teresa, who is hooked up and captive in a battered La-Z-Boy. Jocelyn is smiling a crinkly, sympathetic smile.

"I heard about your condition," Jocelyn says, moving to put her hand on Teresa's shoulder, then thinking better of it. "We've been through so much, haven't we? I've learned a lot from this experience, though. Have you?"

"Oh, yeah, sure."

"I've learned to be more emotionally forthcoming. I tell my husband and children that I love them — oh gosh — maybe ten times a day now. I must be so annoying. I can't help it, they're all so wonderful and lovable. And you know what? I'm lovable, too! What about you? What have you learned?"

Teresa looks hard at Jocelyn. Mean retorts flit through her head then fall like dead birds. What's the point. Jocelyn lives, Teresa dies. Game over.

"I've learned that I'm going to die. I've learned that life is very cruel. I've learned that nasty people get to keep their hair."

"Teresa. Your anger. Your anger is the cause of your hardship, have you ever thought of that? Have you ever considered that your anger is what's killing you? That maybe — forgive me — this is God's way of clearing the way for your husband and your sons, so that they might have a chance at real happiness? I don't know. I'm free-associating here, if you know what I mean. Don't mind me. Take good care."

Teresa is vibrating. This won't do, this will not do. Jocelyn cannot say such things and get away, unpunished. Addled and weak as she is, Teresa must think of a way of destroying Jocelyn's loving, lovable life.

As the tiny nurse sings along to Lisa Stansfield on the radio, Teresa ponders her strong suits. What is she known for? Apart from raising nice kids and cost-cutting impressively through constant use of coupons and rebates, what has she done especially well, in her life?

It comes to her, just at the start of the second chorus of "All Around the World": in her life, Teresa has been especially successful at being a good-time girl. Men — many men — have told her that she made them feel good. She has wooed all kinds of guys: boozy, philandering guys, but also shy guys, nerdy guys, guys whose lives revolved around attic CB radio chatter, around stamp collecting, around church. Hair or no hair, she is almost certain that she has one last boozy, sloppy seduction in her. And if she doesn't, she can still make a formidable mess. But she's pretty sure she can still seduce; like the CB radio guy said to her in his attic, it's not so much her looks as how she looks at you. "Let's just wait and see," she whispers to herself, finally.

13

HIS MOTHER LOOKS BAD. SHE is jaundiced and thin, in her hideous red wig. Her handsome face is now lopsided, almost like she's had a stroke. One eye and brow are markedly higher than the other, so that she appears at once exhausted and intensely curious.

They should be able to cry together, Joel and Teresa, chummy and candid as they have always been with each other. But he cannot cry; his mouth stretches into an inane air hostess smile, his eyes go glassy and unblinking, like a doll's. He can't control it. And his mother responds in kind: she beams and throws her arms open showily, bending slightly into a hammy duck walk as she moves in for a hug. Only his father's face betrays sadness. His face is not so much expressionless, more like it has switched itself off, to save power until the next crisis arises. Smart of him. He's not too bright about a lot — he's often been defiantly unbright — but he has always known what is best, or at least most preservative, for himself and, here and there, for his family.

"How long was the bus ride?" his mother asks, hanging on his arm. "You must be exhausted. You look a bit fat in the face. You've probably been going to Taco Bell every day. You know, there's nothing wrong with soup. When we get home we'll give you some of that pork soup that Grandma Sal made and then you'll go straight to bed."

They settle into the car, and Teresa starts in with recent town gossip, recent town funerals. With her yellow face and the fringe of her head scarf flicking about in the icy wind she is spectral, bony fingers aflutter, an old raggedy-winged moth darting at any available light. Joel cannot begin to envision what is to come. He has some idea, naturally, but he can't imagine how Teresa, specifically, will contend with this sickness: if she'll remain her nerveless self or turn into a wistful, wan lump.

They drive past Tilly Lake, snow-covered but for plentiful patches cleared away for skating. Joel thinks of the three kids who fell through the ice during his childhood: Brendan, the preteen skid obsessed with Sammy Hagar-era Van Halen, drowned and not found for weeks; little Bev, from the trailer park, who fell through in a pink parka overtop a tutu, and whose death so undid her mother that she forgot how to speak; and Mark, a kindergarten friend, who fell through and was quickly fished out but was, thereafter, peevishly anxious where once he was gregarious. At last check Mark was a virgin, lived in his mother's basement, and did clerical work at the jail.

"This is good, then, eh?" Hugh says, slowing into an early yellow light. "You and your mom can keep each other company while I'm at work. I know you two can gab the day away, no problem."

"Yeah," says Joel.

"Yeah, but no," Teresa says pointedly. "I've got things I've got to do. I don't want anybody in my hair all the time. Jolie, you know Mom is glad to have you, but I want you to get a little job or something while you're here. It'll be good training wheels for when you go back to Thunder Bay — or Toronto, I should say. 'Kay?"

"Sure, yeah. Fun."

"It was in the paper that the museum — you know that Donald Tait is a queer, or a gay, I should say — they're looking for someone to stand around, sounds like. That would be ideal, I think."

At home they eat pork soup and crusty buns. Teresa makes a big show of enjoying her food — "everything is just so flavour-ful!" — as if to reassure Joel that she still has life left in her.

"So what's your game plan now that you've dropped out of university?" Hugh asks, looking at his soup.

"I'm not sure. It's a transitional time. I'm trying to figure things out and not be too hard on myself."

"So you're gonna go on welfare."

Teresa drops her spoon. "Jesus God, can we not have a nice reunion dinner for a half an hour without all the bitching?"

"Absolutely. Absolutely. Just trying to take an interest."

Teresa is about to launch in, acidly, but she looks at Joel and lets it rest. Joel feels for his father. Hugh is a kind man, given, when the coast is clear, to lovely gusts of childish awe: once, leaning against the car at Dairy Queen with Joel and Dallas on either side, Hugh saw a goose fly past; "there goes a goose!" he exclaimed, waving at the back of the bird with his ice cream cone.

His already plucky wife gained some tooth in motherhood; she grew brassy and bossy, her girlishness fell away altogether—what was he to do with this new, turbulent, cackling shrew? It has really only been his propensity for awe that has kept him in this marriage. Because Teresa is confounding, mean, relentless … In the main, for better or worse, even now, awesome.

"Have you gone ice fishing yet, Dad?"

"No."

"When's Dallas coming down?"

"Well, he's got that double murder to deal with in Thunder Bay. He's working eighteen-hour days. I sure as hell couldn't do it."

"And let's not forget that goofy girlfriend of his," Teresa chimes in. "He says she jogs two, three hours a day, even now. That can't be good for the fetus. You watch — she's gonna give birth to a milkshake."

Even missing a member, the family always divides into teams. Teresa and Joel versus Hugh and Dallas. Teresa and Joel would watch *Knots Landing* upstairs while Hugh and Dallas played ping pong and Donkey Kong in the rec room. There wasn't any enmity between the teams; it was simply a prudent way for dissimilar people to share a small house. Joel's brother is an oaf, with his inexplicable red hair and blurry maple leaf tattoo. He once threw Joel off a short cliff at Rushing River when the family went camping, August of '86.

"I hope he can make it," Joel says. "I haven't even met Shary yet."

"Oh, she's something, all right. Real nervous. Walk, walk, walk, talk, talk, talk. We met up with them at Polo Park Mall in the fall. You shoulda seen her run up the escalator stairs with her stick legs, flap, flap, flap, just like Irene Ryan in *The Beverly Hillbillies*. But she's a nice girl, at the end of the day."

Joel's face burns from exhaustion; one of his eyelids has started to twitch. He gives his mother a squeeze and goes to his room in the attic.

Everything is as he left it. His pillow, the thinnest, smallest pillow that has ever been. His water-stained Suzanne Vega poster. He takes off his stained, stinky track suit. Presses his face to the cold window. That fat rural silence, so deep that he once needed to hum against it, thrum a finger on the sill, is here still, worse than ever, if possible. The city has reduced his immunity to it. He cracks the window and listens for the smallest sound, a little girl five doors down lazily playing a triangle, anything. Nothing. He goes to the basement, hauls up an old, angry, iron fan. It's good white noise. He sets it up on the night table and falls instantly asleep.

It's noon when he awakes. His mother's not in the house. She can't be that far gone if she's still such a busybody. On the kitchen table is a note: *Don't forget to call about the museum job — 468-5110 better yet just go there 98 Park Street, don't know when I'll be home xoxo mom.* Why is she so insistent on this stupid museum job? She never used to care whether he had a job before. He used to pass whole summers just watching her chain smoke on the patio.

He wants to make his mother happy; despite a long-standing fear of Donald Tait, he'll go to the museum to see about the "standing around" job. It's a fifteen minute walk.

When Joel arrives, Donald Tait is in the lobby on the floor, rooting through a cardboard box and smiling to himself. His hair is much longer than it once was and is pulled into a ponytail. Joel says hello. Donald startles. Styrofoam packing peanuts go flying.

"Oh! My heart! Give an old man some prior warning!"

Joel apologizes. Donald Tait is probably sixty, but apart from a slightly slackened jawline he looks like a man twenty years younger, well-rested and ruddy. It occurs to Joel that he has never actually spoken to Donald Tait, nor has he even looked him in the eye before.

"Sorry to bother. I'm here about the job in the paper. I can come back if you want."

"You're the first one to respond who isn't eighty. I need a real pack mule, not some dotty fossil. Come and see my buttons!"

Joel is almost certain that he has heard a version of this line before, but Donald Tait's eager, wholesome expression tells him that these "buttons" are, in this case, well and truly buttons.

He edges up to the cardboard box. Donald reaches in and offers up a couple of cellophaned, antique opal buttons, mounted on bits of bristol board. They are quite pretty, the buttons, not run-of-the-mill. Clearly they've been handpicked after much deliberation. Joel finds that he is honestly interested in the buttons; he instantly understands Donald's enthusiasm for them, although he isn't sure why he understands.

"I've been picking through people's buttons for fifteen years. My mother gave me this box of buttons, and as I sorted through them — this one dirty brass, that one cut glass, another some crap plastic one off of a Woolworth shirt — I became very emotional. It was a mystic moment. My mother also gave me a box of forsaken dentures around the same time, but the dentures didn't resonate in the same way as the buttons."

"Huh. Wow."

Joel is still honestly interested, but a part of him is also concerned that Donald Tait might be one of those musty, benignly insane people who won't stop talking about something arcane and then starts screaming or falls asleep suddenly.

"You must think I'm mad."

"Not at all! I get the fascination, totally. I can't wait to see what you're going to do with them."

"Neither can I, because I have no idea what I'm going to do with them. I can't just do a button festival, can I? So few people come to the museum as it is, even in the summer. God, even when we snagged Princess Grace's hats in '88, we had to throw in free hot dogs out front. I love my town, but it's not exactly a sophisticated city. It's not exactly Berlin."

"Yeah. No."

"Regardless, we'll figure something out. I'm Donald, what's your name?"

"Joel."

"Joel what?"

"Price. I've been considering taking a stage name, though."

"Price ... Is your mother Teresa Price?"

"Yes."

"I quite like her. So plucky. She sold me my LeBaron a few years ago. Kept telling me how sexy I looked in it. I didn't believe her for a minute, but I still bought the car. I guess that's good salesmanship. So! See you tomorrow?"

Joel nods. He forces a smile, but Donald Tait has already gone back to his buttons.

TERESA IS HOME when Joel returns. He tells her the good news; "good, good, yes, yes," Teresa says all distracted and blasé, as if she's trying to get off the phone with her monologist mother, Hazel. When Joel asks Teresa where she was earlier, she is equally dismissive. "Errands, boring, boring errands," she says. "It's so great to have you home. Let's watch *Out of Africa*."

When *Out of Africa* is over they sit and listen to the tape rewind. He asks her how she's feeling. She says she's feeling like she doesn't want to talk all the time about how she's feeling.

"But guess what Shary's last name is."

"Who's Shary — Oh, right. I don't know. What is her last name?"

"It's hyphenated; her parents had her out of wedlock. 'Spaz-Monk.'"

"No way!"

"I'm telling you. Isn't that the best? 'Shary Spaz-Monk.' I told

Dallas to marry the poor thing, if only to get rid of that awful name."

His mother's endless, only slightly cruel curiosity about life's small phenomena: this was something he took for granted until he moved to the city. Not everyone takes an interest like his mother does; many people prefer to overlook the little curios of a given day.

It's night now, and Joel is in bed flipping through an old *Rolling Stone*. The house is hot; the fan by the bed whips out a small, hot wind. That was the trade-off of Joel's special, attic room: it's his own private space, but it's hot as fuck in summer.

He hears a dog bark once. He is back home, in the bush, once again. He could have a brain hemorrhage, or get snuffed out by some psycho trucker passing through, and nobody apart from his immediate family would know or care. His burgeoning romance with Edmund, his art — well, his *process* at the very least, his obvious, formidable process that could only lead to art, or something — all of that would be buried in the bush. This thought, along with an odd, looping mental picture of Donald Tait's face made into a button, with buttonhole punctures in his drawn cheeks, brings Joel's breath faster and faster; his heart hammers, he bolts out of bed, all sweaty now, dancing about in full frightened flight.

He calls Edmund, who answers on the first ring.

"It's Joel. I'm back in northern Ontario. I know you're a night owl so I thought it would be okay to call you. Is it a bad time?"

"Umm. No. Well, I am expecting a call, but I have call waiting, so it's fine. How are you?"

"I'm feeling somewhat anxious. I don't know why. I really needed to hear someone's voice. To hear your voice. I'm still savouring our night together. It so blew me away. I have this buzzing sensation in my head and I'm afraid I'm about to have a brain hemorrhage. How are you? You sound much more perky."

"I am more perky. I feel great. I feel like I've turned a corner."

Someone on Edmund's end yelps out the chorus to "That's What Friends Are For."

"You have company. You should've mentioned."

"I have a friend staying with me. He's very musical."

Joel's chest tightens. He pictures Edmund on the phone in bed, being spooned by his perfect, new lover. Was it too much to expect fidelity from Edmund after one date? Yes, probably. Joel is devastated just the same.

"I'll let you go," says Joel, "so you can resume lovemaking with your friend."

"Oh, you. Too funny. Yeah. Why don't you give me your phone number, and I'll give you a ring when I'm free."

"That's okay. I'll be okay without your pity call."

Edmund laughs distractedly. "You're too funny. So we'll talk to you really soon, then."

"Maybe. If I'm still alive."

Edmund hangs up. Joel hurls himself onto his bed. He is without a lifeline now. He longs for eternal sleep. But first he eats three bowls of Honey Nut Cheerios and then beats off, to the thought of hands again. Cruel, faithless, roving hands.

14

THEY'VE BEEN AWAKE FOR THREE days, Edmund and Binny.
Binny came back with the crystal, but he wouldn't smoke any
until Edmund agreed to try it. Edmund hadn't heard a lot about
crystal meth, but the way Binny touted it — "crystal turns my ass
into the Cookie Monster! So hungry! Double penetration, fists
right up to the shoulder, fuckin' *whatever*! More! More! More!
Andrea True realness!" — he would've been a fool not to give
it a go. And, he figured, if he didn't like it, the high would pass
quickly, like with coke. This is what he figured, three days ago,
before he smoked crystal.

Happily, he liked it! It was life changing, a glimpse of a fun,
fleecy-faced God at work, apparent in the underside of every
breath, every eyelash, every slat in the closed blinds in every
room of his cozy, sexy house! Instantly Edmund was lucid and
keen as he hadn't been in years, if ever; as Binny spoke at length
about his stable of divas, how each one represents different
aspects of his personality — Diva Tina is Binny's strength and

resilience, Diva Foxy his brazen sexuality, while Diva Whitney is all about "P 'n' P" — which, in Binny parlance, stands not for the customary "Party and Play" but "Pretty Nippy Part-tays." Edmund found himself rapt, hanging on every word as though he were at the foot of the Buddha.

A deep, dense, unceasing fog of sex enveloped the both of them. Made impotent by the meth, they zipped over to Church Street to buy a huge double-ended dildo. Together they lay on Edmund's increasingly greasy bed, feeding the thick thing into themselves and talking, talking, talking.

Binny wept briefly and involuntarily as he described childhood hurts — neglect and solitude in various foster homes, rape, something about a burning curling iron pressed to his forearm. Edmund pushed, but he wouldn't say more. Edmund was thrilled by this sudden trust, this accidental closeness; he could tell it wasn't shtick or hustler hard-sell — he'd glean that falsity instantly. No, this was real and so heady that Edmund has had to break periodically and catch his breath in the walk-in closet. Binny's confessions aren't all moony and speculative like with the boy from the phone line; Binny is only relaying the grimy facts of his hard life, no embroidery.

Edmund was moved to share some of his own childhood pain, baroque shit that took Dean years to extract from him: he found his morbidly obese father dead on the toilet when he was eight, after which his already delicate mother all but surrendered Edmund to their housekeeper, a German woman who hauled Edmund to church with her daily and often made him pray for the soul of "that poor man who only try to help make

things nice" in World War II. Binny immediately put his head-
phones on, and sang along with the CD until he saw that
Edmund's mouth had stopped moving. It seems that Binny is
only able to cope with his own tragic narrative at the moment.
Edmund could listen to Binny talk forever: his jerky cadence,
that hectic head of his, always seeking a way to tie the present
moment to his inner trove of high-heeled celebrity advocates.
Who cares if it's all the product of speed and mental illness.
It's rare that you find someone you don't want to stop
talking.

Edmund has come upon a wonderful, rushing relationship,
just when his life had turned to rot. He has only good things
to say about Binny and crystal meth. The palpitations and
sporadic anxiety are fair trade for the euphoria and the sexual
glamour.

He's pacing the study as he muses on the magic of meth.
Then he notices that Binny is gone. He goes downstairs. Still
no Binny. He hears a whipping sound, like clothesline laundry
on a windy day. He finds Binny in the basement; he's pretending
to be a toreador, with a damp, pink bath towel for a cape. When
he sees Edmund he stops.

"Eddie, I've been waiting and waiting and waiting," he says.
"Who were you talking to on the phone?"

Edmund waves a dismissive hand. "Some kid I met off a
phone line. He's such a sad case. I feel bad for him but I just
can't take responsibility for his —"

"Whatever. I don't want to talk about it. As long as she knows
that you're MY man, 'cuz this time I know it's for real, Diva

Donna, God made AIDS because he thinks homosexuals are gross realness. Does he know that? Did you, how you say, *establish* that with him?"

"Yes, oh, definitely. Everyone knows that you're my love interest. Or he does, anyway. I don't think anyone else knows, because we haven't really left the house yet."

"Right on party cool. Now, I have something very important and private that I need to share with you. Are you ready?"

"Yes. No. Wait. I'm feeling a bit barfy. Fucking Crixivan."

"What is that? Are you hiding some party favours from your girl?"

"Huh? No. It's my meds." And then, without thinking: "What meds are you taking?"

"You mean, like, pills, from, like, a doctor? I don't go to the doctor. Last doctor I saw was when my ex pushed me off the roof of Spa on Maitland and I broke all my face. Year ago."

Edmund nods. No one is monitoring this lovely boy. He could have full-blown AIDS. Edmund will have him checked out by his own doctor, get him all set up, pay for his meds. He would be happy to do that for Binny. Grateful, even.

"We'll get you all sorted out," Edmund says. "Once we get you on anti-virals you'll feel so much better."

"I don't want to go on anti-virals. I feel fine the way I am."

"But you might have AIDS. You might have full-blown AIDS."

"So? If I do, I don't want to know about it."

"But you should live."

"I am living. I don't want to start taking pills and shit, and have one of those fucking plastic pill planner things, and go to the grocery store. That's not me. You should know that by now."

"But what about —"

"Fuck, shut up about it! It's so boring. She wants to lead the glamorous life, Diva Sheila, Prince protégé realness. Okay?"

"Okay. I'm sorry. It's just that I really like you and want you to be around a long time so I can get to know you better."

"You can get to know me better right now." Binny finds a metal folding chair and scrapes it across the concrete to the centre of the basement. He sets the chair up and sits on it, crossing his legs demurely. He holds his head at an angle, then contorts his face into a silent scream, less terrified than emphatic. He says nothing.

"I'm not sure I understand," Edmund says.

"I'm showing you myself, my dream self that can never be," Binny says, dropping, then resuming the scream face.

"Thank you."

"Oh my God, what's your problem? I'm sitting on a bare chair, singing my heart out."

"So you want to be a professional singer?"

"I want to be a female professional singer, and songwriter, like, a Canadian treasure like Diva Buffy Sainte-Marie, I breast-fed my baby on *Sesame Street* realness."

Edmund wants desperately to understand Binny, at exactly the slant Binny intends, but it's almost impossible. "So you are a transgender woman who wants to be a famous Canadian folksinger."

"I am *so* not a tranny."

"I'm sorry, Binny. I'm a dumb guy. I want to know what you

mean, I really do. Could you just spell it out for me, like you would for a moron?"

Binny pauses and gathers himself. This is the most meditative Edmund's seen him.

"Okay. I want to be a famous singer-songwriter, but only if I could be a famous *female* singer-songwriter. A born-female singer-songwriter. I'm not a tranny, or a drag queen. I enjoy having boy parts. I only want to be a famous female singer-songwriter, and I only want to be female when I sing. So it's, like, a no-win situation. It's sad. I was dealt shitty cards by the god of war or whatever."

Edmund doesn't really know a lot about gender issues; he's only hung out with white gay men, whose issues mostly revolved around "learning to feel" and "daring to love again after the death of a dog." There was the time he met up with a guy off one of the phone lines who, when Edmund got to his place, was wearing lingerie, full makeup and a wig, and bore an uncanny resemblance to Maureen Stapleton. The guy got angry when Edmund declined: "I told you I'd be *dressed* when you got here," the guy huffed. "I thought you meant leather," Edmund replied. That guy was simply a cross-dresser, though; this is the first time that someone Edmund is deeply in love with has declared himself as ... a situational trans woman.

"It's totally fine with me if you want to identify as a woman."

Binny snorts with disgust. "I don't want to! Do not make me smash your face in! Fuck. I'll take it from the top. I want to be —"

Doorbell! Someone's at the door! Who could it be? The doorbell never rings! Edmund, spooked, looks at Binny; Binny lets out a worried whinny and runs behind an old sofa propped up on its side.

"Who is that?" Edmund whispers.

"How the fuck should I know? It's your fucking house. Oh my God — did you call the AIDS doctor? I told you I didn't want no AIDS pills!"

"When could I have called the AIDS doctor? We've been together this whole time. Could it be the drug dealer? Did you give the drug dealer my address?"

"Fuck you! I told you I didn't give him your address! Thanks for trusting me!"

"Okay," Edmund says, attempting a deep breath. "I'll go see."

"I'm not here! I'm so not here!"

Edmund hugs the wall as he heads up the stairs; he takes a quick peek into the foyer, like a cop in a shoot-out. Finally, on the fourth ding of the doorbell, he makes it to the peephole. Lila.

As he opens the door he sees she holds a deep dish, still steaming. "I'm pathetic! I'm so bored at home, I couldn't stand it. I made you that meatloaf with bacon that I made you that one time."

"You sweet thing!" he says, not moving.

"Is it a bad time? Is it gay-sexy time? I should've called."

"No! It's not a bad time! I'm just puttering!" He should let her in. He lets her in. They go into the kitchen. She puts the meatloaf on the counter.

"It smells extraordinary! I'm so excited to sample it!"

She studies him. "Eddie, are you okay? You seem really anxious."

"I'm great! I'm great. I drank too much coffee. Things are going really well. How are you?"

"Oh, fine. Not really. I'm so precarious emotionally these days. Marci ... I mean, she's great, but sometimes, the way she keeps talking about the baby — how it's our top priority, the only thing that matters is the baby — sometimes I feel like I'm just an incubator to her, like ... like that woman who had those babies for Michael Jackson. See, now I'm going to start bawling."

Edmund hugs her, and she bawls into his shirt. "You're not an incubator, sweetheart."

"I know, I'm just ... Are you sure you're okay? Your heart is racing."

"Hellooo!" says Binny, behind them. Edmund whips around.

"Binny! Don't creep up like that!"

"I did not *creep up*. Fuck you."

"Who is this person," Lila asks Edmund. Binny slides his way into their open embrace; he pulls at Lila's hand to shake it.

"I'm super rude! My name is Bernard. I'm so very pleased to make your acquaintance." He does a campy curtsey.

"Hi. Lila."

"Hi, Lila. I love your hair. It's very Diva Suzanne, my name is Luka realness."

"Thanks. Eddie, could you help me with something in the bathroom?"

"Ooh, I know what that means!" Binny hoots. "I'll be right here."

In the half-bath off the kitchen Lila grabs hard at Edmund's arm. "I know this is really classist of me," she whispers, "but that person looks really rough. I don't feel safe in his presence."

"He's fine. He's a friend. We're having a really nice time."

"Are you? Are you — doing, you know, hard drugs together?"

"No! My God. Well, he might be, but I'm certainly not."

"Are you sure? Because you also seem somewhat altered."

"No! Well, he may have — I hope he didn't slip me something."

"I think we should call the police."

"No! He's really a very — he's not an immediate threat. I can handle it, definitely. I am going to handle it very shortly." He opens the bathroom door and tugs at her.

"Was that fun?" Binny asks. Edmund nods vigorously. He offers Lila some of her own meatloaf; she says she's nauseous and should get home before Marci does.

"It was so fantastically wonderful to meet you, Lila-Suzanne," Binny beams as she leaves. Lila's eyes narrow. She hunches into his face.

"I want you to know — I am aware of you. And I will be checking in. Should anything ... transpire, *you are being watched*."

"What do you mean? What does she mean, E? What did you say to her? Did you tell her that I'm some sort of — fuckin' — psycho freak?"

Lila's and Binny's lower lips tremble in tandem. Edmund churns. This is all so unnecessary. And now the neighbours can see.

"Everyone is great," Edmund says. "Lila is a dear old friend who is overprotective. And Binny is a dear new friend who is not psycho, who is so dynamic and not a threat at all. Okay, so you head on home now, Lila. We'll talk to you real soon."

"I'm just trying to be a good friend," Lila insists as she shuffles off the porch.

"You don't even know about friendship, ya fucking bitch!" Binny yells as Edmund closes the door.

Binny is shivering violently. His teeth chatter. Edmund hasn't seen him like this. He wants to wrap his arms around Binny, but he's afraid.

"Did you say mean things about me to her?"

"No. Binny. No. I'm so sorry. She's not herself. She's pregnant."

"I'm not a bad person, you know. I try not to hurt people. Just because I don't have very much money, or just because I am sometimes an escort and I party — I say 'please' and 'thank you'! I'm not mean in my heart."

Binny. Trembling bit of tinsel in a furious storm! Edmund will do anything for this lovely bit of tinsel.

"My beautiful boy," Edmund says, cupping Binny's face in his hands. "I know you're not mean in your heart. You're gorgeous in your heart."

Binny settles a little. "Only in my heart?"

Edmund can't help it, he must draw himself close to the boy and nuzzle him, nose-to-nose. "You're beautiful all over. You are. Let's smoke some more."

So begins Edmund's new love affair. They go to the house where Bernard has been staying, an almost-empty two storey place owned by a tall, gaunt piano lounge performer best known as Toronto's Peter Allen, because he only plays Peter Allen songs. Toronto's Peter Allen leans against the fake fireplace in his bathrobe, smoking, as Binny and Edmund stuff clothes and CDs into garbage bags. Peter Allen clucks his tongue and tosses his lank bangs; he attempts contempt in his commentary but can only muster a listless, almost automated play-by-play: "That's right, you put your stuff in garbage bags. That's right, you carry your garbage bags out to the car ..."

Now that Binny has officially moved in, he is much more relaxed, given to smiling, lolling, making the bed as best he knows how. Tenderness with the new Binny is comprised of spooning, and rolling around while spooning, both of them wired as hell but earnestly attempting tranquility. At these times Edmund believes that he has never known such shattering intimacy. Binny and circumstance and the healing properties of meth have combined to permit Edmund a glimpse into a hallowed world known only to ecstatic nuns. He knows it sounds overblown, and he isn't a hyperbolic person, but even as Dean lay dying in his arms he still felt a remove; despair and empathy, yes, but also a sense of procession and duty not commensurate with the intense yet sidelong love he felt for Dean. This thing with Binny is ... big.

At some point Binny runs to the 7-Eleven for more Diet Coke. Edmund finds himself, pen-in-hand, making a list.

1. *Binny — what's he all about, at the end of the day*
2. *How can I set about helping him become a biological female pop star*
3. *Failing that ... how do I create the right environment for him to discover himself as a singer-songwriter in his own right*

4. *You must leave no stone unturned! He is an emissary from a world of love*

5. *He keeps talking about realness because he is really real*

6. *What is the strategy? How will you make him happy? You must make him incredibly happy if you do not you will only know burning torment forever*

7. *REMEMBER TO CALL LILA!*

Binny returns, with his Diet Coke and one of the heavy, yellow glass tumblers that Dean got in Italy. Those tumblers are tucked away in a drawer in the dining room — has Binny been rooting through his house? Whatever, it's fine. He's allowed.

"I'm so glad you're back, you. What are we going to do today?"

"I don't know … party? And do, like, home things?"

"Sounds like a plan!"

15

THURSDAY, THE FIRST DAY OF her plot against Jocelyn Walsh, Teresa slathered on layer after layer of foundation until she looked less like a cadaver and more like an embalmed cadaver with makeup on. She found a pair of earrings she didn't know she owned, way at the bottom of her jewellery box: silver fish, caught on the hook that hooks through the earlobe. She briefly considered doing the big shave down there, or at the very least her legs and pits, but quickly decided that things wouldn't go that far that fast. She also waffled on the wig. Would the average man be more grossed out by an obvious wig or by an obviously bald head wrapped in a scarf? At least with the red wig he might perceive her as both sickly and cheap, rather than simply sickly.

Car keys in hand, she hesitated in the front hallway as she looked herself over in the mirror by the door. Was she delusional? What man could want her, the condition she's in? Didn't matter how good a flirt she was, nobody wants to fuck the terminal. And what grown-up woman — a wife and mother!

a composter! — makes it her dying wish to fuck up somebody's marriage because they said something mean? Why couldn't she rise above?

"Shut up," she said to herself. "Just keep going." Better to be a vengeful person who finishes what she starts than to be a radiant person who doesn't do anything.

She drove to the town hall. She'd never been there; it was surprisingly small, more like a town bungalow, one big main room encircled by tiny offices. At the entrance to the main room was a receptionist, on a call. She had a lovely, if slightly frantic phone manner: "Thank you so much for calling! Thank you so much for asking me that question! … I just hope my answer was helpful. Was it? Was it helpful?"

When the receptionist finished with the call, Teresa asked her who she'd need to speak to about a fireworks permit. She shimmied slightly in her seat and told Teresa how much she loved fireworks. So late in the year, though — was Teresa planning a winter carnival type thing? Yes, Teresa said. Exactly that. A winter carnival. The receptionist produced a thick stack of forms for her to fill out. Teresa quickly realized that the fireworks permit tactic was probably not the best strategy.

"Is my buddy Digger here?" Teresa asked musically. "The fireworks are for Jocelyn's surprise birthday party. We're planning a real big whoop-dee-do for her in my backyard. Why the hell not, eh? You're only sixty-three once." Whimsically tacking on twenty years to Jocelyn Walsh's age made Teresa's fake smile briefly real.

"Oh!" squeaked the girl. "That sounds so romantic. Mayor

Walsh and his wife have such a fairytale marriage. Mrs. Walsh always tells me my prince will be right around the corner if I would only get my lazy eye fixed. I've told her that there actually is no treatment for my eye condition, and she said she would pray that medical science will have a breakthrough so I can have my eye fixed and look good for a man. She's so nice."

"She is. So is Digger in his office? I'm just going to pop in."

"Mr. Walsh is currently not in the office," said the girl. "I'm not normally allowed to tell people where he is when he isn't in, but seeing as you're a family friend and this is such an exciting party idea —"

"Exactly, yes."

"He's down at the Kenwood, having his lunch."

"Of course, the Kenwood. I should've known that. Oh, the times we've all had at the Kenwood. Thanks so much."

"No problem. Can I just ask — is Mrs. Walsh really sixty-three? She looks so young."

"I know. It's a miracle, what they can do for the aging woman these days. She's had everything done. Her nose is made of shark cartilage. Her dentures are state-of-the-art."

The sweet, goony receptionist smiled warmly at Teresa as she turned to leave. The news that Jocelyn Walsh might wear dentures seemed to soothe the girl.

Digger Walsh was at the bar with a burger and fries, chewing and chatting with the bartender. Teresa paused inside the door to study him. He'd put on weight since Teresa last saw him; his stomach strained against his white dress shirt, and his wedding ring made cleavage in his chubby finger. He still had his appeal, though; his jaunty manner and basic charm made Teresa think of President Clinton, who could eat crackers in her bed anytime.

She'd practised this initial encounter over and over in the bathroom at home. Digger would be wary of her, given their history, and she would need to defuse things fast. She decided, in the bathroom, that tearful earnestness was the best way to go. Teresa had never been socially calculating like this; there was a time when such wily pretension would've made her nauseous. (How many girlfriends had she ditched in high school for exactly this kind of thing — one minute mooning over Cat Stevens' long lashes and perfect buns, the next acting the stupid ingénue to woo some dolt?) But she was not ashamed of herself. She was exhilarated. This would be a bit of play-acting, something fun.

She wove her way up to him. Put a pale hand upon his vast shoulder. He startled.

"Oh! Hey, Mrs. Price. I'm just having lunch here. I — I don't want any trouble."

She shook her head vigorously, as though she were innately incapable of trouble. The act of shaking her head made her unsteady, and she clutched the back of Digger's chair. She took a moment to contain the tremendous emotion she was faking.

"Mr. Walsh, I don't want to upset you in any way. I just saw you through the window and had to pop in. So much has happened to me in the last while. You probably know that I'm coping with serious illness."

"Yes, I am very sorry about that. You've had a rough go. But you look good. Your nice hair and all that."

"It's a wig. But it's a nice red, and God knows I'm nothing if not a naughty redhead. Still, I know the truth is I look awful, I do. I run out of steam easily. And it's also very challenging as a big-breasted woman, having to lug these gigantic things around when I already don't feel that strong to begin with."

Digger Walsh studied a French fry pierced by his fork. She was losing him. She had to stop with the leering breast talk. Digger Walsh, Digger Walsh, what did she know about him? He played drums. He seemed to always have a sunburn. His wife was a first class bitch. And he was a born-again Christian; he got baptized in the Lake of the Woods at the harbourfront, a couple years ago. She'd try that angle, the faith thing.

"Anyway. That's the least of it. It has been a struggle, definitely. But one day this warmth came over me, and I instantly knew that I was being penetrated by the Holy Spirit, and I loved it, it was great. It felt so good. I no longer wanted to kill myself. I only wanted to cultivate my friendship with Jesus. I bring all this up because I know that you're also good friends with Jesus. So I know that you can relate. I'm a new woman. I've accepted him as my personal Lord and Saviour. It's so exciting. I've never known such peace. I've forgiven all those who have trespassed against me. I'm sure you and your wife must yap away night and day about how amazing Jesus is. I know I sure can't shut up about it."

"Actually, Jocelyn hasn't yet accepted Christ into her heart, but I'm definitely working on it. She says that she has, but she doesn't worship with me. A believer can spot a non-believer in a heartbeat. I can spot a believer in a heartbeat, too, and I can tell that you have definitely been transformed by God's love. I am really happy for you, Mrs. Price. He saved my life, that's for sure. There's no reason why He can't save yours."

"You know what? I don't even care about that! If I croak, if I end up dead on a slab in six months, big deal. I've got Jesus. Ooh, and please call me Teresa."

The bartender looked uncomfortable, like he'd stumbled into an impromptu revival meeting, which, approximately, he had. Teresa smiled at him and asked for a glass of water.

"Where do you worship, Teresa?"

"Mostly in the basement at home. It can get kind of lonely, worshipping alone in the basement, but oh well. It's just that I've been hesitant to pick a place of worship. I'm afraid I'll pick the wrong one. I know that St. Alban's is kind of dodgy — the little inspirational messages they put on that front marquee are almost always about praying your way through drug addiction or overeating. I don't want to, y'know, sully my faith by going to a trashy church. It's so hard to know where to worship."

Digger put his last bite of burger down. A convert had turned to him for guidance, and he knew he was obliged to do his best to help.

"I go to Knox United," he said simply. "Reverend Griffin has a real simple, sincere way with a sermon. I always come away feeling refreshed, ready for the week ahead. I also go to Bible study there on Thursday nights, as well as AA meetings, naturally. You can't come to the AA meetings, but you are more than welcome to Sunday service and Bible study. I would be — yeah, sure, sure I would be — honoured to have you as my guest."

"Really? I would love that. Should I wear something formal?"

"You can wear anything, Teresa."

"Anything? Ooh! What about pasties and a G-string? Ha ha ha!"

He didn't laugh along. He didn't want her. She was no longer sexy, was only shrill and pathetic. She would need to abandon all her old tricks. Her only play was to pretend to love Jesus.

"I'm so looking forward to Sunday service. It's been so lonely, praying alone in the basement. What's today? Friday?"

"Thursday."

"Right. Sorry. It's the drugs. I don't mean *drugs* drugs, just morphine. I'm so happy. Jesus is so … Yes. I'll see you Sunday!"

She extended her hand to shake his. He went to shake, then took her stiffly in his arms. How nice, to be held by a man who wasn't Hugh for the first time in months. *There we go*, she thought he said as he held her, or possibly *here we are*; his mouth was muffled by her wig.

THEY GOT JOEL at the bus depot the next day. He looked tired and oily. His hair was a mess of shoots and whirls, and she could've sworn she saw a small cockroach dart about in it. Still she pressed his head to hers. He smelled faintly of urine. He whispered how happy he was to see her. They both inhaled sharply, in unison: their way to keep from weeping in public. Showing emotion in public, she always said, was something only crazy people did, or tourists.

Her instinct was to groom him with the palm of her hand, take him to task for smelling like pee, and then, once Hugh was out of earshot, tell him all about her campaign to ruin Jocelyn Walsh's life. Joel didn't know the lengths to which Teresa went to extract justice, or at least an apology, from Jocelyn Walsh on behalf of her monstrous middle son; he didn't know about the gummy bear incident or the attempted hit and run or any of the other, lesser confrontations. So were she to spill the beans now, it would sound to him like the mad tangent of a sick person, rather than the work of art that she means for it to be. She'd wait a while to tell him.

And she was tired. Even an extended hug could sap her now; her limbs were heavy and defiant as she walked back to the car. It was all she could do to toss her purse on the back seat. So be it; later there would be time for Joel, and the giddy stretches of chatter they both so enjoyed. And if there wasn't? Maybe Teresa had, in her vendetta, a more pressing maternal matter. Maybe Joel would better benefit from this last stand of hers, against pure evil in the form of Jocelyn Walsh, than from any ambling kitchen conversation about horrible perms, past and present; she could see him carefully carrying this under-standing of his mother-as-warrior for the rest of his life. He would share this story, The Time His Dead Mom Did a Bad Thing for a Good Reason, warmly and widely with friends, lovers, maybe even — it's possible, although incredibly unlikely — his own children. She could see this great story turning him into an adult at last, hardening and honing him, pointing him toward an honourable manhood.

She knew, in considering this, that she was only slightly full of shit. In fact, she felt herself straighten slightly in her seat at the thought of this parable-in-progress. She was not full of shit. She was having a vision. She had not had a vision before, but surely she could still know a vision when she saw one.

When they got home Joel had some cereal and went straight to bed. Hugh kept his shoes on and said he was going for a walk around the lake. Since when do you go for walks around the lake, she asked him. He didn't answer.

Hugh had been very quiet, more than he usually was. She twice walked in on him watching television with the sound off. He'd started spending a lot of time in the bathroom, also silently, ten or fifteen minutes there, several times a day. She thought it was quite witty of her to ask if he was having an affair with the sink. He said he was just taking his time, doing his thing. But Hugh didn't have a thing; he wasn't a reflective person. He was never one to *take a step back*. He was a sturdy, procedural person. That's why they'd got along, all these years.

But they used to shoot the shit, before, carp about expenses and their insurmountable line of credit. They used to worry aloud about the boys — well, about Joel, really. He would enumerate the many reasons why Joel would probably end up homeless, and she would agree, and then tack on a hopeful "still ... maybe ...," and Hugh would go silent, his version of solidarity. He wasn't an awful father.

They've always slept in separate beds, with Hugh's shift work, but he would tuck her in, or lie with her, in his work clothes, as she awoke or drifted off. Maybe once or twice a year, New Year's, Canada Day, they'd get hammered on the back deck and she'd give him a half-assed blow job or he'd beat off on her tits. It wasn't a great, soaring affair, the thing between them. They were chummy, though. They liked each other.

If he was going all sloppy on her, this late in the game, she wouldn't have it. She needed him to stay the way he'd always been. She didn't have time for her own feelings, let alone his. There would be no *processing* nor would there be any *holding each other through the storm*. There would be no *healing power of sensual massage*. There would be no *talking*, no *listening*. Like the other day — the newspaper, folded at the crossword, at Hugh's place at the kitchen table, with only "one down" done, which filled her with affection for his total lack of pretension, his inability to think to pretend that he knew more than he knew: that was a poignant moment. There would be none of those.

Sunday came, and Joel wanted to go to the marina restaurant for pancakes, like they used to years ago. Teresa would take the boys there after she'd been out all night Saturday; this wasn't a constant occurrence, by any means, but it happened often enough that she'd feel compelled, with her face flecked with mascara and her Jontue smelling less like gardenia and more like bug spray, to make it up to Joel and Dallas with a fun breakfast, and to let Hugh sleep as late as he wanted.

But now she could hardly keep anything down, and today was the day she was going to church with Digger Walsh. She didn't tell Joel about the Digger Walsh part; she simply explained that she'd been investigating her spiritual side since he'd been gone, and that an hour or so of church was worth a big vat of morphine in terms of true pain management. Joel laughed at this. The one time they'd gone to church for something other than a wedding or funeral was when Patsy Gallant gave a Christmas concert, and even then Teresa made them leave after twenty minutes, when it became clear that the whole thing was going to be in French and that Patsy would not be doing any of her disco hits, in any language. When Joel reminded Teresa of that debacle she cursed Patsy Gallant — after all these years Patsy's refusal to perform "From New York to L.A." and "Sugar Daddy" still rankled.

"This is something else altogether, though, Jolie. That was a concert. This is religion."

"But you don't like religion."

"I've never said that. I haven't liked the religion I've experienced up to now, but that was only because my sample was small. Now I've found a religion that really works for me. I've found God." (She regretted her inadvertently blank delivery of "I've found God"; the way she said it made God sound like a misplaced eyebrow pencil that had suddenly emerged from her purse.)

"That's great, Mom. Really. What is it about this church that speaks to you?"

"Oh, y'know, this and that. Everything, really."

"That's so vague. What's your favourite hymn these days?"

Smartypants Joel, always probing, needling, sniffing out deceit. It's an aspect of his personality that Teresa enjoyed and encouraged, as long as it wasn't aimed at her.

"My favourite hymn. That's a toughie. "Bohemian Rhapsody," maybe? Or "Amazing Grace."

He eyed her suspiciously. She went upstairs to change.

She put on the teal two-piece, skirt and blazer, the one she wore when Dallas graduated from the police academy. It was form-fitting then. Now she was lost in it; it looked like the hand-me-down of a giantess.

Before she left, she asked Joel how she looked. He said that her outfit was ill-fitting. Apart from that, she said. He said she looked great, apart from that.

"Why don't I come with you?" Joel asked. "You've made me all curious now."

"I'm thrilled that you're curious, really. But this is something I need to do on my own. It's me time."

Joel appeared hurt, which tore at her conscience, made her want to throw her housecoat back on and forget the whole thing.

"Can I get you something while I'm out?" she asked him. "A nice pie or something for dessert?"

"No. Go. Have fun or whatever."

DIGGER WALSH WAS waiting for her on the steps of Knox United when she pulled up in Hugh's old yellow half-ton. There was a man standing with Digger, a tall, broad black man she'd not seen before. And she would've remembered if she had; there were only a handful of non-white residents in town, not counting Cathy Meeker, who refuses to acknowledge that her father is black, allowing only that the Meekers are "a real tanning family." The man was smiling and beckoning her over. Digger was also beckoning, but a bit more hesitantly, not quite so shopping-mall-sample-girl as the black man.

"I made it!" Teresa exclaimed, slightly winded from the walk up the steps.

"Welcome aboard, nice lady! What's her name again?"

"Teresa. Price." Teresa and Digger said in spooky unison, same pause between first and last name and everything.

"Hi there, Teresa! Are you ready for some heavy-duty fellowship?"

"Heavy-duty fellowship. Yes, I think I'm ready for that, at last. What's your name? It's so nice to see a black person in Kenora."

"Hey, it's so nice to *be* a black person in Kenora!"

"I'm sorry," Digger interrupted. "This is a very good friend of mine, Monty Dalva. He bought Mrs. Saxon's old place way out by the airport."

"Ooh, I love that house! It looks like it's made out of gingerbread. She made him build her that house after she found out he'd been going to Thailand to get teen girls pregnant on purpose. That was his kinky thrill. Oh, she was a hard-looking thing; she looked like a mug shot, not friendly at all. They're both dead now. I guess you must've paid an arm and a leg for that."

Monty simply kept beaming. Teresa instantly saw her mistake. Asking someone how much their house cost wasn't churchy. Gossip was probably a no-go, too.

"My first real church service," she resumed. "I feel like a newborn. I wasn't even baptized, you know. That's quite scandalous, I think. My mother's a real character, that fucking old ... Sorry. I wish her peace, really. I'm so looking forward to this. I loved *Hymn Sing* when it was on CBC. Remember *Hymn Sing*? What about the service itself — are there going to be people screaming and passing out? That's always so stirring."

"You watch too much TV, Teresa," Digger said gently. "It's pretty calm. No speaking in tongues. You'll see. Let's go in."

Monty and Digger walked slightly ahead of Teresa. Monty glanced at Digger. Teresa read suspicion into that glance. She worried that Monty already saw her for what she was: a raging, conniving floozy on her way out. She couldn't waver, she couldn't act on any of her typical impulses. Because she was immediately attracted to Monty, as much if not more than she was to Digger. Another place and time, Teresa would've pursued Monty relentlessly, the way that she has always pursued men: sweetly, insistently, occasionally brazenly but never desperately, always just this side of desperately. There's a long scar on the back of Monty Dalva's arm; she could just imagine what he did to get a long scar like that. The men she's known have seldom had long, earned scars like that.

The church was packed. You could just hear the organist above the friendly chatter. She knew almost everybody. Kath Milley, Mona Minna from grade school, the entire McMehen family, the entire DuBois family. Poor, wrecked Clara Peck, who's only ever been on welfare, was sitting next to the Stepaniuks, who own a cottage with an elevator. People who would ignore each other in Safeway were greeting each other, even hugging. Teresa found the whole thing at once touching and annoying. Why couldn't Mrs. Stepaniuk hug Clara Peck in Safeway? Why couldn't she ask after the fate of Clara's five bastard sons and one daughter-by-incest the other six days of the week?

The organist stopped playing, and the people stopped talking. The music resumed, louder now, and the congregation stood and sang. To a person, they knew by heart all the words to this mystery hymn. She looked at Digger and Monty. Digger's eyes were closed; Monty was looking up at the ceiling, or heaven.

The minister was a squat, ruddy man wearing tiny, wire framed glasses that strained across his wide face. Reverend Griffin welcomed the flock and the flock said something back; Teresa was busy watching Digger and Monty.

The minister paused, straightened papers. "As always, we welcome lovingly new visitors to our little church," he read. "Today we say a warm hello to Jill and Kevin Follows, all the way from Bemidji, Minnesota, and to a local friend, here for the first time, Teresa Price."

Her mouth fell open. What the hell? Digger didn't mention that she was going to be introduced from the pulpit. Suddenly voices all around her were saying hello; she felt hands gently touching her shoulder, her back, her wig. She wanted to tell them all to get the fuck away from her, but she knew that wouldn't be a churchy thing to do. And only now that they'd been given permission, they were all acknowledging her? She smiled and nodded, murmured pleasant-sounding, nonsense syllables, at once patted and subtly swatted the welcoming hands. Jocelyn must have put Digger up to this, she reasoned. Jocelyn had found out about Teresa's spiritual quest and wanted to make her first worship service as mortifying as possible, so she made Digger tell the minister to officially welcome her, a sick woman who is desperately grabbing at religion, sans husband and children, accompanied by two strange, pious men who'd taken pity on her. Well, two points for Jocelyn: Teresa was suitably mortified. Good for her, that nervy bimbo, Jocelyn Walsh. Still an idiot, but a formidable one. Monty Dalva was attempting to high-five Teresa; she quickly looked the other way. It would be so much tidier if Teresa could just electrocute Jocelyn, or whip her off a bridge. This was getting to be quite the production. Teresa was starting to deflate. As the minister prattled on, and the children scurried off to Sunday school, Teresa pressed her dry tongue hard against her front teeth. To others it would look like she was staving off vomit.

Finally, finally the hands all withdrew and they turned, smiling faces faced front again. Griffin's sermon began with rhetorical questions: We are all tired at the end of a long workday, but does that excuse us from our constant job as a loving helper? Are we doing enough? What will our legacy be? Did we stop growing at a certain point and not notice?

He seemed to be looking right at Teresa as he spoke, and she felt exposed. Did Reverend Griffin fashion a sermon especially to ridicule Teresa, on the orders of Jocelyn Walsh? He came across as a kind man, with his white perm and apple cheeks; surely she was being paranoid. Dizziness overtook her, a narrow inner sway that caused her to clutch at the pew and forget where she was in her mean scheme. Who was ruining who? Teresa felt thwarted, outsmarted from every angle.

Maybe she was simply not capable of this grand deception of hers; she never could conceal her feelings, even in health. She considered getting up and leaving, but they were packed into the pew, people to the left and right of her. Digger and Monty were both rapt in the sermon. She didn't want to vomit on them.

"What is prayer?" the minister asked. "I'd like to propose that we all reconsider our understanding of prayer. When we pray, do we come away refreshed? If that is the case, then I am going to step out on a limb and suggest that we're not doing it right. Prayer is a dynamic thing. I emerge from prayer drained, like I've been running on a treadmill. Prayer is not a haven. Prayer is powerful. Jude 1:20 says, 'Build yourselves up in your most holy faith and pray in the Holy Spirit.' Build yourself up, like an athlete builds muscle! And how do you build up muscle? You build it up by first tearing it down. Prayer is exercise! Prayer is pain! No pain, no gain!"

She'd just about had her fill of Reverend Griffin. Prayer is pain! What the hell did he know about pain? Before the morphine, she couldn't sit without crying. When she got the bad news, that night at the motel, she curled herself away from Hugh in his bed and pleaded for something, some feathery technicality that would give her more time, more time to be bored or annoyed, more time to think, to be ignorant of this pummelling terror. She felt she needed to say the words aloud, that night, so she struggled out of bed and into the fluorescent bathroom. "Please, just this once," she said to the mirror. And when she emerged from the bathroom, she was somewhat soothed. Hugh's sleeping form comforted her. The shadows in the room grew less hard, more gauzy. According to Reverend Griffin, however, the peace of that prayerful blip didn't count. She was supposed to feel like hell after talking with God.

She found herself panting in the pew, her vision dimmed by black, darting sparks. Beside her Digger was rapt and Monty was weeping. She pressed herself against the back of the next pew and shuffled, knee by knee, into the aisle.

In the entrance to the church she fell into a red velvet throne of a chair. A wave of the awful fatigue came upon her, that mucky stupor that squeezes out all feeling but dejection. She bent forward at the waist and grabbed her calves. How bad would this death be? Hugh's brother's late wife, sweet Sally, hung on for two years after a diagnosis of lung cancer; at the end her cheekbones came through her grey flesh sharp as origami folds. She cursed her loved ones, Sally did, that gentle woman who made her own Christmas cards and saw Amy Grant in concert twice; she wished aloud in a reedy voice that her husband and twin daughters knew first-hand the pain she was enduring. It could go that way.

Digger came out and knelt beside her. He put a hand on her back.

"I'm sorry," she said through her skirt. "I shouldn't have come. It's not what I thought it was going to be. I can't breathe."

"Should I call an ambulance?"

"No, no. I don't mean 'I can't breathe' I can't breathe, I just can't breathe. I don't feel well. Apparently I've been praying the wrong way. I feel awful. I feel worse than I did when I was going to hell."

"Don't say that, I can promise you, that is not true. The minister's sermons can be a bit — daunting, I guess, if you're not used to them. You'll come to really treasure him. You are richly deserving of God's love."

Teresa looked up at Digger.

"You're so full of shit," she said, staring back into her lap again. "We both know that I don't know what the hell I'm doing. I've made a godawful mess of everything I've put my hand to. I'm weak. I'm a weak person."

"Don't say that."

"Stop telling me not to say things! You don't know. You don't know me. I'm just the crazy lady with the gay son. You don't know what goes on inside. You know what goes on inside? Not very much. You know what my boy — not the gay one, the OPP one — once said to me, out of nowhere? 'You don't scare me. You want to, but you don't.' He thought I wanted to scare him. He thought that's what I was going after, as a mother. 'You don't scare me,' he says. And then the other one, the other one is just —"

"We don't need to go back over past arguments, Teresa. I haven't had occasion to see your younger boy for a few years now. I'm sure he's — What is his name again? Joe?"

"Joel. I call him Jolie. Although I shouldn't. He liked it when I called him Jolie, but I shouldn't have."

"Joel, well. He's okay for what he is, you know? He's fine."

"He's not. He's not fine. I coddled him, I even — I made his goddamn bed for him every day, and now he doesn't know how to look after himself. When he came home he smelled like pee.

I can tell right now he's going to end up in the gutter. With AIDS. And that'll be all my fault. One of them I scared, the other one I didn't scare enough. So there you go."

Digger began to hum. It was a high, faint sound; Teresa thought at first that he was responding to gastric upset. Then he started singing words and phrases: "Oh my Jesus," "I walk with Him," "What a friend He is," "Oh, my hand in His." Sounded like a compost of every gospel song Teresa had ever heard. At first she was slightly frightened, but when she looked back at Digger his eyes were closed and his chin was quivering. This made her chin quiver. She watched as the features of his face — the long fall of his nose, the cliff of his forehead, the peak of his cheekbone — appeared to dissolve slightly then reassemble, melt and remould, his face made molten by faith.

"Teresa, do you want to make a positive difference in the life of your son and, by extension, your own life?"

"Sure, yeah," she said, crying now. "Yes. Of course I do. You know I do. How though? I don't see how."

He put his hand on hers. This is where the previous Teresa, the one who wanted to destroy Jocelyn Walsh, would've silently celebrated such a step forward in the seduction, the hand-on-hand bit. That seemed so long ago, the previous Teresa. She felt transformed, but not in any gusty, ecstatic way; she'd lost all continuity, she'd forgotten herself and was now small, paralyzed, terrified. This must the presence of the Holy Spirit, this sense of being hunted by a hateful, unflinching marksman. Her breath slowed slightly. Nothing could be done.

"Reverend Griffin wasn't pulling your leg about prayer power.

It's not a soothing, lullaby thing, prayer. It's a major agent for change. It blows your mind, when you see what prayer can do."

"If you're gonna tell me I can cure my cancer you can save it because that ship has absolutely sailed."

"Maybe so. But there is still a hell of a lot that can happen. Please let me help you."

"And you promise this isn't part of some plot your wife has hatched to humiliate me?"

"Sorry?"

"Never mind. Yeah, okay. I'll pray with you. You're a nice man."

"We're all nice men."

We're all nice men. Teresa sometimes thought that herself. There were lots of awful men, of course, but in her experience, most of the men she's met have been, well, not *nice* necessarily, but definitely not awful. Women, too. He probably meant women, too, when he said "we're all nice men." Or did he? Teresa was about to ask about the status of women who aren't also nice men, but just then Monty joined them.

"What's going on? Are we all good?"

"We're better than good, Monty. Our friend here is about to embark on an adventure in prayer. Will you join me in guiding her through?"

"I would be honoured. Terry, you will not be disappointed. My prayer adventure has been … gosh … like an African lion safari. The stories I could tell … I'll spare you the gory details. Suffice to say, if I can have transformation through the adventure of prayer, anyone can."

"Actually," Digger said, raising a thoughtful forefinger, "I think Teresa here may benefit from some of the gory details. Make it real for her. Would you offer some testimony, Monty?"

Monty instantly went from happy to solemn. "My dear wife and I had a wonderful life together in Iowa City. Then our girls left for university, and my wife got very depressed. I was at the store seven days a week, and she was lonely. She lost her way. In due course I came to discover that she had started abusing all sorts of pills. Oxycontin, Valium. She'd crush them all up and snort it. I confronted her and she crumpled like a rag doll. However — and I shiver now at the memory of God's hand in our lives at that moment — at the exact same time that I chose to confront her about her drug abuse, she'd also chosen to confront me about the fact that I had been abusing crack cocaine at the store for several years."

"What kind of store did you have?" Teresa asked.

"High-end eyewear. I was a terrible workaholic. Crack kept me going. It wasn't a party kind of a thing for me. Listen to me, preening like I'm not the hopeless drug addict that I am! I'm sorry. The point is: my wife and I faced each other as addicts, asked God for instruction, and He manifested in the form of a crystal palm tree in the middle of our living room — strike me dead if I'm lying; Anita saw it, too — and instructed us to sell everything, pick up roots, and move here. Well, He said Newfoundland, but it's so damp there all the time. So here we are. And we're okay. Day by day. I still sometimes worry about Anita, especially since the knee surgery, but that's just me. Things are good. Oh! And I also have to insert that I have not had a herpes outbreak since that holy moment in the living room, three years ago."

"Thank you for sharing your story," Teresa said. "It was very moving."

"Teresa," Digger said, "would you like to share some of your story?"

"Right now? But I haven't had my transformative God moment yet like Monty had."

"That's okay. You can just talk about your life and where God might be helpful to you. What are your problem areas?"

She mentally flipped through the pages of her life. It didn't take long. "Well, I was always a rowdy, I've always liked to have fun, and maybe having fun sometimes got in the way of being a good person. I like sex, unlike a lot of women my age and older. For my mother, sex was something revolting she had to endure so that my father would fall asleep after instead of beating her. The only advice she gave me before I got married was to just lie there and pretend that you are paralyzed from the neck down. Maybe she had the right idea, though, because she's still alive, and I'm a loose woman who's dying. So I guess I'd like help from God in that department. I'd like to know what I'm doing wrong. I guess that's it."

"We have got our work cut out for us!" Monty said brightly. "Don't you worry about a thing. By the time we're finished, you'll know all about your bad self. And your good self, too, naturally."

"Sounds great," Teresa said.

THAT WAS TEN days ago. Since then Teresa has been twice to Bible study, and to a second Sunday service. She can't concentrate for very long, but what she does manage to absorb is quite interesting. Above all it's nice to have this sudden community — Bible study especially, because the fair-weather, otherwise snooty Sunday churchgoers don't care enough to attend, leaving only the diligent, careful faithful, all of them soft-spoken and considerate, crossing their legs at the ankle, leaning intently when someone else speaks. It's nice, to be a part of that. But it's not enough. Where is the power and glory? Where's that feeling, the one she had in the church foyer, of being pummelled by God? Surely that feeling won't come about from these small sessions of coffee and bunwiches and the cautious dissection of the most popular parts of the New Testament. She'll keep going to Bible study, of course, but surely there has to be another, more showy way of meeting the Holy Spirit. When she dekes out apologetically to smoke during Bible study, she thinks of Ouija boards and séances. But that kind of thing wouldn't likely summon God; she'd probably end up with some shitty, dumb spirit with no pull. There must be another way.

16

SHE'S BEEN ACTING STRANGE FOR a while now, his mother. He's
pretty sure it's not just the disease and the morphine. She's
remote, preoccupied, sighing and muttering like she does when
the car in front of her is doing the exact speed limit. She's mean.
He came home one afternoon, all aglow over certain of the
buttons he had handled that day at the museum — one a cres-
cent moon fashioned from a jagged yellow gemstone — and she
narrowed her eyes and said, "Buttons. Well. There's a future
for you. All your potential and you've got a job playing with
buttons. That's the kind of thing they get retarded people to do
so they won't pull their hair out or run into traffic."

Joel, already fretful about his sudden, fey vocation, had to
beg off to the bathroom to cry. Teresa always did know how and
when to dig the knife in, but before it was done with affection
and levity. Now, if he didn't know better, he'd think she hates
him. He's trying not to take it personally, her angry rapport with
her illness, but still. Moving through the house he's caught her

eye a couple times, and the new hardness in her face made him feel like he did the first time he took the subway in the city: all but trampled, altogether resented as a cloddy obfuscation.

They've not talked about it at all, the cancer. Twice Joel has asked his mother her thoughts on her diagnosis, and she has slapped away the topic: "I don't have *thoughts on my diagnosis*, Joel. Who has *thoughts on their diagnosis*? This is Kenora, this isn't Toronto. I don't feel good, period. Nothing more to say. Do you have *thoughts on your wipeout as a grown-up*? Anyway, my faith sustains me now. What sustains you?"

He had no answer. What had sustained him had been the knowledge that, despite the many cosmetic liabilities he forced Edmund to enumerate and his allergic response to higher learning, his mother loved him. With that gone … And she won't call him "Jolie" anymore. She only calls him "Joel," pointedly, sometimes twice in the same sentence. *Joel, adult people do not put a Holly Hobbie rag doll between their knees to go to sleep, Joel.*

She's gone Thursday nights for Bible study. She'll often head out other nights, too, anxiously gathering her purse and smokes, for emergency prayer circles. Joel, trying to indulge, has suggested that perhaps the prayer circle could be held at their house. Teresa dismissed that out of hand — she didn't want her prayer friends seeing her KISS CDs and Labatt 50 ashtrays.

He even went hesitantly to his father, who was taking apart a cuckoo clock with a butter knife in the basement. Hugh didn't look up when Joel said hello.

"Do you think we should be letting Mom do all these prayer things?"

"What prayer things?"

"You know how she's gone all the time now? How she announces that she has to go off to prayer thing and then goes?"

A gasp of fluty *cuckoo*. His father's twirling butter knife came to a stop.

"You mean all that horseshit with Digger Walsh and all them? I don't know. She likes it. What am I supposed to do about it?"

Digger Walsh? Joel hadn't heard that name since high school. Teresa would frequently, spontaneously insult everyone in the Walsh family: Digger, Jocelyn, Craig and even blameless, little, bespectacled, special needs Michelle ("does she have to be so fucking poignant all the time?") so often that Joel, while grateful for his mother's protective ire, sometimes told her to give it a rest. Now Teresa was clasping hands with the man.

"Digger Walsh — like, mayor/homophobe-who-we-all-hate Digger Walsh?"

"I never said I hate him. I like what he did with the harbour-front. And he always sounds real down-to-earth when they have him on the radio."

"But what about how he defended his son for tormenting me? What about that?"

"That was years ago."

Joel drifted across the hard planes of his father's face, the long, twisted nose. It seemed that a very long time ago, possibly in Joel's infancy, he and his father had silently agreed to ignore each other or, when forced, to treat each other with a thin, boarding-house courtesy. Even so, it stung when Hugh casually belittled his past hurts. More than a few times Joel had caught himself wishing illness out of his mother and into his father.

"So you're okay with the fact that your wife is totally bonding with some guy?"

"You know your mother. She goes her own way. If this brings her some peace, then good. Better that than ... I don't know ... smoking drugs, I'd say."

This made Joel go back up the stairs. How anyone could be so blasé about a spouse's wanderings he couldn't fathom. When he was a boy his mother would occasionally arrive home, in something with spaghetti straps, just as he was having breakfast. His father would murmur pretend concern that someone was certainly burning the midnight oil, then spoon a blob of brown sugar off the top of his porridge and into his mouth. As a boy, Joel thought his parents had a deep, secret but incredibly fun friendship; Teresa would boom about on one topic or another, Hugh would smile slightly, Teresa would fall back contentedly. Now he knows: his mother is a self-obsessed old whore and his father is a gutless non-person.

She left the house right after lunch, and it's now nearly eight o'clock. Joel sits in her seat at the kitchen table, smokes her smokes, waits for her. It doesn't matter that she's dying. If she is friends-in-prayer with Digger Walsh, she has betrayed him.

She takes almost a minute to ascend the four stairs from the front door to the kitchen.

"You've been gone for, like, ten hours," says Joel from the darkness.

"That is none of your concern, mister. Turn a light on. We don't sit around in the dark in this house."

He hears her rough fingers fumbling along the wall for the light switch. She finds it. They both squint in the sudden light.

"Are you hanging out with Digger Walsh?"

"Who told you that? Your dad? Jesus Christ, I might as well be married to a fucking newspaper. Well, yes, I am. Turns out that he is actually a very warm, spiritual man."

"Who begets homophobe terrorists."

"Oh, dry up. There's a nice little thing known as forgiveness, you know. You should try it."

It's gone to her brain. That must be it. Her eyes are glazed with delusion.

"Can you even hear yourself? You would be so, so grossed out if you could hear yourself. It's quite sad."

"There are some big changes for this family coming on down the pipeline. Long overdue. And you are going to thank me. A year from now, when I'm rotting, you're gonna look back and silently say, 'Hey, thanks, Mom. Thanks for putting the brakes on and turning around my crappy gay life.'"

Joel stands up, and his chair goes soaring on its rollers. He waves his hands in showy rage. He is angry, and he is also aware of the dramatic potential of this anger scene. He shakes out long, pretend hair, he snorts and gasps and does a small shimmy of disgust. Teresa weaves slightly at the sight of Joel's antics, bowing and shaking her head, like a nun forced to witness anal sex. This only makes him more animated. He stalks into his bedroom, hissing nonsense.

He heads to bed, lies there fully clothed with the door open. He listens to his mother muddle around. "I don't know who you are anymore," he yells at her.

"I know who you are, though. Better than you know yourself. Always have, always will."

"Shut the hell up. I know who I am."

"No, you don't."

"Fuck off. Yes, I do."

"Okay, fine, you do. But you don't."

"Whatever! I am now sleeping. I have fallen fast asleep, you bitch."

17

"SHE SAYS I HAVE A 'crappy gay life,'" Joel says to Donald, as they flip through Donald's three-inch-thick book of stencils.

"That's quite reductive, isn't it," Donald says, not looking up.

"Can you imagine? What would you do if your mother said you had a crappy gay life?"

Donald stops, brings his palm before his pinched-up face like it's a small mirror. "My mother would never say such a thing. Why would she? The life I lead is neither crappy nor gay, thank you very much. I am a gently-spoken gentleman; I live for beautiful, dignified things. I am a good neighbour, friend, and son. I have never done anything to cause anyone to regard me with derision. Let's get that straight."

"Of course. Sorry. I just assumed that you were gay."

"Well, I may very well be, but I've never been the kind — I just have never seen the use of jumping up and down and screaming 'Hooray! I'm drawn to penis!' It's so ... pedestrian."

They flip through a few pages. Donald traces an ornate letter

"B" with a slightly too-long forefinger nail.

"I mean," he continues, "I can say that you're a somewhat attractive young man, but have I ever behaved in a salacious way towards you? Have I ever — groped at you, cupped a buttock?"

"No. But, like, you could, and I wouldn't be totally grossed out."

"How generous of you. Noted and filed."

18

MONTY DALVA'S LIVING ROOM IS filled with huge, redwood furniture that, Teresa guesses, must have been a real bitch to move: a
long, uncomfortable couch not unlike the pews at Knox; two
high-backed chairs with thin silver seat cushions; a long,
long coffee table at which a dozen dwarves could hold a board
meeting. There is also a tatty, plush easy chair, draped with
an ugly quilt festooned with octagonal children holding fat
hands. Teresa was offered the easy chair, but she refused; Anita
Dalva, tall and beautiful, sturdy but fine-boned, has just had
a knee replacement, and Teresa helped Monty ease his wife
off her crutches and into the chair. Teresa caught the scent of
Anita's tight, shiny chignon: gentlest hint of lilac, real lilac,
not the sickening chemical stink of the hair products they sell
around here.

This is the first time they've gathered at the Dalvas's, and
it only makes sense that they should continue meeting here;
the way the three of them tended to bunch up and break off

during Thursday Bible study was causing church whispers that Digger and Monty were either getting stuck up, or were interpreting the Bible in newfangled and possibly inappropriate ways.

They start with pleasantries; Teresa is introduced to Anita, who has been housebound because of her knee. At least once a minute she cries out in conversational pain: never simply "ouch," always "ooh, my knee!" "I never thought such a teeny, weeny body part could make so much pain. But that's what you get for playing tennis on cement for — ooh, my knee! — thirty years. I'm trying to avoid the use of painkillers, given my past issues with Oxy. I'm in agony. If pain is a teacher, I must have a great, big lesson to learn!"

Teresa relates the story of her mother's hip replacement; a full two years after the procedure her mother still described herself as convalescing, just to get out of doing her own vacuuming. "Some of us need so much, some of us don't need anything at all," is Anita's response.

Digger asks Teresa how she is feeling. Teresa says that she senses her body faltering, that there were times, the past few days, where she has had to tell her legs to stand, to walk.

"I'm not good with weakness, never have been," Teresa says, training her face on Anita, who nods knowingly. Anita is both imperious and maternal, a combination that Teresa, weakened, finds comforting. Teresa can lean on Anita and know that Anita, bad knee or no, is inexhaustibly strong. How fulfilling it would be, to have Anita as a close friend. She's already more candid with Anita than she's ever been with another woman. "I tell you,

Mrs. Dalva, Anita, that I would rather be buried alive than be wheeled around by Hugh."

"Who's Hugh?" Anita asks.

"Her husband," say Digger and Monty in unison.

"Well, we should pray that Teresa's husband finds his heart's replenishment, so that he can proceed from a place of strength and shepherd dear Teresa through. Father God, thank you for —"

"That is super nice," Teresa says, tactful but dismissive. Anita, interrupted, glares and huffs. "I am so, so sorry to interrupt you, Anita. I just really don't want to pray about Hugh. He's a good guy and everything, but he doesn't need praying over. He's fine, and he'll be fine when I die. He's like a cactus tree, or that kind of thing, you know? He doesn't need much attention. When I go he'll hook up with one desperate widow or another, and he'll do his ugly woodworking and be happy as a clam. Same with my older boy. He's got his 'damage,' as he would call it, but nothing that's going to bung up his life. It's really my one boy, my younger boy who I'm worried about. I really mangled my one boy."

Teresa holds tight to a coffee table leg to keep from crying. Digger offers a thoughtful poke to the shoulder.

"I told you about Teresa's son, Joel," Monty says to his wife in a sympathetic whisper. "There's some concern that he is a homosexual and also not sanitary and a layabout. We've all been praying hard for him."

"Boys are a real ordeal," says Anita, shifting in her chair, clearly in pain. "I'm so glad we didn't have boys. We have twin girls and they really gave us — ooh, my knee! — no trouble. Our youngest by six minutes, Kaila, was maybe a little obstinate in high school, a bit — ooh, my knee! — lippy, and she liked the fake hair and the fake nails, and she liked to pretend that she didn't come from Iowa City, that she was somehow ghetto. I thought 'oh, no, she's going to end up a prostitute,' but then she and Thea both got into Iowa State and they're doing great. Kaila doesn't wear store-bought hair anymore."

Teresa nods and smiles and pretends to be happy for Anita's happy family.

"One way or another," Anita continues, "babies are always going to rip your heart out. We know this. When the girls went off to Iowa State I fell into the darkest depression. It literally felt like a bereavement, a double bereavement. There was no centre to my life all of a sudden. I wanted to just die. I started snorting pills. Ground-up pills, of course. I was laid so very low. It sure wasn't the middle age I had envisioned for myself."

Teresa, moved and thrilled by this exchange, wraps her wasted arms around herself. "I had my first at 19," she offers, sensing the opening for her own story. "I always wanted babies, even when I was a little girl. So when I met Hugh — he was nothing to look at, even then, but he had this dog, this sad old thing with one eye, all patchy fur, and Hugh was so sweet to that ugly dog I thought for sure he'd make a good father."

"And was he?" asked Anita.

"I guess so. I mean, he never beat them up or anything. He was good with Dallas, my first boy. Dallas was a real *boy* boy, from the get-go. He screamed non-stop the whole first year. And then dirt bikes and Lego and judo. He couldn't stand spending time with me. So when Joel came along, and he was all dreamy and gentle — he loved to sleep, I'd have to wake him up when he was a baby — well, I just gobbled him right up. He was always hanging off me. We'd lie on the couch and read *Family Circle* and *Chatelaine* together.

"What's *Chatelaine*?" Anita asks.

"It's a women's magazine here in Canada. It's my favourite. It's for the more sophisticated woman."

"And you read these with your son?"

"Yeah, so, when he was in kindergarten he'd come home every day and tell me which boys he was in love with that day. In kindergarten! I should've … I should have, I don't know, spanked him or something, but he was just being himself with his little face and his little arms and legs."

"I hear what you're saying, sister. But we know that evil quite often assumes a pleasant disguise."

"He is not evil! I mean, I understand where you're coming from and everything, but please don't call him evil. He's not evil, he's just ass-backwards. And that's my fault. I've coddled him, because — like you said, Anita — he was someone who seemed to need so much. I thought I was being a good mother, but I wasn't. I've been a bad mother. I have."

Anita slowly rises, unassisted, from her chair. "She's standing up!" Monty whispers excitedly. Anita palms the air downward, as though pressing down folded bedding to make more room in a drawer. Teresa isn't sure what this gesture means; she decides to stop talking and wait for further instruction.

"I came up Pentecostal. My girlhood was burnished in that beautiful faith ..."

"Yes, she did and yes, it was," Monty affirms. "Burnished like a brass chalice."

"... and I am so grateful to have had that foundation. Where would I be had I not had that foun — ooh, my knee! — dation?"

"Nowhere, is where. Nowhere, without a map!"

"Since then, I've travelled the world with my dear husband. We were most often the only black faces, wherever we went. This place is no exception. Little babies stare at us in the gro-cery store like we're monsters from space. And that can harden a person. I'm a bit hard. But I'm also a whole lot soft."

"Hard and soft," Monty seconds.

"Please stop rephrasing me, Monty. We're not the Shirelles. In my faith we believe in the basic goodness of a person, but we also believe that goodness can be overwhelmed by evil. Now, we can wring our hands over this, and try to figure out what went wrong and when, and wonder if maybe we should bring in a psychiatrist. There is only one solution. We know what that solution is."

"Oh, Anita, please don't," Monty whimpers. "Our friends here aren't ready for that yet."

Anita glares at Monty, who folds himself up on the floor by her feet. "I respectfully disagree, dear husband. I think you underestimate our friends. I think they are ready for that."

"What? Ready for what?" Teresa asks anxiously.

"The only hope for your wayward son is exorcism," Anita says, grave as a doctor delivering bad news. "I've seen a madwoman become a kindergarten teacher; I've seen a killer transform into a kind and patient gardener. But all of this, all of it came through exorcism. These people still write to me — *thank you so much, Anita. I don't where I'd be without my exorcism.*"

Digger looks at Monty with disbelief. Even in a state of grace, Digger has no time for foolishness; he keeps rotating his wrist-watch, tapping the heels of his cowboy boots together. Monty looks at his quaking wife.

"When we say exorcism, we aren't talking about heads spinning around and all that crazy stuff from the movie. It's more of a stylized prayer. Wouldn't you say, Anita?"

"Yes, although there have been some terrifying supernatural incidents along the way."

"I'm definitely up for anything that might help Joel," Teresa offers. "But demonic possession — I don't think we have that in Canada. At least not in Ontario, I don't think. Anyway, I think it's really, really unlikely that Joel will consent to an exorcism. And what sort of demon presents itself as slow-moving and dreamy and sentimental?"

"Doesn't have to be a demonic possession, could just be a powerful, negative influence. Did your second son fall under the sway of someone when he was very young?"

Digger Walsh tucks his jean shirt deeper into his jeans. Teresa can sense his impatience. She feels bad that the exor-cism conversation is making him restless, but she can't stop.

"I think I'm gonna head on out," Digger says, standing. "This is a bit much for me. This isn't the way I worship."

"Oh, please stay," Teresa pleads. "Please? I need your

strength and prayer, more than ever. Please. Please?"

Digger considers, then slowly sits with a sigh. "All right," he says. "But the moment you all start throwing chicken bones on the floor, I'm out of here."

"Chicken bones," Anita says, surveying the words carefully as though looking for structural damage. "So you perceive me as a practitioner of voodoo, do you? Because all powerful black ladies practise voodoo, right?"

"I didn't say that."

"But you wanted to say that. In your eyes I'm just another uppity — ooh, my knee! —negress, doing uppity negress things."

"Anita, I have never seen you as an uppity negress. I didn't even know the word 'negress' until now. Come on. We're friends."

Anita considers a response, decides to let it go. She returns her attention to Teresa. "We were talking about negative influences. Think hard: what negative influences were there in your son's childhood?"

"Umm, negative influences. Well, his grandma is the biggest suckhole of all time, and she never missed the chance to ride him about using moisturizer, but she wasn't around very much, thankfully. I know that he was a big fan of Farrah Fawcett when he was small, went on and on about how he wanted to grow up to be her."

Anita weighs the evil sway that Farrah Fawcett might wield. She doesn't look convinced.

"Okay, Farrah Fawcett. Yes, for sure. Anybody else? Really concentrate. A neighbour. A teacher who maybe turned out to be a molester. A wandering vagrant. Really think. Monty, go get those Percocet and some water. I'm sorry, I cannot stand this pain one more minute."

Monty's head flops to the side in disappointment. "You don't need those pills, Anita. You've been doing great without them. Just keep breathing through the pain."

"Monty, my pain has become unbearable. The doctor pre-scribed me those pills because he knew I would be having extreme pain. I am having extreme pain. I am not going to relapse. I am not going to crush and snort. Please go get my Percocet!"

He slowly makes his way to where he's hidden Anita's pain pills. "I'm sorry about all this," Anita says. "It's a sad state of affairs when your own — ooh, my knee! — husband treats you like a dirty junkie. Well, he'll get his. I shouldn't say that. We'll pray on it. What were we ... Oh yes. The dark forces that may have taken over your child. Any other ideas? Take your time. I'll sit down again and — ooh, my knee! Ooh, my knee! — wait."

Teresa Price is a skeletal woman, kneeling on a beige shag rug, trying to think of causes of corruption in Joel's childhood.

"Wait," she says after several minutes of arduous reflection. "When he was really, really little — three, four — all of us would sit together, me and Hugh and Dallas and Joel, and listen to records really loud. Dallas next to his dad, Joel on my lap. This would've been, Christ, '81, '82? Those were good times. Supertramp, the Eagles, Fleetwood Mac. And I remember, when we played Fleetwood Mac, their big one — *Rumours*, I think it was, yeah, *Rumours* — Joel would stare and stare at the back cover, and kiss the blonde lady's picture. Not the pretty one who sings "Dreams," with the goat voice. The other one. It was the oddest thing. Her, of all people. Oh, what the hell is her name?"

She looks around the room. Digger isn't listening. Monty, back now with a pill bottle and crystal goblet of water, only shrugs. Anita pops a Percocet. And another.

"We're strictly a jazz and classical family," Monty says. "Ask me who wrote *Moonlight Sonata* and I could help you. Wait. Who did write *Moonlight Sonata*?"

"Don't get me more gummed up than I already am," Teresa snaps. "God, now this is gonna really bug me. Hold on, Hugh will know."

She gets up and picks up the phone on the end table beside her. She calls Hugh. He answers with that amputated, surprised *hello* of his: *'o?*

"Hey. What the hell is the name of that girl from Fleetwood Mac, not the pretty goat one, the other one. Christine McVie! Right."

With that she hangs up.

"Christine McVie."

Anita nods, slowly. "Okay. So nobody from real life? You can't think of anyone who's not famous? You sure he wasn't molested? Even a little bit?"

"No, he wasn't at all."

Obviously annoyed, Anita rolls her eyes, then closes them. Eventually, she makes a satisfied, sighing sound, as though she has slipped into a hot tub.

"I'd like to begin with a room-cleansing chant that I learned from a First Nations documentary I saw recently. It'll prepare the space. Monty, go get that paper that I wrote that First Nations thing off the TV on."

"Where is it?"

"In the bedroom, by the TV."

"There are no papers by the TV in the bedroom."

"Well, unless you moved it — which you so often do, even though I've told you a thousand times not to move stuff around, ever — it'll be beside the TV, because that's where I left it. Go and get it!"

Teresa and Digger look at each other. Anita keeps her eyes closed, muttering about how useless her husband can be. Monty can be heard in the bedroom, cursing Anita and moving stuff around. He returns with the piece of paper. Anita snatches the paper from his hands. Another long pause as she studies the words before her.

"Hey-a hey-a hey-a hey-a hey-a hey-a — ooh, my knee! — hey-a hey-a hey-a hey-a hey-a hey-a hey-a hey-a hey-a hey-a hey-a hey-a hey-a hey-a hey-a — ooh, my knee! — hey-a hey-a hey-a hey-a hey-a — ooh, my knee! — hey-a hey-a —"

"You've gotta be kidding me!" Digger barks. "Wrap it up already!"

Anita's earrings start to shiver. "How. Dare. You. Interrupt. My. First Nations. Cleansing. Thing."

"I'm sorry, Anita, but come on. I have been the honoured guest at powwows that were shorter than that."

"You're lucky my Perkies are starting to kick in, or I would start again from the beginning. Hey-a hey-a hey-a ho. Now, what was the name of that girl that you didn't know the name of again?"

"Christine McVie."

"O, Christine McVie," Anita incants, grave and sincere. "Your dark reign is over, do you hear me? Ooh, my knee! Study war no more. I cast you out of Teresa's younger son, Christine McVie! Get out of that boy! Run! G'wan! Shoo! I want to hear your hooves clacking, demon Christine!"

Digger stands again.

"Well, that finishes it for me," he says, stepping around Teresa. "I'm sorry, but how stupid can you get. How and why would a pop star lock herself in some pansy boy who smells like piss? Wouldn't her friends notice that she was missing? Wouldn't the rest of Fleetwood Mac notice?"

"I don't mean the corporeal body goes into the person," Anita snaps. "We're talking about — ooh, my knee! — soul exchange, essences and things like that."

"It's the Percocet, Digger," Monty mouths. "She's not normally this — theatrical."

"Yeah," Teresa says, "actually, this exorcism isn't really working for me, either. Anita, isn't there maybe another prayer we can do? Something more earthy?"

"I am not a jukebox," Anita says, turning away, deeply offended. "I am a fifty-three-year-old woman in great physical pain who is trying to save a stranger's son from further — ooh, my knee! — torment. But now I feel like an intruder in my own home. That is not a pleasant feeling."

Digger huffs out. Monty follows him, in an antsy sidestep. "That's it," Anita calls after them. "You run along now. We don't need you. Either of you. You've turned us both bulldagger!"

She lines herself up with her chair and falls into it. "I'm just kidding about being a bulldagger. I witnessed first-hand, in my own church when I was a young girl, the torment of the sissies and the bulldaggers, and it is not something I'd wish on a dog. They would all hang themselves if they had the courage, but they don't, so they kill themselves slowly. Did you know that? The sissy, he will insert absolutely any object he can get his hands on directly into his anus, and he will retain it, store it in there until AIDS takes place. Such a sad affair. Whereas the bulldagger, she eats. She'll eat and eat and eat until she can no longer move. This then sends out a signal to other bulldaggers nearby. The other bulldaggers come zipping in their power chairs to her house and feed her to death, and then they move on when the next immobilized bulldagger who needs killing sends out her signal. It's a tragedy, any way you slice it. Nobody wants that for their child."

This is all nonsense. Even Teresa in her shaky state can see that. But she's come too far to forsake this crazy woman who might also be saintly, able to conjure transformation for Teresa and her fallen son. She crawls to Anita, sits at her feet in the same spot Monty occupied, wants to place her face in Anita's lap — some gesture of surrender to the stronger woman, a physical declaration of Teresa's own voided maternity. She gently places a hand on Anita's knee.

Anita shrieks.

"I'm so sorry! I'm so sorry, Anita! I touched your knee. I can't believe I did that. I'm so dumb. I'm sorry."

"It's okay," Anita says through gritted teeth. "Ooh, my — I'm okay. I'm all right. You're a believer. That's a rare thing. You think my Monty's a real believer? He's not. He says he is. But at the end of the day he dismisses me. All my life, all I've ever wanted is to help people. I was a good, dutiful daughter, granddaughter. I was a great mommy. What can you do. That's all over now. Mommy time is over. We're old and alone. Our men — all men! — are weak. Weeeeeeeak. We have nothing to live for. Might as well be lez-been bulldaggerssss 'n' eat ourselves to death, know what I sssayin'?" Anita is slurring now. Teresa senses that Anita may not be lucid for much longer.

"Anita. Anita? Anita!"

"Hey. Wuz goin' on, ladyfrien'?"

"I want you to exorcise me. Well, I don't want you to perform an exorcism on *me*, I want you to exorcise me, from my son. I think that is probably what you were getting at from the beginning, wasn't it?"

Anita's head has slipped off to one side. Teresa bangs on the coffee table. Anita rouses.

"I'm the dark presence that invaded my son's soul when he was just little. It's not anything to do with gayness. It's me. I'm the problem. I'm the demon."

"I need to lie down for a little bit. Come and lie down with me for a little bit."

"Please, Anita, I know you're in pain, but please try to focus. Please exorcise me from my son. Please, Anita. Please, now. It feels very urgent."

"Quit riding me, woman. Am I in my pyjamas?"

It's no use. As Anita sways in her seat Teresa realizes that she will have to do this — whatever this is, this self-exorcism aimed at a remote target? — on her own.

19

She has shuffled into the living room, picked up the remote and turned off the television. Joel is not in the mood. He learned how to use the debit machine at the museum gift shop today, as Donald's shit breath billowed into his face in sighs of impatience, and now he has a headache in his right eye. His mother has yet to apologize for her last outburst; Joel does not know how to contend with the fury of his favourite person, who is wasting away. And now she has interrupted a rerun of *thirtysomething*.

"I know I must leave this house. It's not like I'm having a great time. I'm thinking of maybe giving Montreal a go. I feel like I could gestate there. Not that you care."

"No, you must leave now. I don't care where you go. You're out. Get out."

Joel looks around at the other faces he imagines in the room, all of them as incredulous as his.

"Why don't I help you get settled into bed?"

"I don't want to go to bed. You think I'm joking. I want you out. Now."

"Where am I supposed to go? It's nighttime."

"Be resourceful. You need to be resourceful. The cord has been cut. I don't care anymore."

Joel goes to his father's room. His father is starfished on his stomach in frayed grey briefs.

"Who's there?" Hugh shouts when Joel shakes him from his sleeping pill coma.

"She wants me to leave the house this instant. Should we call the doctor? What should we do?"

Hugh squints. He can't come to this quickly.

"Hey? Leave the house. Maybe go stand outside on the lawn for a while?"

"I don't want him on the lawn," Teresa pipes in, "I want him out!"

"It — Who?" Hugh asks his pillow. "Oh. Right. I'll drive you to Hazel's, then."

"I don't want to go to Granny's. This is wrong. Mothers aren't supposed to throw their children out of the house. Isn't that, like, illegal?"

"I'll take you to Hazel's; she'll take it all back in the morning. Your mom's haywire right now."

Joel puts his Walkman, a pair of underwear, and *The Book of Rock Lists* into his backpack. His mother, when he passes her in the kitchen, is grey and tearful, but still juts her jaw and sets her mouth in a pantomime of piety. He tries to think of something broken to say, something he would've said before, to disarm her: *Guess what? I love you! Oh, you! You're my favourite person!* But the thought of saying such things makes him nauseous.

JOEL DINGS HIS grandmother's doorbell for a good five minutes before her beady eyes appear in the window. Hazel Hannigan is eighty-two and, apart from the burgundy rinse in her sparse hair, looks every minute of it.

"Who is it? I've got a goddamn rifle!"

"Hi, Granny. Sorry, it's Joel."

"The hell it is. He's in Toronto, I know that for a fact. Who is this?"

"Gran, it really is Joel. Joel, who was too effeminate to eat Christmas dinner with you two years ago. Remember when you said that?"

"Joel? What the hell do you want? Where did you come from?"

"I've been in town for a while. For Mom. But she made me leave the house. Can I maybe come in?"

"Oh, for Jesus Christ," she hisses, fiddling with multiple locks.

Joel hugs his grandmother, who does not hug back. Hazel is infamous for her bile and total lack of tact. Most people hate her, including her children. But Joel has this dim recollection of once, as a child, making Hazel laugh, in spite of herself, laugh into her shoulder furtively, so nobody could see her experience happiness. So Joel retains a fondness for this hateful woman.

"I'd fallen into a nice sleep for the first time in years and you come and startle me. So is she — gone?"

Joel, jostled from the night's events, doesn't understand the question. And then he does.

"No, she's still alive. Sort of. How did you know she's sick? Mom said you guys haven't spoken for months."

Hazel sits, lights up a Black Cat, sucks it with her anus of a mouth.

"I'm still her mother. A mother knows when her thing — her child — is in pain. And the girl who comes in to do my hair seen her downtown and said she looks like hell."

"You really should go and see her. It won't be fun, by any means. But you'll really regret it if you don't."

Hazel laughs, a clammy bramble of a laugh, which dissolves into coughs. "Don't talk to me about regret, mouthy. I was married for forty-four years to an animal. He broke every bone in my body, he threw me through a window, he threw me off a Ferris wheel, he pushed me down the escalator at Polo Park Mall, and I am to this day convinced that he rigged the bathtub somehow in an attempt to boil me. But I stayed, for the benefit of my children. Then my daughter tells me she'd rather I aborted her than raised her. How do you like that? My whole goddamn life has been one big regret. And now I've got my *gayandlesbian* grandkid scratching at the door like a raccoon. Christ, *I'm* the one that should've been aborted."

Hazel cackles. Joel looks at the limp plastic Christmas wreath on the wall above the toaster oven. That wreath has been there always.

"So is it okay if I just, like, sleep on your chesterfield tonight?"

"No, it is not okay if you sleep on my chesterfield. What if someone looked in and seen ya? They'll think I'm running a flophouse. No, you can sleep on the floor in the basement. Well, there's a loveseat down there, you can lay on that. For tonight. Then I want you out of my hair."

Joel descends to find that Hazel's basement is actually quite homey: chintz curtains on the windows that look out onto black brick, a well-kept navy area rug, a glass-and-brass display cabinet in the corner, filled with ballerina dolls of all sizes. He hasn't seen the doll collection before. Ballerina dolls, mid-dance, swirled in white and yellow and even black tulle, with real hair pulled into tight buns.

He snoops around his grandmother's basement, on this bleak, absurd night. On top of the television is a VHS tape: *Estrella Plant's Ballet and Jazz Dance for Seniors*, it says on the box, which also features Estrella Plant smiling strenuously while doing the splits. On the floor by the loveseat is a book: *Never Too Late: Inspired Life Change at Any Age*. He flips through it; it's a workbook, with blurbs by old people who have hurled their craggy bodies out of airplanes or reached their very first orgasm, with a much younger partner. There are exercises and questionnaires. Hazel has filled out only one.

Q: Describe the forces in your life that may have discouraged you from pursuing a goal, and possible ways of addressing those negative forces so that they no longer hamper you.

A: I always wanted to be a ballerina, but when I told Daddy that I wanted to be a ballerina he said that only whores become ballerinas and also I was plain in the face. I got married and that was that.

This negative force no longer hampers me because Daddy capped from a stroke in '79. At the funeral I cried along with Dot and Peg but we were all secretly relieved that he had finally capped.

GRANNY DECODED AT last, Joel thinks, triumphant. All these years Hazel's been torn between dance and domesticity, just like the girl in *The Red Shoes*, and her thwarted passion has expressed itself as crankiness.

He runs upstairs. Granny's in the bathroom. He knocks.

"G'wan! I'm taking a shit!"

"Granny, I understand now."

"Understand what? I'm taking a shit. And it's my first one in a week so don't wreck it for me."

"No, I mean, I understand about your — your bitterness over not being a ballerina."

No response. Joel calls to her twice. Finally, a flush. Hazel opens the door. Her face is all veins and menace.

"Have you been snooping around in my things?"

"No! Just what was lying out in the basement."

"I don't have nothing lying out in the basement. You went through my personal things. I feel like I been raped."

She puts a hand against the hall wall. Joel can't tell if she really needs the wall for support or if it's just for show.

"Granny, I'm trying to say that I understand. I'm torn between artistic expresion and romantic fulfillment also. Like in

The Red Shoes. Have you seen the movie? Have you heard the Kate Bush record of the same name? So good."

"You get out of my house! People don't talk to other people about their personal ballerina things. I never felt so raped. Even when I *was* raped!"

"I'm just trying to reach out. I wasn't trying to rape you, Gran."

She pokes him. Pokes him down the hallway and through the kitchen.

"Out! Out! Out!"

"Please don't throw me out. That would be twice in one night. I'm starting to feel really … not seen, and not heard. Please? I love you, Granny. I love your passion for ballet."

"Stop. It's like a knife up my privates! You go and get your cruddy knapsack and get the hell out of here. You got five minutes."

Hazel staggers to the back of the house, slams a door and locks it noisily.

In the basement Joel finds a heavy, black rotary telephone and calls Edmund. Edmund answers with his usual "Edmund speaking."

"It's just Joel, hi. I know it's super late and you've moved on with a new lover, and actually I've also moved on in a big way, so that's really great, but I just had an argument with my grand-mother and I feel all — Yeah. I continue to experience crisis. How are you?"

"I'm great. Busy. It is truly astonishing, how much there is to do and get done, when you really inspect your life. They're doing some construction next door, so my days and nights are punctuated by pounding and sawing and drilling, all day, all night, 24/7, which you'd think would be illegal, but. Wait. You said you're in crisis? When you say 'crisis,' do you mean *crisis* crisis as in 'Hey, I'm in crisis, where is the ice cream truck right this minute?' or do you mean *crisis* crisis as in "I'm in crisis, turn me over, what about Linda?' sort of thing."

"I don't understand what you're saying."

"Really? Oh no!"

"Edmund, are you okay? I'm worried that you've — have you had a stroke?"

Edmund whoops away from the phone. Joel hears a circular, swooshing sound; Edmund may be swinging the phone around by its cord like a lariat.

"'Have you had a stroke?' she says! That's one for the photo album of all time. No, I have not had a stroke. I think laterally these days. My whole thought process is much more intricate and mystic. It's been a very expansive time of late. Now I sound like something that fell out of Grace Slick's purse. Forgive. I'm going to stop talking now. Now. No, now. Shhh. Tell me about your crisis."

Joel hesitates to speak, fearful of fuelling Edmund's mania. This yapping loon is so unlike the slow, lilting man he first knew.

"My mother, who is insane and totally dying, threw me out of the house for no reason. So I went to my granny's. And now my granny is throwing me out of her house for being supportive of her lifelong dream of being a ballerina. I'm homeless. I don't know what to do."

"Hmm. That part of Ontario is quite pastoral, isn't it? Why don't you camp out?"

"I don't know how to camp. I was hoping that I might be able to come and stay with you. I have enough for the bus to Toronto. Even if I could sleep in, like, a closet or whatever. I know you have a new love interest, and even though that destroys me I'd still be grateful if you'd have me."

Edmund hems and haws aloud, like in a radio play. Granny bangs on the ceiling.

"Or even in your backyard? Seriously."

"You know, Joel, my life is so busy these days. My house is a hive. I really don't think you'd be comfortable here. And, as you said, I really am so immersed in my new relationship. You'd be better off camping in the bush."

"No, I wouldn't."

"Or take shelter in a church."

"Please? Please, Edmund?"

"Please don't — say my name, tenderly. I can't. Whoa, yeah. I'm off now. There's a pie. I need to make. Talk soon."

Edmund is off the phone before Joel can try to plead in an untender way. He grabs his knapsack. He is homeless in his hometown. He tries to picture himself pitching a tent, making a fire. He can't.

20

OLD FRIENDS IS WHAT IT'S all been about of late. These past weeks, darting here and there with Binny, getting the meth from the meth people, finding new meth people when the usual meth people run out, doing the meth, nude amid candles and dildos in this condo or that — Edmund keeps encountering acquaintances he hasn't seen for years, men he'd assumed were dead. But they aren't dead; they're on disability and meth. Hollow-cheeked, dentured, prone to edema of the lower legs, stocked up on fancy groceries that go uneaten, breathless, fidgety, forever pushing pampered cats out of the way with fat, slippered feet, these guys are all in pretty rough shape, but it's great to see them again. As they leave these candlelit condos after three-day binges, Edmund will fill Binny in on who these men are, or were. *That guy was almost the mayor, twice. That guy used to have his own cooking show.*

Yesterday, might've been the day before, but definitely recently, Binny pulled Edmund into somebody's bathroom and declared his love and loyalty. "I'd die for you, I'd fry for you," he said. Edmund returned the vow, in a high, disco whisper. He isn't sure that he does love Binny, but they get along magically well when they party. He thought he definitely did love Binny for a stretch there, when they came together in Edmund's many rooms, all giggly possibility. As the days went on — days of getting high, speeding for forty-eight hours or more, then crashing, sleeping, trying to stave off the pummelling despair as dopamine levels flatlined — their relationship suffered. It's impossible to enjoy another person when your only thoughts are of suicide, or more meth to eclipse those suicidal thoughts. They are an affectionate couple, bound together by meth. Maybe that's not the optimal foundation for a relationship, but it really could be worse. It could be based on duty, or guilt. That kind of relationship is truly sick.

And the sex is … well, not technically extraordinary, what with everyone impotent from the meth, but the aura of erotic possibility is constant and powerful, and it insists that Edmund and Binny abandon all else in pursuit of marathon group sex. This is an arduous task; there has to be at least one guy in the group amenable to either taking Viagra (which means no poppers, lest they have a heart attack) or fucking straight while everyone else is fucked up. When the details all line up, though, and marathon group sex does happen, you instantly know that this sex, with these people, on this drug, is the sweet spot of all mortal experience.

During these sessions, in dark apartments made muggy and hot to counter cold hands and feet, Binny becomes a squalling primate, while Edmund babbles. Binny becomes insatiable, endlessly able to accommodate cock after cock, while Edmund becomes not so much insatiable as insatiably interested in the topic of sex. He talks non-stop about sex. As Binny is penetrated by a procession of people and objects, Edmund curls up like a mermaid on the side of the bed and colour-commentates: *How does that feel? Surely that's far too large for even you to take. What an achievement. I don't think I've ever seen a sparkly dildo before. Wow. Look at that. Oh my goodness. And that is not a small fist, either. Well done. Way to go.*

They've met up with some S&M tops. Binny found them too polished, with their leather outfits and prissy rules — when one of them launched in on the dangers of bipolar currents near the heart area during electric play, Binny screamed at him to just shut up and plug in. If there is no real threat that Binny might be maimed or murdered he starts to lose interest. He likes it rough. Brutally rough: no cloying cat-o'-nine-tails for him; he wants the shit thoroughly kicked out of him, by an amateur with a real grudge. This tall order has been almost impossible to come by; there was one guy, a paunchy older guy with a big mole on his forehead like Aaron Neville's, who delivered one punishing backhand to Binny's face before going soft (on all fronts) and apologizing profusely.

Binny tries to goad them, exhort them to really slap, really punch, really choke, he can take it, he's a nasty boy who needs killing. They've often been asked to leave, the torture bottom and his yapping pimp. All those long, ear-popping elevator rides, the two of them silent, panting and studying themselves in the mirrored walls and ceiling.

When they crash, they crash in unison and sleep for two days, always two, rising periodically to chug orange juice and maybe stand for a moment, vertiginous at the sight of the stove, the sad stove, and the fridge, the sad fridge. At one point, they're both up at the same time; Binny asks Edmund if there would be any way Edmund would consider beating him up a bit. This annoys Edmund. He's feeling the same dejection that Binny is, but he's sleeping it off, not begging for a beating. "Bear the brunt!" he barks at Binny and goes back to bed.

Finally Edmund is lucid again. There's a voicemail from Lila.

Eddie, it's Lie-Lie. I was just going to say "I have some bad news, please call me," but I behaved so atrociously last time we saw each other, I realized you have every reason not to want to call me. I'm so, so sorry for the way I acted towards your friend. I was judgmental. Forgive me. Not just because you're a very dear friend but also because — I — we, we lost the baby. They saw that all of his organs were on the outside of the body and his little spine was all twisted. I gave birth to Israel. He came out sleeping. He'd already passed away. We're hurting, Eddie. Please call me. I love you.

He calls. He gets Marci. He tells her how sorry he is for her loss. She thanks him — is it just him, or is she being chilly? — and hands him off to Lila. Her voice is small and froggy, a cried-out voice.

"Oh, my Eddie, are you still my friend?"

"Always, always! How can I help?"

"Just come see me. Please come see me. I need to see a friendly face. Marci — I think Marci's mad at me."

"That's not true. She's just grieving."

"Can you come over today? Please come over."

"Definitely. Just give me a bit. I'll be there as soon as I can. Is it okay if I bring Bernard?"

She pauses. "Umm, sure, of course. I owe him an apology."

After they hang up Edmund runs a dishrag under the faucet and wipes down the kitchen surfaces. He thinks back to his old, fallow life after Dean, before Binny. Quiet days, the long slats of winter light that fell across his body as he watched television — what was so sad about that? The lassitude, the small gnaw he felt then was blissful compared to the cold immobility that now binds him to his bed between binges. He would like to see Lila. A nice visit could be curative. She'll get the chance to assuage her conscience with Binny, and he'll get the chance to brush against his old life. He would have to be high, though. Lila and Marci and Lila and their dead baby. He'll have to be high. Binny has to be there. He doesn't do anything without Binny now.

"We're going to Lila's," Edmund says to Binny, who is flossing his teeth and watching porn with the sound off.

"Who's Lila? I don't generally like to party with girls."

"Lila, you know, who you had that unfortunate run-in with a little while ago. She feels terrible about the way she acted."

"That fucking bitch. Good, I'm glad she feels terrible. That really fucked me up."

"And she wants to see you so she can apologize."

"What, she wants me to go to her like a fucking royal subject? Fuck that. She wants to apologize to me, she can come see me."

"Binny, she lost her baby."

"Where?"

"No, I mean, she miscarried."

"Oh. Well, that's shitty, but still."

"She would be grateful to receive your wonderful, positive energy."

Binny loosens a little. Edmund feels a pang of guilt for homing in on Binny's need for approval.

"Did she really say that she thinks I have positive energy?"

"Yes."

"Okay. Maybe I'll make her something. A 'get well' thing or something."

"That's a lovely idea. Why don't you write her a song?"

"I've never written a song."

Edmund suddenly has a vision of Binny in the basement, singing into a microphone, amplified by an amplifier. Binny will learn to sing as himself, drop the crutch of some amorphous female alter ego, hone his skill, write a plaintive song for Lila, and everyone will feel a whole lot better.

"If I buy you a state-of-the-art microphone and amplifier, will you come?"

"Really?"

"If you make use of them. Will you commit once and for all to your music?"

"I don't have any music, but yeah, totally. I think I need like a keyboard, though, too."

"Do you play keyboards?"

"No. But I want to be able to look over at the keyboard while

I'm singing and think 'oh hey, there's the keyboard,' know what I'm saying?"

"I think so."

EDMUND REMEMBERS DEAN mentioning a store called Gunn Music; he had a funny experience there but Edmund can't recall the particulars. He knows it's on Bloor.

They cab it over. The store is big and well-stocked, but oddly empty of shoppers. Binny picks out a microphone, a stand, and a keyboard. He mouths the words to something histrionic into the microphone, running his hands salaciously up and down the mic stand. The salesman looks uncomfortable. It would appear that he has not yet had to deal with a tweaking, gay, fake soul-singing star before. Edmund smiles empathetically at the salesman, who quickly looks away. Edmund is wearing terry cloth slippers and a yellow silk shawl wrapped several times around his neck. A couple times recently he's caught a glimpse of himself through other people's eyes — this salesman, the Filipino housekeeper who interrupted a lazy orgy at some guy's house one morning, exclaiming, "Good morning. I can't see anything! I'm a blind lady!" and, almost every day, the old man at the corner store, who still smiles but no longer says hello — and has desperately wanted to leave this brisk, blazing madness, call the whole thing off, bundle up his current state as one big, strained practical joke, go home, vacuum, reside in silence. It's too late for that.

"Eddie," Binny beckons. "Come and hold this guitar. I thought I hated guitars, but now I think I love them. I really feel this one. So amazing. Come and hold it."

"I'll be right back," Edmund says, walks to the other end of the store and stands behind a stack of drums. Sometimes he stops liking Binny. Sometimes Binny is too loud, too upper case. There is no breeze to Binny. Edmund wants the best for him, wants to help him as he has helped previous lovers. He would happily bankroll a course of study, even a small business, for him, but this dingy, day-to-day friendship has got to stop. Binny is less and less endearing. Edmund decides, behind the drums, that affairs with turbulent boys are not what he needs, not after Joel, the moony pest, and Binny, the kid twanging an unplugged electric guitar.

He reluctantly returns to the scene.

"This is the one. I'm in love. I need this one. I need this one so bad. I need it like Diva Annie, 'I Need a Man' realness."

"I see the connection between you and that piece," says the salesman. "I should let you know, this guitar, without the amp, is $2,600." He sounds sincerely cautionary, not like a salesman, more like a guidance counsellor.

"That's a deal, probably, eh? That's probably a deal. I don't know the first thing when it comes to what's hot and what's not in guitars. Anyway, it's only money, eh, Eddie? I sing for the things money can't buy me like Diva Stevie, Klonopin Street Angel realness. Let's ring it up with all the other stuff."

"Binny, I would like to be the one who announces 'let's ring it up,' if you don't mind."

"Well, sore-eee. Sorry for enjoying myself and having a nice time shopping with you. I thought we knew each other. I thought there was love and trust going down. I see now that I was wrong. I was so, so, so, so wrong."

"Binny, don't be melodramatic. You can have the guitar, I'd just like to be acknowledged in the transaction."

Binny gently sets the guitar back on its rest.

"I don't want it anymore. I hate it. It's gross."

The salesman briskly begins unplugging things.

"Hold on," says Edmund. "I want to buy the guitar. It's a nice guitar. You can have it."

"I don't want it. You hurt my feelings, and now the guitar has bad vibes."

FOR TWO HOURS Binny has made good on his promise to carry his gear, or at least his microphone, wherever he goes. The kitchen, the bathroom, the den. He's trying hard to improvise songs; so far his best work is the word "you," spread across several short, discordant notes that sound like a cat scampering across piano keys.

Now it is time for Edmund and Binny to get ready to go comfort Lila. Edmund picks out a set of black silk Chinese pyjamas that Dean sometimes wore. He doesn't know how to dress anymore. He doesn't know his body. He has lost some weight in the last few weeks. Twenty-five, thirty pounds, maybe. He puts on the pyjamas. He is swimming in them. His face is gaunt — but not scarily so. His face has definitely been gaunter — is that a word? Really, were it not for his ashen complexion he could almost pass for an endurance athlete.

Binny wants to bring the microphone and amplifier to Lila's.

Edmund points out that Lila and Marci are grieving the loss of a child and probably wouldn't appreciate a house guest setting up electric musical equipment in their living room.

"But I was going to sing a comforting song to her, remember? It was your idea."

"Was it? Oh. Well, I'm having second thoughts." Edmund changes the subject softly. "Wait — I've just had a flash of inspiration. Why don't we both wear Chinese pyjamas to Lila's? It'll be charming. You can leave the mic and amplifier at home, and we'll both be charming and delightful in our pyjamas."

"I'm not going to wear silk pyjamas. That's too 'show tune' for me. Props to Diva Liza, Pet Shop Boys Don't Drop Bombs 12 inch remix, hip replacement realness, but I don't go there personally. And I'm not going to abandon my mic, no way. You know that. I don't want to hurt its feelings."

"Please?"

"No. Nope. Sorry."

Edmund ponders what would make for the ultimate bribe. "If I promise to arrange the ultimate dom top sexcapade, the ass-kicking of a lifetime, will you go to Lila's without your microphone?"

Binny makes a big, campy show of thinking it over, searching the ceiling, pulling at a phantom beard. "Who did you have in mind for this ass-kicking of a lifetime?"

"Leave it to me. You won't be disappointed."

"Cool. Yeah, okay. But he better be psycho."

"Let's do a bit of you-know-what," Edmund says, reaching for the little square of tinfoil on his night table. Binny hands him a lighter; Edmund runs the flame back and forth beneath the foil.

21

"SIX O'CLOCK. FIVE-THIRTY IF you know what's good for you," Teresa calls after Hugh, who's out the door on his way to the legion. He goes to the legion every day now. Teresa doesn't care one way or the other; in fact, she always encouraged him to drink: he was borderline fun when drunk. Today, though, she wants him home in time for dinner. Monty and Anita are coming over, and however much she may have disparaged her husband during prayer sessions, she still wants him to make a good first impression. She's excited to show Hugh that she can make new, wonderful friends, even this late in the game. Monty and Anita have their quirks, certainly, but she thinks Hugh will like them both. He likes characters and go-getters and people who like to talk, because he is none of those things.

She gives the living room the once-over, then the dining room, the bathroom, other conspicuous nooks Anita might see. She's always been house-proud; even when the boys were little and she was working, the house was immaculate, dustless, smelling of pine and maybe of makeup after she'd done herself up for the day, but never, ever of excitable boy or damp man: you'd never know the place housed three males from the sight or smell of it, and if that has maybe caused Hugh to sometimes feel like he's been erased from his own home — oh well. He'll have the run of it soon enough.

It's time to get dressed. She'll leave her nightgown, first time in days. Lifting her arms above her head is a long, tough task. She said she'd make a lasagna. Why did she say she'd do that? There's no way in hell she can make a lasagna, the shape she's in. Anita will understand. Their friendship already goes deeper than any lasagna. Anita certainly has no bones about making her husband do all the housework, with her bad knee; that said, she hopes Anita won't take Hugh to task for not preparing the lasagna, because he would have, had she not shooed him out of the kitchen. Maybe she should call Anita and explain that there isn't going to be lasagna, but that Hugh isn't lazy and is actually a really good cook when it involves things he's just shot. She's getting carried away. They'll get nice takeout, chicken balls and wings from the Ho Ho. Anita will like Ho Ho takeout. Hugh's eyes glaze over with pleasure whenever he eats a Ho Ho chicken ball.

She sits at the kitchen table. Turns off the radio. Joel's been gone four days. Hugh went to the museum the day after she made him leave; Joel's staying with Donald Tait at his house downtown. When Hugh told her this, she screamed that she didn't want to know of Joel's whereabouts, but she was relieved to know he was safe and not caught in the talons of his monster grandmother. All she wants is her boy back home with her. She needs his wide, flat feet padding around (what a hard time she had when he was small, finding shoes to fit those feet, as wide as they were long!) and his smell — not the piss smell he came back from Toronto with, the mint and wood smoke smell that he was born with, a smell she never had to spray away like she did with anything Dallas or anything Hugh. What a huggy kid he was — he is! It's rare to come across such an affectionate kid, boy or girl. She hopes he won't lose that, after this reformation; hopefully he will become a strong man who is still capable of affection. What if she'd had two boys like Dallas, who swatted her arms away almost as soon as he could walk? She couldn't imagine. She wouldn't have lasted, all these years. She would've fled in the night with a stranger, any stranger.

She wants Joel home with her. She wants what is best. Her bones pulse with pain. The pain remains, even with morphine; the drugs make it so it doesn't consume her, she can walk past the pain in its cage but she knows it's there, panting, all claws. She turns on the radio. She'll feel better in a bit. Anita will come over, and she'll be grand and wacky, and Teresa will be bolstered by her, diverted.

She lies down in the living room. She turns on the TV. The TV and radio together create a soft, gabby hum that pacifies her. She nods off.

Someone's at the door. Nobody ever comes to the door. She'll ignore it. But what if it's Joel? Or Hugh, with Joel lying dead in his arms? She's able to sit up by the second ring, stand by the third. She can see a purple kerchief on a grey head through the window. She hates that purple kerchief. That head.

"What do you want?" She cracks the door open as she would for a stranger.

Hazel's face starts to scrinch into its default setting — resentful raisin — but she tries her best to tame it.

"I took a taxi all the way from Keewatin to see yous, which cost a small fortune, so yous sure as hell better be nice to me. Oh, Teresa Beryl, look at you. I don't think I can hack this. The skin is just hanging off you. Don't you look like particular shit. My God. Surely — Can't they fill you up with air or something?"

"I'm sorry to scare you. I'm between visits to the air-filler guy. Would you be able to stomach me if I put on my fucking Little Orphan Annie wig?"

"Oh, now. I'm here now. Mom is here. I brung some popcorn I didn't eat last night. Oh, and I brung you this book I got — this magazine, I should say — has some nice pictures of Princess Margaret in it. They have a before-and-after type thing. Gosh, she was so pretty, and now she's so bloated and red in the face, eyes all slitty, looks like a real end-stage alcoholic. The article says all she does is drink and have enemas. So sad. But the queen wouldn't let her marry that guy she liked, and she was never the same. That's what you get when you take away a woman's dreams, though, eh? Let me in the goddamn house!"

Teresa doesn't move. Hazel shivers showily. Teresa winces, lets her pass into the house. Still that smell of her mother, of mould covered up with cheap perfume. Hazel mounts the front stairs, Teresa gasping after her.

Hazel looks around the kitchen, with particular notice to the new fridge, the newish table, the matching cans for the flour and sugar and coffee. Hazel, when she's over, always looks around for new objects acquired since her previous visit.

"New fridge, I see," she says. "Must be nice. My fridge doesn't work at all. You put a fresh bag of carrots in the crisper and they're rotten and black by morning. What did you do with the old fridge?"

"I don't know. Hugh got rid of it."

"Oh. Would've been nice if I knew about the hand-me-down fridge; I would've taken it. All the food in my fridge is rancid. Everything I eat is rancid."

"Sorry."

Hazel gripes quietly about the lost chance of a better refrigerator, until it's out of her system.

"So?" she says.

"Yeah? What?"

"What've you been up to lately?"

"A lot has been happening. But I honestly don't have the energy to get you up to speed. We haven't spoken in months."

"Whose fault is that? I called you — I think I did, anyway. And I sent you that nice birthday card."

"No, you didn't."

"Yes, I — Oh wait, I sent a birthday card to Mister Charlton Heston. Was it the one with the parakeet on the cover?"

"How should I know? You sent it to Charlton Heston."

"I'll find a nice one for you. I'll do that first thing tomorrow."

"It's okay. My birthday was four months ago. Let's leave it, okay? I don't have time to chat. I've got guests coming over for dinner."

Hazel laughs, all scorn and phlegm. "Guests coming over. Since when do you have guests over? You don't do that. Unless — Is this a dinner for all the men you've been with?"

"Yes, that's it exactly. A sit-down dinner for twelve, followed by one last gangbang. Nothing gets the motor running like chemotherapy."

"Well ... what the hell are you going to make for this dinner?"

Teresa so begrudges civil, neutral conversation with her mother — really any conversation that isn't recriminatory; she has a limited supply of conversational niceties and doesn't want to waste them on Hazel.

"I was going to make a lasagna."

"No. I've had your lasagna. It was gritty, like you put sand in it. Don't make lasagna."

"I'm not. I don't have the energy to cook. I thought we'd order in from the Ho Ho. I don't think my friends have had Ho Ho yet, so it'll be a treat for them."

"The Ho Ho! Oh, no. You know you can't know what you're eating from that place. Oh sure, they've put up new wallpaper and that new sign out front, and they've hidden away that old Chinaman woman who used to squat in the corner and peel things. It looks fancier now, but they still use cats and dogs in all their meat dishes. What, don't make that face, it's true. Helga out on Second Street there, she saw the Ho Ho people break into the house next door to steal the poodle. Yes. Garbage cans full of little collars and noses out back. And they've been using the same vat of fat for twenty-five years. The old, squatting woman and her daughter are always at bingo. The Ho Ho! No No! I'll make something. What have you got in the fridge? Nothing, I bet. Let's take a look."

Hazel roots around in the fridge. Teresa stares at her bony ass in red polyester. "I just want to say ..." says the bony ass, which then becomes impossible to hear.

"I can't hear you with your face in the fridge, Mom."

Hazel slowly withdraws from the fridge, straightens up, but won't look her daughter in the eye when she says, "I just wanted to say that I think it's real horrible that you have this sickness. I feel real useless because there's not a damn thing I can do for you. If I could take away your sickness and bring it on myself to suffer and die, I would."

Teresa thinks on it. Her mother has made this kind of generous, heartfelt statement before: once, right after Teresa's brother died, Hazel pulled her aside to say that, while she did love Teresa's brother more than Teresa, that didn't mean that there was no love at all for her daughter. And then Hazel hugged her, and said that they would just have to try harder to get along and love each other. But they didn't try harder. A few days later Teresa caught her mother stealing all the bills and coins from Teresa's wallet, and they didn't talk for many months after that.

"It's nice of you to say that, Mom. Means the world."

Hazel hauls out an onion, a saran-wrapped package of ground beef. Slams around, in the hunt for pots and pans. "There's not a lot to work with here," she says. "But it'll be better than dog meat."

Anne Murray on the radio, the song where they don't have any money but she's so in love with you, honey. Joel was a baby when "You Needed Me" was big; Teresa was always so exhausted that she'd burst into tears whenever that song came on the radio, and when Joel saw Teresa burst into tears he'd also burst into tears. She had to be super careful around little Joel that way. He was such a sponge, emotionally.

"What are you going to make?"

"Wouldn't you like to know. It'll be a surprise."

"Oh God. That's what you used to call that fried glop that you always fed us on Fridays. Remember when Daddy got food poisoning from it and he had to go to the hospital?"

"Christ, he was so mad when he got out! Thought I was trying to poison him. I wasn't, though. Not that time, anyway. Ooh, he was mad! I can still see that big vein in his forehead."

"He beat the shit out of you that night. He smashed the toilet with a baseball bat. That was the day he broke my wrist."

Hazel bangs a bowl on the chopping block. "Do you not have a spice rack? What kind of person doesn't have a spice rack?"

"It's on the wall above the dishwasher. He hit my wrist with a hammer. I had a cast."

"I don't remember that at all. He saved his violence for me. You had a carefree childhood. We should all be so lucky to have such a carefree childhood."

"I had a cast. You sat and watched them put the cast on me."

"You fell out of a tree; you loved climbing trees."

"No, I didn't, and no, I didn't."

"I'm eighty-two, get off my back. Christ, turn the record over.

We all had tough times. Someone mistreats you, then you spit on their grave and curse them to hell and you get on with things. You know what you do need to be concerned about is that goofy boy of yours, wandering the streets. He's a goddamn menace. A tenderizer — terrorizer — terrorist, I should say."

"I've got things under control with Joel. There's a long-range plan in place."

"What horseshit. The only long-range plan for that kid is drugs and then jail for life. Whose house is he stealing from now?"

"He's staying with —" She stops herself. Hold the line. Stick to the holy plan. Hazel doesn't need to know anything. "I actually couldn't tell you who he's staying with right now. He's in the wind, as they say. Haven't a clue."

22

JOEL SETS THE WORLD'S SMALLEST table for dinner. Donald Tait's tiny house was never meant for guests. Joel could only find one fork; he put it with Donald's plate, took a soup spoon for himself.

At least he's in off the veranda. At first Donald would only let him in the house to warm up. Then he'd make Joel go back on the veranda with a space heater. When he did finally allow Joel to stay in the house, there were several provisos: don't touch anything — including the countless, teetering stacks of newspapers, file folders, magazines, three-ringed binders, and hundreds and hundreds of books — never knock on Donald's closed bedroom door for any reason, ever; don't comment on the condition of the house or its perceived uncleanliness — ignore the toilet bowl, porcelain gone brown from years of untended piss, make no mention of the fur balls, ossified cat turds, old, inkless pens, thumbtacks and pennies on the curling, tiled floor; and, if at all possible, avoid eating, drinking, moving about, urinating or having bowel movements. So far

Joel has mainly made good on these promises.

Donald enters with a plate of buttered French bread. Joel greets him with a smile.

"It is my intention," Donald says, "that we have a pleasant meal together this evening, but I really do not want you to get accustomed to this. I don't have dinner parties. I lead a very intense interior life. A life of the mind. I don't socialize very much. I do hope that you are actively organizing an exit strategy, because I may very well need you to leave at a moment's notice."

Joel nods. Donald goes back into the kitchen and returns with a burned shepherd's pie.

"So," Donald continues, sitting, "what is your exit strategy?"

"I'm almost definitely going to go back to Toronto. I'm going to really be more — forceful, I guess."

"Forceful. Regarding what, exactly?"

"My work."

"Right. Yes. Sorry. What exactly is your work again? You may have told me, I just can't remember."

"I perform my — I have these — I write — I perform my poetry, except it's not really poetry, it's more like — statements, that I recite in a really emphatic way."

Donald nods, flips his braid from his front to his back, forks off a bite of shepherd's pie.

"Which artist would be a comparable reference point? Ginsberg?"

"Umm, I don't know. Sort of like Sandra Bernhard, but more stark."

"Sandra Bernhard ... Do you mean, Sarah Bernhardt?"

"No. I don't think so. Or do I?"

Donald daubs at a crumb in his crumby beard.

"Why don't you perform something for me."

Joel goes red. Giggles. Mentally sifts through his repertoire.

"It's been ages since I performed. This will probably be totally awful. Should I stand?"

"If you like. Yes, why don't you stand. Just be mindful of the Sears catalogue collection immediately behind you."

Joel stands, regards the seven foot stack, moves to one side. Takes a breath.

"This is a recent piece. I haven't actually written it down yet. I'm still workshopping it, hardy har. Hoo. Woo. I'm nervous. Okay.

> *"She threw me out of the house*
> *I can't even believe it*
> *She threw me out*
> *Part of me says, 'No way!'*
> *Part of me says, 'Yes, way!'*
> *As if.*
> *Seriously!*
> *My stone pillow. Poison. Oh my God. Wow.*

"Obviously it's still very rough. But you can sort of get an idea of what I'm going for. The, like, visceral — impact."

Donald looks into his plate, then starts to laugh. Tears stream from his face, his shoulders dance. He can't stop. Finally, fingers splayed on the table, he contains himself.

"You did not tell a lie. That was totally, deliciously awful. Oh, my stomach!"

"When you say 'totally, deliciously awful,' do you mean the subject matter?"

"Yes, the subject matter, the text, the delivery. All of it. Good on you for sharing that, though. I haven't laughed like that in years."

Joel looks at the stack of catalogues. This is nothing he doesn't already know about his stuff. Sure, it's aggressively conversational, wilfully naïve, and his delivery is halting, but there's still a kernel of — something, in there somewhere, isn't there? He hadn't been giving his performance art much thought of late, with all the upheaval, but now that he is: there is a certain something there, isn't there? Everyone has a certain something.

"I'm glad that I was able to make you laugh, but I don't think it's fair of you to condemn the efforts of a young artist. It's a real struggle, being a young artist."

"I'm sure it is. You don't have to worry, though, because you're not an artist."

"That's mean. You don't know that I'm not an artist. Sometimes it takes a long time for an artist to find their voice."

"Absolutely. And sometimes it takes a long time for a person to realize their natural facility. Isn't it better to know now that you're not an artist, so you can discover your true vocation?"

Joel glares at Donald. He realizes that Donald is saying reasonable things, in a pleasant tone of voice. He is still hurt.

Shit-breath, ponytail man doesn't know what he's talking about. Or, if he does know what he's talking about, you'd think he'd be able, as a mentor, to frame the conversation so that Joel could feel real hope for his future, rather than the ringing futility that makes him want to curl up on Donald's veranda and cease breathing.

No. It isn't fair that Joel should have to start from scratch, fret and toil, while Donald Tait gets to continue with his tidily untidy, cozily uncozy life of the mind. Donald Tait needs to be reminded of the pain of personal turbulence.

Joel puts a palm to the stack and pushes it hard. It tips and falls into a stack of binders. The binders go flying. A flurry of loose-leaf fills the room. The three barren birdcages on the buffet clatter to the floor.

Donald scans the wreckage. He opens his mouth. A high, blurry note comes from his throat, a sound like a deaf person learning to speak. He gets up and looks at the long-buried places in the room now uncovered by the paper landslide. Still the keening deaf sound.

"I'm sorry," Joel says. "I just really needed to express —"

"Shut up!"

Donald moves to the spot where the catalogue stack was. Stuck deep into the carpet is some torn construction paper. He kneels there.

"The nudes," he says. "I haven't seen these in thirty years."

"Nudes of who? Of you?"

"Could you please not interrupt my reverie?"

Joel kneels next to Donald. He is silent for the sake of

Donald's reverie. On the torn paper is a charcoal sketch of a fleshy, reclining male.

"Dan the Fisherman drew these. I was your age, younger even, seventeen. Look how lovingly he drew me. He loved me. I loved him. We were in love. It was — alchemy. I sound insipid."

"No, you don't. What happened to him?"

Donald goes quiet. "He was murdered. By a bear."

"Really? Oh, no. Were they lovers, too?"

Donald is aghast. "Were they lovers! It was a bear, a brown bear. And this was long before the Marian Engel novel."

"Oh, sorry. By 'bear,' I thought you meant a hairy gay guy. That's horrible, I'm sorry. A bear, gosh. But an actual bear can't commit murder, in the strictest sense, can it?"

"It most certainly can, in this instance. Dan the Fisherman was a woodsman, a seasoned camper. The bears were his friends. And then one of them eviscerated him, ripped him limb from limb. What would you call that?"

Respectfully, Joel says nothing. Donald pries the drawings from the rug. He spreads them out, six sketches in all. They study them awhile.

"You were kind of chunky back then, heh? What was your weight-loss secret?"

Donald scowls. He looks at Joel's earnest face. His scowl dissolves. He laughs, not the wracking cackles of a few minutes ago, but a soft, friendly laugh. He playfully thwacks Joel on the side of the head. Joel's temple stings but he takes it in stride. Maybe, he thinks, this new, smiling Donald will actually lend him a proper pillow tonight.

23

"EDDIE, PLEASE TAKE ME WITH you. Please just leave with me right now!" Through the crack in the door Lila grabs at Edmund, then looks behind her, terrified.

"Who is that, Li? Is that Edmund and friend? Let them in."

Lila's eyes fall shut in despair. She opens the door all the way. Marci is standing in the hallway in a sweat-drenched, baby blue leotard. "You just caught me doing yoga in the basement. Lemme freshen up and I'll join you all in a bit."

"Marci," Edmund says, "this is my close friend —"

"Hold that thought," she says, putting a hand up. "I want to be properly introduced. Back in a minute."

She bounds up the stairs two at a time.

"Wow," says Binny. "You guys have a really nice house, eh? How come there are towels covering all your paintings and shit?"

"Those are mirrors. It's a custom in Judaism, after a death. I'm sitting shiva. I don't care what Marci says. She says you can't sit shiva for a miscarried baby, it's not permitted, it's tacky and maudlin, but I don't care. My grief is my grief. You watch, when she comes downstairs she's going to pull down all the towels off the mirrors. I don't understand why she's being so hard and bossy, like more than usual, at a time like this. We've just lost our baby boy, and she's acting like I tracked mud in, or broke a vase or something."

She sighs the sigh of someone completely depleted and leans into Edmund.

"She's mourning in her own way, Lila," Ed offers, stroking her hair.

"Well, she's mourning in a stupid gay way, I say," Binny says. Lila looks up at him.

"Aren't you a sweetie! I'm so glad to meet you again. Please forgive me for last time."

"Aw, group hug!" Binny throws his arms around Edmund and Lila. "You really are so pretty, Lila!"

"I tried to tell Marci what you said about my hair, it was so charming, but I couldn't remember exactly how you said it."

"About your hair? Your hair is very Diva Suzanne, solitude stands in the doorway realness."

"Yes! That's it. I love it, it's like you're talking in a gay, umm, patois. It's like that wonderful documentary about the black drag queens."

"*Paris is Burning*! That movie saved my life! You saw *Paris is Burning*? Work!"

Lila smiles. Then it fades, and she gropes along the wall into the living room.

The walls of the living room are covered with posters from films that Marci has worked on. She's a line producer or project manager, something like that; Edmund can't remember. None of the films are familiar; one poster features Nancy McKeon dressed as a nun, another Melissa Gilbert in a blue wig, holding a butcher knife. Above the television is a black and white photograph of Lila and Dean. Edmund isn't sure when it was taken, but Dean has a beard, so it had to have been close to the end.

They sit.

"I should've brought food!" Edmund says. "I absolutely should've brought food."

"That's fine, Eddie. I know you're not a food person anymore. Besides, Marci made a whole bunch of food. I told her not to, but since we're not officially sitting shiva, she went hog-wild and made munchies."

Binny shakes his head disgustedly, like he knows all about sitting shiva. "That's awful," he says. "What a bitch."

"Binny, you shouldn't call Lila's partner a bitch."

"Yeah, you'd better not. I don't mind so much, but if she catches wind — look out."

And here is Marci, in navy velour track pants and a flimsy pink peasant blouse, hair raked away from her face by a plastic headband. Now that she's close up, Edmund notices a faint rash covering the left side of her face, roughly in the shape of South America. She immediately extends her hand to Binny, but says nothing until he catches on and stands up.

"Marci Laylor, great to meet you, welcome."

Binny hangs a heavy hand from Marci's, tugs it once, then sits again. "Binny. I'm sorry about your baby."

Marci shrugs, almost jaunty. "Well, these things happen. It's part of the process. We'll try again."

"So this last one was on purpose?"

Marci looks around with disbelief. "Well, two monogamous lesbians can't accidentally have a baby, so yes, it was on purpose!"

"Cool. And so who were you pregnant for?"

Lila starts to speak but Marci barges in. "We weren't pregnant for anyone, other than each other. We used an anonymous donor."

"Cool. I guess you can't, like, get a refund?"

"Why don't you bring out those plates of hors d'oeuvres you made, Marci?"

Marci offers her blazing grin and gnawing jaw. She wordlessly goes into the kitchen.

"She's intense, eh?" Binny whispers. "Is she — She's not tweaking, is she?"

"What's tweaking?"

Edmund's gut seizes. Binny, stop talking, say no more, shut it. "Marci has an incredibly demanding job; I don't know how she does it. She's an iron lady."

Marci returns with two blue plates. She sets them down on the coffee table.

"Don't those look wonderful," Edmund says. Little round flaky things topped with white stuff. Long, slick black things drizzled with red stuff. Edmund used to consider himself something of an epicure. Now he can't even put a name to — what is that white stuff on the flaky thing? Goat cheese? Must be. He takes one of the flaky things and holds it in his palm.

Binny asks if he can smoke in the house. Marci says no. Binny says he understands, totally no problem.

"So, Binny," Marci says with a strained smile, "what do you do?"

"What do you mean?"

"For a living, or for fun?"

"This and that."

"Sounds mysterious! Like what?"

"Why you on me? I've never been in jail. I know how to sit and chat and be nice. I'm not going to steal your shit. Sorry, I think I do need a cigarette."

He bolts for the front door.

"I'm sorry about Binny," Edmund whispers. "He's a bit volatile. He's quick to take offence. He comes from trauma. He's really a very gentle soul. He's a big fan of an assortment of black female singing stars and black female rappers. I think he might be quite talented."

"I wish I hadn't been such a fucking snob last time," Lila says. "It's only natural he'd be defensive. God, you know, we all present ourselves as uber-sensitive to issues of class and privilege and, you know, the sex industry, but when you encounter an actual representative of all that stuff, it's so easy to fuck up and say something stupid."

"I totally support your friend in his journey through his — issues and — experiences," says Marci. "But I feel the need to make it clear that our home must not be considered an injection site. I'm sorry if that sounds harsh, it's just that the last thing either of us needs to cope with is a needle-stick injury."

Edmund laughs, looks at the round flaky thing in his hand, puts it back on the blue plate.

"I completely understand. You guys are the sweetest people. Binny doesn't do needle drugs. He's really very grounded. At the most all he does are very light party favours."

Now Lila's all concerned-looking. "Okay. Party favours? Tweaking? Is this just more of Binny's gay patois or is this drug lingo?"

"Oh, you. I'm not sure — a bit of both? It's all in good fun. Binny and I are really committed to fun. It's a time to heal."

"You can't — you cannot — do drugs, Eddie," Lila says sternly. "Your health is fragile. Please don't do drugs. What would Dean say if he were still here?"

This irks him. "First of all, Dean is not here; he left a long, long time ago. It's been just me for a while now. Secondly, I don't think it's appropriate for you to be invoking the name of Dean, because he was mine, he was the love of my life, thanks very much, and anyway, he was the biggest coke whore in Toronto when he was alive, which you know full well. But all of this is irrelevant, because I am not doing drugs."

Binny returns. "Hope you bitches didn't do a bulbie without me!"

Marci cocks an eye at Edmund: more drug lingo?

Edmund asks Binny what a "bulbie" is to save face. Binny,

annoyed, says Edmund knows damn well what a bulbie is — they did one in the bathroom at Wendy's a couple days ago.

"So why don't you tell us exactly what a bulbie is, Mister Drug-Free-Fun Guy," Lila says in her angry voice, a monotone falsetto.

He can't keep up the ruse. "It's when you use a lightbulb, a sort of modified lightbulb, to smoke crystal meth."

Lila falls forward at the waist. "Oh, Eddie. Meth. I've read about meth. It's not a light party favour, it's a bad drug. God. Like I wasn't worried sick about you as it was."

This sets off Marci; she jumps up, clucking her tongue, making a weird, Al Jolson-ish fan of her shaking hands around her face. "And there we have it. That is why we are in this shitty situation. You're so worried about your former employer that you couldn't look after yourself. Or our baby son."

"Ooh, girl!" Binny says, leaning in.

"It almost sounds like there's some blame in that statement," Lila says with a quivering face. "It sounds like you're blaming me for the death of Israel."

"What happened in Israel? Is this like a news thing?" Binny asks Edmund.

"That was what they named their baby. Israel," Edmund says softly.

"I'm not blaming you, although if that's how you want to interpret it, fine. I'm working my ass off trying to make a wonderful life for us, for our family. I can't help but feel slightly betrayed, Lila. I feel like I entrusted you with one thing — one thing — and you were unable and maybe even unwilling to come through. Sometimes I just think — do I have to do it all? With everything I've got on my plate, do I have to be the pregnant one, too?"

Lila looks at Edmund. He can't bear it. Cannot. Time to skedaddle.

"Wow," Lila says. "I've never felt more like a fucking brood-mare. How did this happen? Who are you? I feel betrayed, Marci. As your wife, and as a lesbian."

"Me, too, honey," Binny says.

Marci swats at the space beside Binny's face. "Get out of here! This is none of your business. Both of you! Out!"

Edmund jumps up. Binny doesn't.

"Don't tell my friends to leave. I want them to stay. I want witnesses. I want people close to me, who have been through the horrible things I've been through. What have you been through, Marci? What were you doing when we were burying our friends? Getting your fucking master of whatever degree? Playing fucking golf with that fucking chick from fucking *Street Legal*?"

Marci's tiny mouth opens and closes and opens, like a goldfish's. She turns on a bare heel and runs back upstairs, slams a door.

Edmund puts a hand on Lila's damp back. "Go to her, Lila."

"I don't want to go to her. Fuck her! I'm so tired of her stupid goal-oriented bullshit. *Oh, I'm sorry we didn't reach our 1998 target, Marci, but you know what, I would rather stand with my friends sometimes, if I had to choose. Really. I would rather stand with you, Eddie, and with all of our ...*"

He takes his hand from her back.

"There's nothing left to stand with, sweetie. There's nothing here. We're all gone. Go be with your girlfriend. She's not a monster, she's just sheltered. Go hang out with her."

Lila nods slowly. Squeezes his arm. Drags herself up the creaky staircase.

"Old school lezbo realness! So cool. Wow. They should settle that shit for real, with guns 'n' shit."

"Let's go. Now."

"Word."

24

FIVE TO FIVE AND NO Hugh. Teresa and her mother had a screaming match over Mrs. Clemens, the sweet, elderly waitress at the Husky who used to babysit for Hazel; Hazel brought her up in stupid, preposterous gossip, said that a friend told her that Mrs. Clemens was once a prostitute in India. Teresa called Hazel a hateful piece of shit and why did she have it in for such a sweet lady, still forced to waitress at eighty-eight. Hazel said that Teresa's father once said that he thought Mrs. Clemens was kind of nice-looking, that she knows a whore when she sees one. Teresa could only make this long, guttural grunting sound and stomp off into the living room. Since then Teresa has been sitting in the chair by the picture window, watching the lake across the road, pretending that the clatter in the kitchen is not her mother, is only an innocuous ghost. Where is Hugh? Has he been in an accident? Here comes Anita, zipping up the driveway in an old yellow minivan.

"Is that Hugh or the company?" Hazel yells from the kitchen.

"It's my friends."

"Shit! Shit! Shit! My hair looks awful. Oh, look at it! It's all flat on the side. Why didn't you say something?" Hazel runs into the bathroom. Her hair won't look a bit different when she emerges, but Hazel, for all her coarseness, has always been obsessively vain.

It's only Anita when Teresa opens the door. Anita looks tired and unkempt. But she is off the crutches, has two canes instead. Teresa looks around Anita for Monty, but he's nowhere in sight.

"Who're you looking for?" Anita asks, almost sarcastically. "You looking for Monty? Because Monty is long gone. I didn't want to come today, to be honest."

"My God, Anita, what happened? Come in."

Teresa puts an arm around Anita, careful not to bump her canes. "He went to the city, to look for crack. Haven't heard from him in three days. He could be dead, he could be anywhere."

"My God. I'm so sorry. Careful on these steps here."

"He said I triggered him! He said he felt triggered whenever I acknowledged my pain, and then when he saw me using Percocet to relieve my pain, that pushed him over the edge! Isn't that just the most. He doesn't want me to acknowledge my pain, but he also doesn't want me to relieve my pain! How fair is that! *Oh, every time you say "ooh, my knee!" it's like someone is handing me a big rock to smoke ... Oh, you broke our covenant by taking Percocet, now I have to smoke crack,* he says."

"Oh, Anita. I'm sorry."

"Nah, no. I'm sorry to dump all this on you."

Teresa tells Anita to never apologize for reaching out to a friend. She tells Anita that she has never felt closer to another woman. Anita doesn't respond; instantly Teresa regrets her candour. "I mean, friend-to-friend," she quickly qualifies. Anita, clearly preoccupied, offers up a hollow chuckle.

"What a nice home you have. It oozes warmth and love," Anita says wistfully, having lost her own.

"Ha. You must be picking up the love ooze from a neighbour's house!"

Anita asks how Teresa is feeling. Teresa says she doesn't want to talk about it; maybe later.

"I flushed the rest of my Percocet this morning. I'm just now starting to have some breakthrough pain. You do not want to be in my head right now, trust me. I want him to come home, I do. I can't live in this town alone. I am sorry to say, but I really do not like this town. And I'm too old to start over somewhere else."

Teresa smiles sympathetically, but can't help feeling slightly anxious about Anita's desolate, un-Anita-like state.

"I'm sure I must look like hell; my hair is all flat on one side," says Hazel in a stage whisper before she comes around the corner. Anita turns, smiles. Hazel goes pale.

"Anita, this is my — well, mother, Hazel."

"Hi."

"Yes. Teresa, can I borrow you for just a minute? There's something in the bathroom I'd like you to look at."

"I do not like the sound of that!" Teresa laughs and looks to Anita, who is mouthing *ooh, my knee* with a pained face.

"Please? I just need you for one second."

Teresa rolls her eyes, apologizes to Anita, follows Hazel into the bathroom. Hazel slowly, soundlessly closes the bathroom door.

"It's a black!" Hazel hisses, clutching Teresa's upper arm. Teresa swats her hand away.

"What is? Anita? Yes, Anita is black. And?"

"Where did it come from?"

"Stop calling her 'it.' She lives here with her husband, who is also a close friend. They have two daughters."

"But it's — she's as black as night!"

"I will throw you out of this house right this second if you don't shut your trap and pretend to be nice."

"I just — I don't — Where did they come from?"

"Iowa City."

"Oh, Christ! American to boot! You know they come up here and snap up all the bargains at Zellers before we even get the flyer in the mail. It's not right. And I don't have to remind you that I was raped by a black last year."

"You mean that nice old man who asked you to go see *Titanic*. He did not rape you. And he wasn't black."

"He is. Rita Cleave told me — he's a light black; his mother was a full black and his father was a partial black, but he walks by day as a white! I went to the show with him, because I thought he was a white. And when the show was over he grabbed at my brassiere strap like he was pulling on the reigns of a horse. He was getting ready to ride me like a horse, before I gave the go-ahead. I call that rape."

"He was feeling for his goddamn coat! He has one eye!"

"Okay. It's your house. But you'd better sit on your purse and hide your coupons."

Teresa pokes her mother hard in the chest. "You are going to shut your fucking mouth and treat my friend with courtesy and respect. I don't want to hear any more of your stupid inbred friends' theories on who's black and who was a fucking runaway prostitute in India. You are just going to shut up and then fuck off and that will be it!"

Hazel is bug-eyed, but knows better than to speak. Teresa withdraws her finger. This bit of temper has left Teresa weak and barfy.

Anita is flipping through a photo album from the coffee table. It's the one with purple pansies on the cover; pictures of the boys from '85 to '90.

"Hope I'm not being nosey," Anita says. "Now which one is Dallas and which one is Joel?"

Teresa sits with Anita. She smiles at the picture Anita points to, Dallas and Joel in a tomato patch in Fargo, summer of '86. Dallas is thirteen; Joel is eight. Dallas looks at the huge tomato in his hand, Joel straight into the camera, smiling wide.

"Dallas is a real string bean in this one, just like my girls," Anita says.

"He's much stockier now," Teresa says.

"Dallas is a wonderful person ," Hazel interjects. "He's OPP. He's real natural and normal, a gentleman. So handsome. If he wasn't my grandson I'd tell him to climb aboard!"

"Mom! That's disgusting!"

"Oh, ease up, sober-sides. I'm just saying that I like my grandson. He's really made something of himself. Not like that other one of yours. When's Dallas coming down to visit? I'd love to have you all over for a nice dinner."

Teresa doesn't want to add to Anita's dejected mood in any way, so she decides not to remind her mother that she's never made a nice dinner for anyone.

"Him and Shary and the baby are coming down next week, supposedly. They've been saying that for a while, though."

"Have you met your — ooh, my knee! — great-granddaughter yet, Hazel?"

Hazel ignores, or doesn't hear, Anita's vocal tic, but does seize on Anita's easy sympathy, which comes through even in Anita's grumpy state of withdrawal. Hazel acts all forlorn and grabs at an invisible pearl necklace around her throat. "No, unfortunately I have not," she says, eyes downcast. "My son had no children before he passed away, so this will be my first great-grandchild. I'd love to see her, but ... I tend to be treated very badly by my family. I've cried until my tears ran dry."

Anita nods sympathetically. "I'm sorry to hear that. There's nothing worse than a loving family torn apart by dark forces. I worry that our girls will have nothing to do with us after — ooh, my knee! — they find out their daddy relapsed and their mommy also had her own ... hiccup."

Teresa changes the topic. "So, hopefully a nice visit from Dallas and Shary and Misty will revive me a bit and —"

"They called her Misty? That's a dog's name! Why didn't they just call her Lassie? Good God," says Hazel, unable to keep up the sad act for more than a minute. Teresa asks her to go check on whatever's cooking in the kitchen. Hazel reluctantly leaves the room, blinking and tittering like a naughty, eighty-two-year-old schoolgirl.

"I'm not doing well, Anita," Teresa says once Hazel's gone. "I'm struggling, and I feel all foggy and weak. I can't handle my mother's selfishness right now. I don't think I can even — I know I'm already so reliant on you, and you've got your own family problems, but I need your strength more than ever."

"I don't have any strength left, sister, but if I did, you'd have it."

"I don't believe you don't have any strength left. You're the strongest woman I've ever known."

"It's nice that you think I'm strong, but I'm telling you I'm not. You think I'm hiding some secret reserve of strength I don't want you to know about? Ooh, my knee! You calling me a liar?"

"No. God, no. Why don't we pray?"

"I'm not really in the mood. But ... would it really mean a lot to you if we prayed?"

"It would."

Anita, all irritation and knee pain, drags herself into conversation with God.

"Dear heavenly father, we address you today from a place of great fear and uncertainty, and a lot of anger — righteous anger! One of us is dying, Father God, and she worries that she's not doing right by her children as she prepares for the final passage. And one of us has had her fill of her unreliable, selfish husband of twenty-five years, and of this bullshit town that doesn't even have a multiplex movie theatre or even a Walgreens. We ask you, Lord, to steady us both. Make my husband stop doing crack and come home. Take away his fetish for personal odour. Soothe my sister Teresa as she journeys towards the golden light of you and Jesus and — ooh, my knee! motherfucker! — heaven. Amen."

Hazel comes running with a wooden spoon in her hand. "Did I hear an 'amen'? Were yous praying, just now?"

"Well, we were trying to, anyway," Anita says slowly.

"Are you from one of those gospel things where they sing and fall down and that?"

"I guess, yeah. You could say I'm from one of those gospel things."

"That's so nice. I didn't have religion growing up. I come up hard. My mom and dad were hard people. I had to sleep in the kitchen sink. My only toy was a clump of hair in a rubber band I found by the side of the road. I think I really missed out. I've been through so much hardship. It would've been so nice to have religion to rely on. Especially later when I had my own family, and it became clear that I probably had nothing to live for. You know that hymn, 'There Will Be Peace in the Valley'?"

"Of course I do."

Hazel's chin starts to quiver. Teresa is made even more barfy and has to clutch at the couch arm to keep from heaving.

"Sometimes I wonder ..." She stops, exhales through her mouth, starts over. "I've lost all my loved ones, and now my sweet daughter is not doing too good ... Anita, do you think that there might be ... peace in the valley for me? For Hazel? For little Hazel and for grown-up Hazel who doesn't have anything?"

"I really can't say one way or another. Sorry."

Teresa can't bear it. "Who cares if there's peace in the fucking valley for you? This isn't about you. Anita is my friend; she's here to support me in my time of need. You've never been to church in your life."

Anita puts a hand on Teresa's shoulder. "Let's take it down a notch, all right? My head is pounding, and your voices are like buzz saws."

"I'm sorry, Anita. But you have to admit that my mother is a vampire. She sees someone else receiving love and support and she tries to steal it. She doesn't care that I'm sick. She only sees that I have a new friend. She won't stop until she's stolen you from me."

Anita's unimpressed. "Hey, news flash — we're not in high school anymore."

"This is what I'm always saying to Teresa," Hazel says. "Grown-up people don't go around stealing each other's friends. Why do you think Teresa acts that way, Anita?"

Anita's face stiches up with annoyance. "How do I know? Is my name Teresa? I've got my own problems."

"What else do you do that's spiritual?" Hazel asks. "Do you read palms, too?"

"Oh my God," Teresa clucks. "You are so racist. Anita sees you for what you are. Don't you, Anita?"

"Shh ... What kind of painkillers do you have? Just the

morphine? I guess I could give that a whirl. No! Cancel that. I do not want to go down that road."

"Gosh, Anita," Hazel says, smiling, showing her remaining teeth, "you are so pretty. Your hair is so nice, and straight. I don't see a single knot. Is it hard to comb?"

"Not really. My hair's not all that nappy, naturally. Back home I used to just let my hair do its thing, but here I make the effort and straighten it."

"It looks so soft," Hazel says. "Can I touch it?"

"Don't let her touch your hair, Anita," says Teresa. "My mother is a racist. She hates all people of colour. She doesn't deserve to touch your hair."

"What a thing to say," Hazel says. "I don't hate anyone. I haven't known very many black ladies in my life — I can only think of Shileen McKean, from when we lived on Myrtle Road, and she could've just been a squaw that got some sun; I never found out — but I'm always eager to meet new people, from lots of walks of life."

"Really, Mom? So you're saying you've never used the N-word?"

"Oh, you do not want to be using the N-word," Anita snaps. "I don't even use the N-word, and I'm allowed to!"

"I don't think I even know what the N-word is," Hazel says. "I just like making new friends."

"This is my new friend, Mom. I made this friend on my own. Can't you just please stay away from her?"

"You'd think I was the fought-over baby in the Book of Kings! Silly women."

Teresa squirms and sighs like a thwarted toddler. She never gets her way; she has to get her way this time. "Mom, I'd like you to repeat what you said to me in the bathroom just now."

"I can't remember. My memory is gone. Anita, I maybe have dementia, and that can sometimes be really hard."

"In the bathroom you called Anita 'it,' and you told me to sit on my purse and watch my coupons. When I was little you and Daddy used to use the N-word all the time at home. All the time. Whenever a black person came on TV. I remember the time Lena Horne came on TV in a fancy gown and you said 'who did that nigger have to ride to get that dress?'"

"And that is my cue to head on out," Anita says, struggling to her feet. "I never learn. That is it. I am out."

"But I'm not calling you a nigger, Anita. I'm exposing my mother. When you leave, she's going to say something along the lines of 'there goes a nigger.'"

Anita shakes her head, shifts her weight onto her canes. "I am in — ooh, motherfucker! — terrible pain, and I'm tired of you people. Do you know how close I came to playing on the WTA circuit?"

Anita sees Hazel's bafflement, which irks her further. "Tennis! I was going to play tennis! Tired of this fucking town; shopping is a nightmare. I'm too nice. I give and give. 'The crystal palm tree is telling us to move to Canada!' he says, and I just pick up and follow him like an idiot. To be honest, I don't think I even saw the crystal palm tree; I was just trying to be supportive. When's someone going to look after me, for once? Do you know how exhausting it is to perform an exorcism?"

Teresa paws at Anita, who dodges her.

"I'd love to look after you, Anita," she says pleadingly. "Whatever you need. Let me look after you."

"Easy for the — ooh, fuck off! — white lady to say when her ass is dying. I don't need your looking after! I need my life in Iowa back. I need my dignity back."

She canes her way through the house. Teresa and Hazel follow, imploringly.

"Where are you going?" Hazel whines. "Don't go. Hey, do you go to nightclubs, where they have, like, the bouncers and the big sparkly ball above the dance floor? I've never been to a full on nightclub. Would seniors be welcome at the black nightclub?"

"Anita," Teresa interjects, pawing at her friend, "why are you being so severe all of a sudden? Please don't lump me in with my mother. I'm a good person. Please? I know you're in terrible pain but I need your support. I could — I would even pay you."

"Teresa Beryl, that is about the most pathetic thing I've ever heard. You would pay someone to be your friend? Christ, I'll be your mother for a hundred bucks a day if you want. Anita, I apologize for my daughter. Can I get a ride with you? I guess — Do you think you'll be going to a nightclub today?"

"Anita, please don't go. I can't do this alone."

"You're not alone," Anita huffs. "You've got your mother." At the door Anita turns around. "I want nothing more to do with you, any of you. I'm sorry. I don't have any compassion left. I'm sick of talking. I'm sick of — Father God, plug your ears, I cannot help myself — right now I am sick of Jesus." She canes her way to the driveway and drives off.

Teresa falls back on the wall. Hazel looks around the edges of her daughter.

"Well, that's that, I guess," Hazel says, resignedly. "She's so tall, eh? Looks a bit like a man. Pretty, though. It was nice meeting her. Do you think she's going straight to the nightclub?"

Teresa slaps a hand to her forehead. This has never happened before. She has never grabbed at a person and begged them not to leave her. This is not how things should go, at a time like this.

"What do you want me to do with supper," Hazel asks Teresa on the floor.

"Why did you do that, Mom? Why?"

"Do what?"

"Why did you try to steal Anita away from me?"

"What? You're goofy — I was just being nice. I like meeting new people sometimes. She was — Once I got over the shock of all the black, she was nice and interesting. You kind of get all swept away when she's talking, eh? I hope she finds her husband. What should I do about supper?"

Teresa thinks on dinner: the countless dinners she has thrown together, distracted, resentful of her loved ones, annoyed by the necessity of food; the dinners that remain, and her annihilated taste buds.

"Just throw it out," she says.

25

JOEL IS ADMITTEDLY GIDDY, AND the way he rushed the first grade class through the museum — making them run from display to display, summing up each one in a few words — was simply an expression of his happiness. The kids had a great time. But Donald is livid. He yanks Joel behind the stuffed moose and the three-hundred-year-old nightie.

"What did I say about our — interlude, right before our interlude began?" Donald demands, wagging a finger.

"Oh, I know, I know. I'm sorry, Donald. I'm just feeling really, like, sprightly and happy, and I can't keep it in."

"That's your challenge as my employee, then, isn't it? Keeping it in. Part of being a grown man involves concealing your emotions at all times." He softens a little. "And part of being a quote unquote gay man is acting like you're bored even when you're not. Yes? I think so."

"Right. But I don't want to be like that."

Donald draws breath to speak, but stops. He lets his long hand come up and cup Joel's full, flushed face. Joel leans into his touch, the delight of a man's hand, any man's hand, on his face. Donald sees Joel's delight and takes his hand away. The museum's still open. Nobody ever just pops in to the museum, but it could happen. Donald tells Joel to start with the invitations to the button opening, sticking the address stickers to the envelopes.

Seven hundred and fifty invitations. Every white collar family in town, a few benevolent eccentrics. Donald is hoping at least 100 will show. Joel starts sticking the stickers. Donald was so thoughtful when they made love, after the stacks fell. Joel warned him of his smallish penis before they disrobed; when Donald saw it he said, "How sweet. If only they were all like that," and, taking it in hand, went on to lament the cult of the big cock. Dan the Fisherman also had a small endowment, and the big cocks Donald encountered after him he found frightening. An enormous, erect penis, Donald said, fondling Joel's small balls, always struck him as silly, inconvenient, out of place, like a garden gnome in the middle of one's bathtub. Donald's own body is what Joel expected it to be: white, slack, flabby in places, sunken in other places. His penis is, naturally, much larger than Joel's, but certainly not silly or out of place, nestled as it is in greying, weedy pubic hair. His knees are quite nice, in Joel's opinion. His knees and his feet, although his toenails, like his fingernails, could do with a good trim.

They ground their bodies against each other. Joel moved to suck Donald's cock; Donald stopped him and said that oral sex wasn't necessary. Joel continued, pressing his face into Donald's only slightly sour-smelling crotch. He set about performing a blow job as he best understood it — up and down, relentlessly. After a few minutes of Joel's up-and-down, Donald thanked him for the attention and asked that they move on to other things.

They kissed! Joel assumed that Donald would turn away from a kiss, but Donald initiated it. The soaring sensation it caused in Joel's chest! It didn't matter that Donald's halitosis made his eyes water or even that Donald insisted on darting his tongue about like a startled wasp. Joel is now among the frequently kissed.

Neither of them came. They touched and kissed for an appropriate length of time, then contentedly withdrew to either side of Donald's bumpy double bed. Donald remarked on Joel's relative ease of being in bed; he's not all hunched and stiff or limp and dead like the other young men Donald has been with.

Since then Joel has been allowed to sleep on a mildewed air mattress on the floor beside Donald's bed. He listens to Donald sleep. Sometimes he'll say things while he's sleeping, little bits of nonsense murmured in a childlike voice. Joel finds this adorable. Confirmation of Donald's tender, evergreen interior.

Joel has asked Donald if he could consider himself Donald's boyfriend. Donald said that Joel could consider himself any way he'd like, but to Donald Joel would only ever be an employee, and besides, sixty-one-year-old men do not have boyfriends or anything else breezy; they have enlarged prostates and gnawing anxiety over the ramifications of early retirement. They were standing in Donald's kitchen. Joel said that a sixty-one-year-old man could have it all: all the anxiety and prostate problems and a boyfriend. Donald told Joel to go stand around out of sight. Joel went and stood in the bathroom. He wasn't hurt by Donald's request that he stand out of sight. He just filed it under "Donald's baffling but adorable little ways," and tried to think of something nice to get him for Christmas.

Now Joel stands in the museum's back office, sticking stickers. He recognizes some of the names on the address labels, old teachers he never thought would show up on Donald Tait's mailing list. Like Mr. Cotton from grade five; could it be that he's gay? Mr. Cotton once told Joel that he was "seriously awry" because of the frantic, squealing way he played badminton in gym class. Mr. Cotton couldn't be gay. Likely he has a wife who forced him to donate to the museum once.

He's almost done the Fs when Donald pokes his head in.

"Your father — well, he says he's your father — is here."

Joel has a sticker on each of the fingers of his right hand. He moves, still stickered, toward the door, then goes back to pick off the stickers and tab them to the table's edge.

Hugh is thin, his pompadour wilted. He sees his son and lifts a corner of his mouth by way of greeting.

"How ya makin' out?" he asks, looking at the case of children's moccasins for sale.

"Awful. Otherwise good. I'm surprised the monster let you out of the house."

"Yeah, I guess I'm in her bad books 'cuz I missed supper with that goofy praying couple the other day. But Dallas and them are comin' down for a visit. You should drop by."

"But I've been banished from the household. I can't just drop by."

Hugh chuckles the chuckle he chuckles when he doesn't know what to say and wants to change the subject.

"That mother of yours is sure something else. How ya makin' out?"

"You asked me that already. How is she? Is she much worse?"

Hugh chuckles the chuckle. "Oh, you know your mom. That hellraiser. She'll outlive us all."

Donald creeps in between them. Joel introduces Hugh to Donald. Hugh extends his hand. Donald touches his palm to Hugh's then withdraws.

"I'm very sorry, but could I get the two of you to stand off to the side so you don't block foot traffic?"

Hugh immediately moves off to the side, while Joel observes that there is no traffic in the museum, ever. Then he moves off to the side. Donald, assured that the coast is clear, recedes again.

"How are you doing, Dad? You don't look that great."

"Yeah. I haven't been sleeping good. I think I need a new pillow. The one I have now has gotten all thin and lumpy all of a sudden. I don't know. And the shift work is getting harder and harder. I don't know. And when I got days off it's like I forget what I used to do on my days off before, so I just end up driving around town, or sittin' at the legion."

Hugh pulls his wallet from a back pants pocket. He picks

out three fifties, slides them across the moccasin case for Joel. Tells him not to spend it on crap.

"I should skedaddle. Your mom'll scalp me if I don't do the groceries. Dallas and them will be here Friday. You drop by this weekend. They said the homecare should start comin' to the house, but if you can't wash your own goddamn wife there's something wrong with you. I'm sure your mom'll be glad to see yous. I don't know if you should bring that queer with yous. He seems to think his shit don't stink."

Joel and Hugh hug in the awkward stickman way they always hug. Joel watches his father get into his blue Pontiac across the road. He goes back to stickering. He thinks of his father's compromised pompadour, his big, bony hands. He writes Hugh's name and the home address on a museum envelope. He'd never come to a do at the museum, but Joel wants his father to know that he is loved. Or at least that he is regarded way more fondly than when Joel was fifteen and hated his father's guts.

Donald silently approaches and stands behind him.

"He seemed like a nice man," he says.

"I've never seen him so fucked up. It's almost like he has Alzheimer's. He's never that ... chatty."

"That's chatty? I thought it was remote."

Joel leans back slightly into Donald.

"Is it okay that I'm sort of leaning back on you like this?"

Donald sighs. "It's not exactly comfortable, but if you feel compelled."

"I do feel compelled, I really do. I'm at a loss, Donald. I love you. I totally love you."

Donald swats Joel on the back of the head. "Why must you say such idiotic things? This isn't a film. We're two unfortunate men passing time. Get that straight."

Joel apologizes, but continues to lean on Donald. Donald lets him.

26

"WHERE'S MY KILLER TOP?" BINNY brays umpteen times a day, ever more insistent. Edmund has thus far failed to deliver. Binny has been fucked a lot — one guy pounded him with such perfect rhythm that Binny started humming along to the sticky beat of pelvis on ass — but he is unbruised, unwounded, woefully well. Edmund has sifted through his tattered address book again and again, looking for hot possibles in between the bricks of black marker that cover the names and numbers of dead people. All the hot possibles are dead. Just now, though, winnowing his fingers into the tiny vinyl pouch on the inside of the back cover, he found several business cards. And one of them is Jim the shrink's.

Big Jim, once so brawny and ebullient, a psychiatrist who somehow managed to maintain empathy and keep burnout at bay, a notoriously kinky fucker with a donkey dick: a major, major catch, a great lay, expert procurer of the roughest, most closeted men. His practice, on the second floor of his six-bedroom house, was at first a bastion to muddled, upper class housewives, fast-lane gay men with arid inner lives, and several professional athletes paralyzed by performance anxiety. Then, when the plague drifted in, his homely waiting room became populated with gaunt, coughing young men, and the housewives and quarterbacks fell away almost instantly.

Jim helped many men contend with the throttling shock of certain death where, just recently, there was only effortless, perfect health. He was a community hero. Then his own lover died, and Jim imploded. Closed up shop and dropped out of sight.

Edmund calls Jim, who answers, with that unmistakable overnight DJ bass voice of his. Turns out Jim is partying a bit right this moment. Come on over, Jim says, the more, the merrier.

His house is oppressively hot; he has the heat cranked, on this warm fall day, and all the windows weep with condensation. Jim is wearing a red flannel nightshirt.

"Welcome!" Jim says, with a bottle of Lemon Pledge and a rag in his hand. "There was a really hot guy here a minute ago, but his wife came by to pick him up — I don't know and I don't want to know! He left his paw prints everywhere, and I keep spraying and dusting but they won't go away. So. I'm sorry about the construction going on next door; the noise is outrageous, it's 24/7. I didn't know you could get a permit for round-the-clock construction."

Apart from Carly Simon's "Let the River Run" playing on repeat, Edmund and Binny don't hear a thing. But they know where's he's coming from; they've all heard imagined construction noise at one time or another.

"How you guys? You guys good? Help yourself," he says, pointing at the pipe and the tiny baggie on the coffee table. Binny helps himself.

"It's been a long time, Ed. Last time was at that ACT art auction thing in — gosh, '93?"

"Quite possibly, although my memory is awful. I'm doing great though, Jim. I really am."

"Oh, me, too. It's unbelievable. I never thought I'd be this great again."

They both stand there, grinning their greatness. It's something of a stand-off. Edmund doesn't know what to say next.

"I need cock like, five minutes ago," says Binny through the smoke.

"I promised Binny a good working-over by a mean top, and I instantly thought of you."

"Ha! That's so sweet. I don't fuck anymore. I'm a bottom now."

"Another Toronto bottom, hoo-ray!" Binny says resentfully. "Another nasty old hole, trying to steal the cock supply away from the fresh young hole."

"He's lippy, isn't he? I can see why you'd want to see him get roughed up."

"Well, I also recall that you've got great connections in the kink community, so ..."

"Yeah, not so much anymore. They've kind of fallen away.

They're not so much into the whole PNP thing. I'm much more a part of the PNP community now."

"The PNP community!" Binny sneers. "Bitch, please! Do you drive the fucking 'PNP bookmobile'? Where the 'PNP meals on wheels' at? Huh?"

Jim puts down the Lemon Pledge. He gives Binny a long look. "You know, now that I think about it, I might have a couple of ideas. Lemme see what I can come up with."

Jim goes off to the back of the house. Binny smiles triumphantly. "See? She gets what she wants when she wants it!"

EDMUND AND BINNY sit and listen to "Let the River Run," over and over. Jim returns; he's found some tops, and the first one will be here within the hour.

They sit and listen to "Let the River Run." Finally Binny, nicer now that cock is en route, clears his throat loudly. "You know, I really am all about Diva Carly, intense stage fright made me have my period onstage realness, but do you maybe have another song, or even a whole CD? I would seriously even listen to that one that got the bad reviews, *Hello Big Man*."

Jim is confounded. "The music," Edmund clarifies. "Do you have any other music?"

Jim bounds up to look through his CDs. This takes a very long time. The top guy arrives before Jim has arrived at a selection.

He is ugly and rather squat, but he has a nice piece. He fucks Binny on Jim's bed for nearly an hour — good endurance for a sober guy, but barely foreplay for Binny, whose face and torso are flushed Kool-Aid red and whose fingers keep pinching at the bedsheet as if feeling for flaws in the fabric. "Fill me up!" Binny barks every two seconds; as soon as the guy announces that he's about to come, Binny yells "next."

And so it goes for several hours. One guy after another, in filthy baseball caps and budget denim, bypassing the two middle-aged men talking at each other in their underwear, en route to the beckoning, bossy bottom boy with his legs in the air.

At one point in the night Edmund notices a familiar object in Jim's living room, a cheap, sparkly, plaster bust of a Roman man.

"Hey," Edmund says, "where did you get that Roman head? I know I've seen it somewhere before."

"The Romans," Jim said.

"What do you mean? Oh! You mean the old Romans, the bathhouse? That's it! That head was right at the front desk. Wow. What a memento. How did you score that?"

"I was friends with the owner. He let me have it when they closed."

They both stop their fidgeting to take a long look at the sparkly bathhouse head.

"I had some amazing times at the Romans," says Edmund. "Remember that little old man, five feet tall if that, who used to stand, fully clothed, in the dark room, and when you walked past he'd say, 'Hi, I'm friendly!'?"

Jim nods. "He actually came to see me a few times. For a month or so, three or four sessions. He was totally fucked. He was worried that his cat was mad at him."

"Aren't you breaching patient privilege or whatever it's called?"

"He's dead. I don't practise anymore. It was a lifetime ago."

"True. So where did you find all these guys?"

"Cruiseline."

"Oh. Okay." Edmund is disappointed: here he thought Jim was this plugged-in sexual maven, and it turns out he's been finding guys through the phone line, like everybody else.

Come sunrise the only guys on Cruiseline are lonely hearts calling in before work. Binny needs more cock and he still hasn't gotten beaten up yet. He lies, nearly preverbal, on Jim's big bed, asshole agape, skinny legs kicking. *Cuck*, is how he's pronouncing "cock" at this point. *Ah nee mo cuck*.

They run out of crystal, and Binny's butt is getting lube all over Jim's pillow shams. Edmund wouldn't mind a change of scenery himself, so Jim calls his friend Julio, who always has party favours. Julio says that Jim's timing couldn't be better; he has a hot top guy there who needs service and won't accept service from Julio, for whatever reason. Jim and Edmund wrap Binny in a duvet and cab it to Rosedale.

Julio answers the door nude. He is deeply tanned. He has had an unfortunate face lift, which has left him looking surprised and mildly annoyed, as though the cable bill has just come and it's a lot more than he thought it would be.

"He's so hot," Julio says, pulling them all inside. "He's from somewhere way in the east end, possibly even Scarborough. He told me when he got here that I was too fat and old to have sex with, and that I had lied about my age. He was really mad. Really, really mad. Scary. But hot."

"How old did you say you were on the phone?" Jim asks.

"Twenty-two."

"But you're fifty."

"I know. I just thought, with only the lava lamps on, he might not notice. I've stopped eating dairy, and I've just been feeling so fresh these days, so … Anyway, I told him I'd give him my DVD player if he'd hang out with me."

"How big his cuck?" asks Binny, bookended by Jim and Edmund.

"Aren't you lovely! I haven't yet seen his pride and joy, but his hands are enormous, so I'm sure you won't be disappointed."

They file through Julio's house, past the obligatory lacquered fans hung on the walls, past the obligatory fat, indolent cat and the bathroom that reeks of aerosol lilac overtop recent diarrhea. The guy is propped up on the bed, fully clothed, flipping through the channels on the huge, squat television. He's massive, longer than Jim and twice as thick, with a beard line that begins just under his small, hooded eyes.

"Everyone, this is —"

"Burt," Jim interrupts. "It's been a long time. How've you been?"

"Good. Shit, what's your name again? John?"

"Jim."

"Right."

"Okay, so we'll all just leave you with Binny for now," Jim

says, encircling Edmund and Julio with his arms. "If you need anything, just holler."

"Great, yeah, 'cuz I was just going to say — I'll do the young one, but I'm not gonna do all you old-timers."

"That is absolutely more than okay!" said Julio instantly. "The rest of us are just going to be in the other room, and maybe we might come in just to watch?"

"No fuckin' way. No watching."

"Absolutely okay. One-on-one can be so special sometimes. We're just going to hang out in the living room and catch up."

"Yeah, you do that. Go do your fuckin' drugs."

In the living room Edmund asks Jim how he knows this Burt person.

"That man," Jim says hesitantly, then stops to ensure that the door to the living room is shut tight. "That man is a sociopath. He's been banished from the leather community. He's overdosed boys on G, fisted them and then left them for dead. And — do you remember Brutus, who owned The Truck?"

"Yeah," says Edmund. "He was murdered. Stabbed, wasn't it? You're not saying that Burt is —"

"Yup. There wasn't enough proof, but everybody knows that Burt did it. A few people have told me they've heard him actually bragging about it in bars."

"Oh my God. Maybe we should tell Binny."

"It's his fantasy. He wanted a psycho top. I personally would never let someone I love play with Burt, but if you want crazy and mean, he's your guy."

"This is so kinky!" Julio exclaims with antic hands. "I feel like I'm in a porno!"

Edmund thinks. As long as he checks in on them periodically, Binny should be okay; he knows how to handle himself, and he is thirty-one (Binny would be furious if he knew that Edmund found his birth certificate in the back pocket of his baggy black jeans). Yes, Edmund will play it by ear.

Meanwhile, Julio can't stop talking. About how hot Burt is, how awesome it is to meet guys who actually have the kind of sex Julio only fantasizes about. About how warm it is for late autumn. About how spunky and sexy Binny is. About how great Julio's been feeling, lately.

Both Edmund and Jim confirm that they, too, have been feeling really great lately.

"It's such an exciting time," Julio resumes. "The possibilities are so endless that it blows my mind. The diarrhea from the meds is almost gone. I was really looking forward to bottoming again, after so long out of commission that way. Then Burt comes over and says I'm too fat and old to fuck and he punches me, and suddenly the diarrhea comes back. How's that for the so-called mind/body connection? This batch of crystal is possibly the best I've ever had. It's such an elegant, thoughtful high. I feel like … like Margaret Atwood, or someone like that, or that journalist who's really pretty — Barbara Amiel? I've finally found a reliable, humane drug dealer. At this point in my life, I strongly feel that crystal is a valid, holistic choice. I pretty much introduced crystal to Toronto, did you know that?"

"No, I didn't," says Edmund. "Thanks for your work on that."

They set up to smoke. Through two closed doors Binny somehow hears the telltale sounds and bolts into the room, feral and splay-footed, intent on the first hit of the pipe. Edmund has never seen someone so given over to the craven, cruel, base, sucking want. Not even in his many laps around the Romans bathhouse. Once Binny is all lit up he barrels back to the bedroom.

"He's so feisty," Julio says. "And yummy. Are you guys an item?"

"No. I don't know. He's — a — he's — someone in my life. You know how sometimes you have people in your life who are — in your life?"

"Oh, sure, yeah, sure. And he likes the pig sex, I guess, also, heh? Seems like he's really into the pig sex."

"He likes to be roughed up — well, more than roughed up, beaten really — during. Does that count as 'pig sex'?"

"Oh, sure it does. Yeah. Hot. Nice. Oh, yeah. Sure. Yeah. Hot."

Edmund and Jim glance at each other. Through the hum of the drugs it needs to be silently said: this Julio person is rather frantic, possibly slightly stupid, clearly unable to handle his high, unlike Edmund and Jim.

"So, Julio," Edmund ventures. "What do you do?"

Julio gathers himself as if preparing to give a speech. "I was seventeen years with Air Canada as a flight attendant. It was a dream come true, until I got sick in '92. I was really bad there for a while. I had dementia. I forgot my mother's name, my phone number. Then the cocktail came along and now I've never felt more — undemented, or whatever the opposite of demented is. I feel so fresh, especially since I had my face ... freshened up, which was the greatest gift I ever gave to myself. I was all set to go back to work when the — tragedy occurred, but you don't want to hear that whole saga," he says, obviously wanting to tell the whole saga. Edmund looks to Jim again. Jim shakes his head to indicate that Edmund would, indeed, be better off not hearing the whole saga. In the silence Edmund can hear Binny's sex chatter, that numb chant of grunts and demands. To drown him out Edmund asks Julio to elaborate on his tragedy.

"I was very close to my parents. We were a little team, just the three of us. They were both small people; my mother was officially a little person — or midget, as she used to call herself. The doctors told her that her tiny pelvis couldn't withstand childbirth, but out I came, right as rain. We were so close. When I came out to them, they just hugged me. For, you know, half an hour. And when I told them about my illness they cried and cried — Dad actually cried until he passed out, but he was sitting down, so he was okay — and then, a couple days later, they vowed to die alongside me when my time came. Of course I said, 'Absolutely not!' — how could you ever condone your parents killing themselves for you? — but the more I thought about it, the more comforting I found it. So it became this unspoken agreement. Can you believe it? Isn't that just so moving, that they'd do that?

"Then the pills happened and I got better. We were all so relieved. Winter of '97 Mom came down with a real aggressive female midget cancer; it was just awful. So Dad euthanized her, and then he — passed away on purpose, also. I was in Palm

Springs at the time. They left a note for me. I went mental. I was so, so pissed off at them for leaving me, for not including me. I was put in the Clarke on suicide watch for several weeks. And now ... I'm all alone in the world. I'm Little Boy Blue, you could say. I'm all alone, but that's okay, because solitude really makes you ... think about everything, and watch movies. I'm so happy. I really am. I get to party and spend time with nice people like you. You want some more smoke?"

Edmund declines the pipe. Julio's story was a buzzkill. He no longer feels sexy. He wants to leave.

Jim senses the shift in mood and lights into Julio for being morose. "That's exactly the kind of downer shit we're trying to get away from, Julio. Why do you always have to tell that god-damned fucking story? Jesus. And there is no such fucking thing as a 'female midget cancer,' so get that straight. Ugh. Let's go see what the other guys are doing in the bedroom."

"But we can't," says Julio. "Burt said we couldn't watch. He already punched me in the face for being fifty. You don't want to antagonize him."

Jim gets up. He gestures at Edmund to come along. Edmund is afraid of what he might see. As they get closer to the bedroom, the yelps and smut talk become more distinct.

"You like getting all fucked up on drugs and having your asshole split open?"

A smack.

"Yeah, I love it. I'm nasty."

"Cheap-ass piece of shit. You're just a hole, aren't ya? Fuckin' street whore cum dump."

"I fuckin' suck! Use me like a fuckin' cum rag!"

"You like getting smacked around?"

"Yeah, pound me."

"You're fucking cheap. I should choke the life right out of you."

More smacks. Then Binny choking, gasping. Edmund cracks the bedroom door open.

"Yeah, fucking DO ME!" Binny says, his voice shredded. "Fuckin' RUB ME OUT! Fuckin' MURDER ME!"

Edmund looks at Jim. "We should probably intervene," Edmund whispers.

"Why? The heart wants what it wants."

Julio comes up behind them. He bobs about for a better look. "Is it hot? What's happening? Is there anal? Is it hot? Is there ass-to-mouth?"

Binny is turning purple. Edmund steps in. "Okay guys," he says, pulling at Burt's shoulder. "Let's have a time-out."

Burt jerks away from Edmund but releases Binny. Binny coughs and coughs. Close call.

"What the fuck, Eddie?" Binny barks when he can finally speak. "You fuckin' ruined it! It was so hot."

"I'm sorry, Burt," Edmund says, sitting on the side of the bed. "Could we have a moment alone?"

"Ah, Christ," Burt grunts on his dismount. "What is this?"

He stalks off to the bathroom. Edmund puts his hand on Binny's cheek; Binny slaps him away.

"Why are you fucking with my sex? It was so amazing!"

"But you were purple. Do you not have a 'safe word'?"

"Fuck that. Fuckin' safe words are for pussies. This dude is for real. He said he wants to take me home and fuckin' put me in a fuckin' box on wheels under his bed, and then fuckin' roll me out to fuck me and then fuckin' roll me under again. It's finally happening. It's really happening. I've just got to go with this."

"But what if he … Okay. Okay."

"Cool. You're the best. Love you lots. I'll, like, call you when it's over."

Edmund rises. He's not sure what has just occurred. Is Binny leaving him for murderer Burt? Or is Binny simply instructing Edmund to go wait in the living room? As Edmund passes Burt on the way out of the room he has the urge to shake Burt's hand, offer some gesture to signify a gentlemanly passing of the torch, but he's afraid Burt might punch him for being old.

"Why don't we go somewhere else," Jim asks Edmund in the hallway. Edmund looks around for Julio. "Bathroom. He's got the runs again," says Jim, sensing. They sneak out of the house.

"Surely you guys aren't leaving already!" Julio says, running barefoot over the lawn to catch up with them. "It's just getting hot. Does the beat-me-up guy have to leave, too?"

"No, no," Edmund says. "He's having a great time. He'll be fine."

"Please don't leave. I don't want to be the odd man out. I have some crack, too … We could smoke some rock and play 'Clue.'"

Jim pats Julio on the shoulder. Tells him they'll be in touch. Thanks him for the party favours. Julio holds out his hands and clamps them open and shut in a gesture meant to convey longing. Edmund mouths a farewell while waving down a cab.

"It's snowing," Jim said. "Where are we going? Are we going back to my place?"

"Sure, yeah, I love your place."

Jim reaches into his jeans, produces a baggie of yellowish chunks that look like mangled teeth. "I swiped his crack. Aren't I a caution?"

"Jim! That's so gutter. You're a homeowner."

"It's wasted on Julio. He doesn't know how to have fun. We'll go to my place and give it a go. 'Kay?"

Crystal is one thing, but crack? Stolen crack? That's quite a commitment to the lifestyle. But there is something disarming about Jim; he has a way of normalizing the most far-flung notions. What to do? Dean said that Edmund's indecisiveness pointed to a fine, rarefied sensibility. Edmund never understood how Dean could glean that conclusion from his dithering over toilet paper brands for twenty-five minutes. He'll go to Jim's.

Back in his living room, Jim digs out a glass stem, different from the pipe they smoke crystal with. Jim lights up. "Interesting," he says, handing it over.

"I will in a minute," Edmund says.

"Our highs will be all discordant, then," Jim pouts.

"You don't think that guy would actually kill Binny," Edmund says.

"He won't kill him at Julio's, I don't think. If he brings him home and does what Binny said he was going to do — What did he say Burt was going to do to him? Bury him under the bed?"

"Put him in a box on rollers under the bed."

"Right. I wouldn't put it past the guy. There's pathology there. I don't know what to tell you."

He doesn't want to think about it. "Hey," he offers, trying to smile flirtatiously, but feeling instead like a rotting, dagger-toothed jack-o'-lantern. "Are we — on a date right now? Is this our first date?"

"One sec," Jim says, breathing deeply, hand on heart. "What was your question? Oh, right. Umm, no, we're not on a date. At least I don't *think* this is a date. Do *you* want this to be a date? I don't care one way or another. What would make this more — *date-like* for you?"

"We could order a pizza," says Edmund. They both rock with laughter: eating pizza while on crystal! Edmund tries to remember the last thing he ate. He only poked at the fancy glop at Lila's house. Before that ...

Jim advances the crack pipe again. Might as well add to the library of drug memories. It tastes awful. And ... his head is going to explode.

"My head is going to explode, Jim!"

"I know. It's great."

They sit. Edmund is flammable. His lips, his fingers, his chest: flaming. His face knits itself inward with the unexplainable images that rip through his mind: mean neon, rash pink, vile yellow; towers of teeth, a grain of wheat, tap shoes that tap upon a lesion. And then, more or less, it's over.

"Weird," Edmund says. "Scary, but fun. Hey, did we ever fuck? I honestly can't remember. I know I've seen you naked,

I'm pretty sure I've seen you hard, and I recall smoking a joint with you once with dried cum on my face."

Jim looks at Edmund, reaches for his pack of cigarettes. "You're shitting me," he says. Edmund offers a confounded face. "Yes, we had sex," Jim resumes. "We had very nice sex. Twice, actually. The four of us did."

Edmund can only continue to look at Jim blankly, unsure of why Jim is suddenly referring to himself in the plural, worried that he might be on the brink of drug-induced psychosis.

"You, me, Ross and Dean," Jim says, slightly annoyed. "We had some nice four-way action, summer of '91. We were all hanging out at Woody's, we were all HIV, lamenting our pariah status sexually, and we decided to have a four-way."

Edmund thinks back. He can only barely recall Dean's jeaned leg bouncing on a bar stool at Woody's. And Ross — *that* was his name, Jim's lover — he can remember, drinking a Stella, looking, with his yellow hair, beaky nose, sharp cheekbones and deep tan, like Martina Navratilova. He remembers Jim's big hand on Ross's knee. And something about a wine bottle. Laughter, and a wine bottle. They were naked, in a blue room, with a wine bottle.

"Did somebody — Did somebody sit on wine bottle?"

"Yeah. You did. It started as a joke and then it got really hot."

"Isn't that odd — I can see the wine bottle in my mind, but I can't see myself sitting on it. What else did we do?"

It's Jim's turn to think back. He smiles slightly.

"We did it all. Like we used to. There wasn't a condom in sight."

"There wasn't? I don't remember that."

"Nope. There was no *mutual JO* or any of that bullshit. We fucked. You loved Dean, I loved Ross. There was no head trip, no jealousy. We had a great time. And we had a great time the next time."

"Yes! That was at our house, I remember. We kept popping porn VHS tapes into the VCR, stacks and stacks of tapes. And the next time, I remember we —"

"There was no next time. Ross came down with toxo and it was pretty much game over. He was fine, and then he wasn't. That was probably the last time we were out socially. All that fall and winter it was one thing after another. I didn't sleep. You know how it was."

"It was … hard." Edmund cringes at the inanity of his response, but he's struggling to listen to Jim. Here is a chance to gab deeply with a comrade at last, to speak and grieve and heal and become young again!

"Gosh," he goes on, "thank you so much for this opportunity to talk and grow. I really feel like you and I are making courageous choices, really hitting out and knowing and — it — my quote unquote pain — I think I can now understand my pain as — a — an enormous — headdress, that I can finally remove."

"I'm sorry — your 'headdress'? I don't think I'm following you."

"I'm butchering this, aren't I? I'm sorry. My main point is that I know both you and I want to — renew, and kind of start over and be young again, so to speak."

"Be young again … Yeah, no. No, I have zero desire to be young again."

"No, I don't mean *young* young, I just mean … young."

"Nope."

"Not young, so much as … you know … fresh."

Jim laughs a mechanical laugh. "Fresh. Like, Julio fresh?"

Suddenly Edmund feels emotionally pedestrian.

"Ed," Jim continues, with therapeutic restraint, "it sounds to me like you're looking for a big, edifying moment that is never going to happen. We've been through a lot. There's no getting over it. There is no renewal. Ross kept coming into new ways to suffer. PML — you don't get over watching your lover's mind go to mush from PML. We do what we have to do to get by, and that's how it's going to be."

Jim's sentiments don't sit well with Edmund; he doesn't believe Jim is truly this resigned and threadbare. He's observed Jim closely all day and night, and he has seen the glint in his eye upon the first hit of meth and crack, his veiled delight at the pairing of psycho Burt and psycho-seeking Binny: Edmund can tell that Jim secretly wants to feel fresh.

Jim, with an exhausted resistance, slow as a centipede, hauls his hand to Edmund's heart. Edmund looks at Jim's hand on his chest. His heart is racing and he feels anxious, but he knows that's probably the crystal and the crack.

"I forget what you're supposed to say when you do Tantra," Edmund says.

"Don't worry about it. You can't really do Tantra when you're fucked up."

"Please? Can we try?"

"Okay. But it'll be anticlimactic. You're not going to feel 'renewed.'"

"Shh. I'll decide that, thank you." They touch each other's galloping hearts. They close their eyes. Jim speaks laconically of an emerald green light, emanating from Edmund's chest. Edmund opens his eyes, but he doesn't see any light or anything.

27

SHARY WAVES THE BABY, ICY and silent in its Santa hat and jingle-bell booties, in front of Teresa's face. Misty is a nice-looking baby, Teresa tells Shary, but as she studies her small body she feels no special connection to her, no twang of understanding that this baby is her first grandchild. She doesn't really know Shary. Her mind is so focused on her younger son's redemption and her own death. She hasn't had time to consider the grandchild milestone. A previous version of Teresa would have been excited about grandparenthood. Teresa tries to ape this previous version of herself for the sake of her son and his zippy, twiggy girlfriend.

"How much did you say she weighed at birth?"

"Eleven pounds. Eleven! It was crazy painful. I have no hips. You can imagine."

"Dallas, were you there in the room with her?"

"Dal had a hockey game in Vermilion Bay, so he couldn't make it. My mom came to see me. And my friend Dar."

"Did you guys win?" Hugh asks Dallas.

"Five to two," Dallas says after a gulp of Export.

"Nice one," says Hugh.

"Dallas, you did not pick a hockey game over the birth of your first child," Teresa says reproachfully.

"What? She said it was okay."

"Read between the lines. No woman wants to give birth all alone."

"Really, it was okay," Shary says, manically tamping down her bangs with her fingers. "He had the team to think of."

"Yeah," Dallas says. "It was special circumstances."

"How much more special a circumstance than the birth of your first child?"

"I wasn't there with you when you had the boys," Hugh offers.

"You were there in the waiting room. And that was the seventies, anyway. If you'd said you were going to go fishing instead I would've set you on fire."

"There will be lots of time to make new memories," Shary says, still tamping. "I lost a lot of blood and almost died, but I'm feeling stronger every day and I don't pass out anymore when I stand up too quick."

Dallas is giving Teresa his stock look of angry confusion. "I'm not a deadbeat," he says. "I'm paying for everything. I hold her. I've changed her."

Teresa smiles weakly at Shary. She *is* quite pale, now that she mentions blood loss and Teresa gets a good look at her. Teresa feels a leap of empathy for the girl. Whatever young hope Shary may still harbour for her impending marriage, she probably already knows that Dallas, like his father, will never be a source of empathy or conversation.

"Is Joel at work?" Shary asks Teresa after a long lull.

"I don't know. Joel — has had a falling-out with the family," Teresa says shakily.

"He never fell out with me," Hugh says.

"Well, he never fell out with me, either," Teresa snaps, scratching at her Annie wig, finally pulling it off and dumping it in her lap. "I was trying something, so he wouldn't end up — I don't want to talk about it. Shary, Joel is … special needs, I guess you could say. Not retarded, but vulnerable. Very sensitive. I've made mistakes with him. I'm still making mistakes with him. With both my boys."

Hugh goes to the kitchen for a new beer.

"What mistakes did you make with me?" Dallas asks. "What's wrong with me?"

"Nothing, Dal," Teresa says.

"Aw!" Shary says, tilting her head against Dallas, who startles slightly.

"You've done just great in so many ways," Teresa continues. "A homeowner at twenty-five! I'm very proud."

"All the insulation was asbestos," Shary says. "We had to get hazardous materials guys to come over to take it out and dispose of it."

Teresa is caught by Shary's words. Asbestos insulation. She sees herself hacking away at the walls in the attic years ago, making Joel's new room. Fibrous white dust everywhere. Was that her exposure, the cause of her lung cancer? What did she know about asbestos? Did anyone know about asbestos in the early eighties?

Joel. Joel, growing up, lolling in that attic room all those years, breathing it in. What has she done? Will he go like her? She can't think about it. She doesn't know for sure that she was hacking away at asbestos. Other, safer stuff can also make fibrous dust. Jolie is fine. He will be fine.

"Owning your own home is a great accomplishment," Teresa says finally when she sees Hugh back with his beer. "I'm proud of you. Joel needs some help when it comes to things like that."

"No kidding he needs help," says Dallas. "He's — Well, I won't say it. Still can't believe I once had to share a room with him. I think it's like a betrayal when you're going along, living in a house with your brother, and then it turns out he's been gay all along. It's like, *narc!* Right? I mean, let him be gay or whatever, but don't lurk in enemy territory, right?"

"There is no enemy territory in this house," Teresa says.

"I know, I don't mean enemy. But we shared a room for a long time. How do I know he wasn't checking me out?"

"That is disgusting, Dal," Shary says, laughing, swatting him on the arm. "That is all kinds of wrong. You know, in high school I worked for a veterinarian, this really, really nice, old lesbian lady. So good with animals. Even the most anxious dog would just go limp in her hands. She had that special touch, you know? Anyway, she retired shortly thereafter, moved to the east coast. I heard just recently that she'd died. The sad thing was that, when they finally found her in her house, they said she'd been dead for approximately two years. Isn't that the saddest thing? Two years she sat there, rotting away, and nobody'd given her a second thought, all that time."

Teresa suppresses a laugh. "I'm not worried so much that Joel is going to go like that — he's a people-pleaser, he'll always have someone around — as much as I am that someone is going to take advantage of him or hurt him." She crumples slightly; her husband pats her on her bald head.

"I had a domestic that was two gay dudes a few months ago," Dallas says. "Great big dudes, too, like wrestlers. One of them hit the other one with a bowling trophy. We asked the one dude if he wanted to press charges, and he starts crying and talking about how him and his buddy 'love hard'! Oookay ... We got out of there in a hell of a hurry."

Teresa has a vision of her older son, in uniform, responding to a "domestic" involving her younger son, who is fat and bearded; Dallas arrests Joel for no reason. Teresa motions at Hugh to help her stand. "I need to lie down for a little while," she says, smiling at her son, his girlfriend, and their ghostly baby.

She leaves the bedroom door open to eavesdrop. Collapses on the bed.

"What a fighter she is. So strong. I can't even imagine. I could never be that strong. I'd just throw up my hands and jump into my grave." The baby moans slightly. "Oh! Someone's hungry!"

"Jeez, is she gonna whip 'em out right here?" Teresa imagines Shary undoing her nursing bra, and then the shocked look on Hugh's face. His intense modesty — she's seen him barefoot, let alone naked, maybe a half dozen times in their marriage.

"Mr. Price — Hugh — breastfeeding is the most natural thing in the world. You're a daddy, you know that!"

"Yeah, but in the living room? Do you whip 'em out when you're walking down the street?"

"When I'm feeding Misty, my breasts aren't breasts, they're — feedbags."

"That's right. I don't mind a little squirty-squirt from the ol' feedbags myself, eh, Shary?"

"Dallas! Oh my goodness! Squirty-squirt is so private!"

"It's just my dad. We talk about that sort of shit all the time. Don't we?"

"No, we do not. You remember wrong. I wouldn't even talk about that kind of thing with a — a doctor."

Teresa lifts her head off the pillow. Silence. It's true: he doesn't think about that kind of thing.

"Anyway, I know your mother is sure glad you guys made it down. How come you didn't come sooner?"

"It's a busy time. I don't like driving far on winter tires. Shary has the baby. I've got a lot on my plate. But hey. I'm sure we'll be back."

"*You're sure you'll be back?* This isn't a restaurant. These are hard times. Your mother could go at any time."

"Or she could be fine for months or years. She doesn't need us, anyway."

"That's not so. You need to be here. We need you here."

"God, shut up about it already!" Dallas's voice gets closer; he must've stormed out of the living room.

"Dallas, where are you going?"

"Out."

"Are we leaving? Should I put Misty in her travel thing?"

The front door bangs against the walkway wall. Teresa hears her son's Trans Am start up. That's what he's always done when he's overwhelmed: he drives around. She lets her head fall back on the pillow.

"He's so upset about everything, Mr. — Hugh. You know how Dallas gets about serious things. His work is hard that way. I try to shield him from serious things at home. I was scared to tell him I was pregnant. He doesn't like things with emotional meaning."

"Well, he better get the hell over that. He's twenty-five. He can't run away from something like this."

"No, he can't. You're right. I don't know what to suggest. I know that a long relationship isn't about happiness at the end of the day. It's about … Well, I don't know what it's about. I'm sure you do, though."

Teresa listens for Hugh's answer. He doesn't say anything.

"Sorry, what were you saying?" he says.

"About what marriage is made of."

Teresa has a coughing fit. When she stops coughing, she hears Shary say, "Aw."

"So, I guess you have homecare coming in now," Shary continues.

"No, I do not have homecare coming in. I'm taking a leave

243

of absence from the mill. We're doing okay. We've got it covered."

"I've talked to Dallas about staying with you to help out. But I know that the baby would probably be a distraction. She can be quite vocal, that's for sure."

Misty is not a vocal baby; she has only made that one, tiny moan since their arrival. Just how far, Teresa wonders, does Shary go to shield Dallas from serious things? Does she drug the baby so it won't annoy him?

"How do you know when she's done feeding?"

"She lets go and dozes off. There we go. Did you want to hold her?"

"That's okay. Excuse me. I'll be right back."

Hugh has come to Teresa's bedside. He sits.

"Hey, you. You sleepin'?"

"Not really."

"I was thinking — that — it would be nice — if I went over to Donald Tait's and got Joel and brung him home for dinner. Would you like that?"

"Maybe, yeah. But he won't want to come. He hates me now."

"He doesn't. Who could hate you? It's Christmas. He's crazy for Christmas."

"Says who? He was crazy for Christmas when he was six. This year he's mad at me, for good reason. So I know that I probably won't see him again."

Hugh touches her fuzzy head, lets his fingers graze.

"Stop that. It feels like lice."

"I'm gonna go get him."

"No, don't. Okay, do. But he won't come. Dollar to a donut. He will not come."

Hugh pats her arm and stands.

"And bring him that marble cake that Mary Beattie brought over the other day," Teresa commands. "He'll gobble that right up."

Hugh leaves, and Teresa lies on her side, studying a nick in the wood of the bookshelf by her bed. She is not a stupid woman; her rationale for forcing Joel to fend for himself was sound at the time, founded in the overwhelming love she feels for him. Now, though, as her body shuts itself down, all she wants is to have Joel with her again, reading aloud from tabloids and women's magazines, lamenting the poor fashion choices of various has-beens. He's fine the way he is. Even so, there is a distinct possibility that he'll eventually get asbestos lung cancer ... "Oh, shut the fuck up, Teresa," she says aloud to herself.

"Did you call for me?" Shary pops her head in. "The baby's out for the count!"

"Honey, are you giving that baby Valium?"

Shary's head darts about like a chicken's. "What? No! My God, no! Nothing like that."

"No? Then what *are* you giving her?"

Shary goes quiet. She listens for any sound of Dallas or Hugh. Bites her lip. "Maybe a Benadryl every now and then? I know, I know. I feel so guilty. She is just so, so constantly screamy. Dallas freaked out. She kept waking him up and then he'd have to go to work. I didn't know what to do. I told my friend Dar, and she said to give her Benadryl. She gives it to both her kids with every meal and they're fine. It's supposed to be harmless. I'm so sorry, Mrs. — Teresa. I don't know what to do."

"Sit," says Teresa, nodding at the chair by her makeup table. Shary obeys and dumps herself onto the chair, slump-shouldered, near tears.

"Dallas was *exactly* that way, as a baby. Scream, scream, scream. It was hell. It's a miracle I didn't just throw him in the freezer and walk away. I thought about it, not *at length* or *in detail* or anything, but it did cross my mind."

Shary nods, clearly relieved to commiserate with another mother who isn't her friend Dar. She nods that grateful nod, just as Teresa did that first time Digger prayed with her in the church foyer. "And what did you do?" she begs, about to tamp at her bangs, then forcing herself to be still. "Did you give him Benadryl?"

"If I'd known about Benadryl, I'm sure I would have. I was lucky — Dallas's dad was so patient and calm. If he'd been high-strung like me or like Dallas, I don't know what I would've done. But sooner or later you're going to have to deal with your kid, and her little personality is going to be so unlike what you'd envisioned; she's only going to become more and more herself, and there's a good chance you may not like the person she's meant to be, but you're stuck with her, so you have to just love her and get used to her. You can't drug her forever. You can't really do a hell of a lot, as a mother. They're going to be who they're going to be, and you can make sure you don't give them food poisoning and get them all their shots, make sure they can read, hug them, and that's about it."

"I don't know if I like the sound of that."

"Yeah, well. Welcome to motherhood. You've got to make your own fun, wherever you can."

"Fun. I don't have fun."

"Oh, I don't believe that."

"I have no complaints. Apart from the obvious ones, of course."

"Which obvious ones might those be?"

"It's hard with Dallas and his crazy schedule. Most of the time I don't know what he's thinking or feeling, or if he still likes me or just thinks I'm a — we're a — burden."

"I know."

"Do you think he still likes me?"

"Who knows. He can be a real blockhead. I don't care how sweet a man is, how understanding: you're going to be disappointed, again and again. But you know, so what? You can always — supplement."

Shary is crying now, and Teresa starts to regret the topic. She doesn't have the energy to prop the girl back up again.

"It's just … if things are hard now … Sometimes, in the afternoon, I'll find myself in the basement, or in the hall closet, or even the front lawn, and I don't know how I got there.

"It's scary. It's like I have two or three lives, running all at once, and sometimes I lose myself between them. I need more support. I've even started hanging out with the francophone lady next door, who only speaks French and is actually kind of mean, but I don't know who else to turn to. I don't ... What did you mean by 'supplement'? I know you're not talking about vitamins or anything like that."

Teresa shrugs a shoulder. "You can't get everything from one person, you know that. So you make new friends: shopping friends, bowling friends, bingo friends ..."

"Yes, of course, right. I do need to make more friends."

"Yeah. And so you'll have naughty girlfriends who you can go the bar with every now and then, and nice men friends who know how to please a woman, who you can have sex with, nice and discreet. It all works out in the end."

Shary is wide-eyed, looking left and right. This is the response Teresa anticipated, but it's way too late in the game to pull punches with the girl your boy's destroying.

"You're not suggesting that I — do adultery."

"Well, not *right away*. Possibly not ever, if Dallas is able to please you thoroughly in, y'know, bed, although to be honest I really can't envision that being the case. So yeah, at some point in time you may come across a nice man who really enjoys pleasing a woman, and I don't see any reason why you shouldn't proceed. In my case — and I'm talking woman-to-woman here — I like a man with girth. Hugh is nice and long, but it's not especially thick. Especially after childbirth, a narrow penis is like a breadstick dipped in a bowl of soup. Not the desired sensation. So ... anyway, I've said enough. Just something to bear in mind."

Shary stands, backs away. "I would never, ever do that. But thank you so much for your suggestions. I promise I won't say anything about what you've said."

"Oh, I don't care about that. Everybody knows I like to supplement. Hugh knows I like to supplement. You'll find that life is so much easier if you take a relaxed approach to that kind of stuff."

She's young. It's pointless, this line of counsel, if it's premature. If the girl believes she hates sex, it's like explaining country music to a table. The best Teresa can wish for young Shary is that she will eventually, even accidentally, find out how to give herself an orgasm. If she knows how to give herself an orgasm, there is hope.

28

JIM'S LEGS REST AROUND EDMUND'S sitting hips, Edmund's legs around Jim. They are deep-breathing in unison. Edmund's entire face itches, and he would dearly love to claw at it end-lessly with his nails. But he staves off the impulse.

"I send you love," Jim says, his hand on Edmund's heart.

"Oh my. Let's not rush into things," Edmund says, giggly, twitchy.

"No, you have to say it back. This is the root of Tantra. Are we doing this, or aren't we?"

"Sorry. Yes, we are doing this. I send you love."

Edmund thinks of a winged valentine wending its way through Jim's chest hair. "I feel awash in sensuality. It's so transcendent."

Jim pokes Edmund in the chakra. "You are not awash in sensuality. Come on."

"I am. God. Isn't it bad form to doubt your Tantric partner's ecstasy?"

"We're high. I've been up for three days. I used to do Tantric sex all the time with Ross, and right now I feel nothing."

"Well, I'm sorry that's your experience thus far, but I personally am awash in sensuality."

"It's the crystal, honey."

"Why are you so afraid of intimacy, Jim?"

"I'm not afraid of intimacy. I love intimacy. I've lived my life for intimacy. This isn't intimacy. This is a farce; it is. Sorry. It's almost ... campy."

"I see. Like it wasn't campy last time we tried it? I had the DTs. And if memory serves, you were pretty over-the-top, yourself."

Jim laughs scornfully. He takes his hand away. He has definitely stopped sending love to Edmund.

"*Over-the-top*? My lover had just died. I was shattered. I assisted in suicide; did you assist in suicide? No, you did not, so shut the fuck up. I had known the ultimate in intimacy, *the ultimate*, and I couldn't conceive of life without that intimacy. So I tried to conjure it with you briefly. But now ... How stupid was I to attempt to fill that void with ... Do you even understand what I'm talking about? I mean, I know you had your thing with Dean and whatnot, but I wonder if it was truly as meaningful as you make it out to be."

Edmund gets up off the floor, using the fireplace for balance. Punky's urn. He could hurl it at Jim; that would be a typically druggy thing to do. But he is not a hurler.

"You're skating dangerously close to 'my relationship was better than your relationship' territory. We don't want to play that game. I'm not going to *attempt* to articulate the depth of my love for Dean. I like you; I liked Ross. I would never diminish your bond. So many people over the years have commented on how showy and insincere you came across as a couple, but I always shut down that kind of talk as soon as it started. I refuse to be snarky."

Jim jumps up onto his knees, like Ukrainian folk dance. Edmund watches his face dart between rage and doctorial remove. Edmund hates himself for this brand of icy cattiness, but once it's underway it's hard to stop.

"Thank you so much for defending us. Similarly, I was quick to defend you when people said that the only reason you and Dean were together was because you paid for everything and Dean was little more than an illiterate parasite and a coke addict."

"Is that supposed to wound me? We joked about that aspect of our relationship all the time. Levity — we had a lot of levity. And you know what? I *would* have paid for the pleasure of having a lover as beautiful as Dean. The same cannot be said of Ross. He was a nice man, but even when he was well he looked like a lesbian dressed up as Tom Petty for Halloween. You have to admit."

Jim's mouth falls open. "You're saying that my dead lover was ugly. Wow. What more is there to say?"

Edmund inches toward Jim, making a petting motion with his hand. "Jim, I'm sorry. I got carried away. I'm not myself. Ross wasn't ugly. Ross was great. Dean was great. We should be dead, and they should be alive. They had purpose. We're shitty. We're flotsam. We should be dead."

Jim walks the length of his living room. He holds his head in a stately way, but his odd, unbroken footfalls make him look like he's measuring for an area rug. "Speak for yourself," he says. "I'll decide if I'm flotsam, please and thank you."

"I think we're still grieving. Do you think we're still grieving?"

"I'm not talking about this with you anymore. I've more than had my fill."

"No, wait. I think — Let's try the Tantric sex thing again. Please? I have this deep, gut feeling that we are each other's only hope for —"

"For WHAT? *Freshness*? Fuck off! You try crying for seven years and get back to me. Then you'll really want to party. You try not bathing for a month, pissing the bed and not caring. That's grief. I know intimacy, and I know grief, and I know futility. You are a dilettante. I'm sick of your face. Please leave."

"I pissed the bed, too, I honestly did. I forgot to do laundry, I was burdened, I'm a zombie. Don't make me leave."

"Buh-bye. Now. Out."

Jim shoos him out of the living room. Where can Edmund go now? The only option is suicide. Or the tubs.

29

DONALD IS READING ALOUD FROM *Great Expectations*, ham-acting all the characters, having a wonderful time. Joel stares out the bit of window not blocked out by stacks of antique cookie tins.

After half an hour Donald realizes that Joel isn't listening.

"Reading from Dickens is very much a Tait family tradition at Christmastime. I'm sorry that you find it so stultifying. Joel. Joel? Joel!"

"Hey. Sorry. I was zoned out. We did *Great Expectations* in grade eleven. I didn't really like it then, but you really made it come to life."

Donald inserts the ribbon bookmark and sets the book on the arm of his chair. He creeps over to Joel. Joel notices; he braces for Donald's brand of affection: fingernails lightly scraped across the back of the neck; his cheek pressed to Joel's; a gentle pinching of Joel's upper arm that makes him feel like Donald is calculating his body fat. But this is how Donald loves, and Joel is grateful.

"Would you like to go into the other room and spoon?" Donald asks, hunched over Joel.

"That would be okay. I need closeness."

"I suppose I can furnish that, as your special friend."

"I can't believe I stumbled upon life partnership in my hometown."

"I don't know that I care for the term life partnership. Sounds like a fundraising form letter. I'll need to think on it."

"If not life partnership, how about — fuck!"

"Now, that's just base."

"No, my dad just pulled into your driveway. What does he want? What if he has her with him? Doesn't look like it. I can't deal. When he comes to the door tell him I'm — out in the bush — looking for a Christmas tree. 'Kay?"

Joel streaks through the house, artfully avoiding the towers and mounds of junk.

"Joel!" Donald says in a breathy shriek. "I can't lie to your father! I'm incapable. I'll hyperventilate and crumple to the floor! Get back here!"

Joel listens behind the bedroom door to Donald greeting Hugh. Donald wishes Hugh both a merry Christmas and the very best of the season. He can hear Donald already panting from anxiety.

"Sadly, Mr. Price, you just missed Joel. He is out in the forest, chopping down a tree for the living room."

"That's a first for Joel," Hugh says. "Well, his mother really wants to see him — she sent for him — so could I come in and wait for him?"

Joel hears Donald's fretful hem and haw; Donald would rather die than have a stranger see his filthy house with its calamitous collections.

"You could come in and wait for him, but unfortunately I have an infestation problem and have just sprayed the house with noxious chemicals. The mist is very carcinogenic."

"But you're in there, breathing it in."

"Yes, I have a gene, that makes me immune to cancer ..."

Joel can't bear to hear Donald's pained improv. He comes out of hiding.

"Hey, Dad."

"Hey, mister. Did ya find a nice tree?"

"What? Oh. No."

Donald sighs melodically and trundles his bulk out of the picture. He gently clangs pots and pans in the kitchen to approximate domestic business.

"Your mother really wants to have you over. She feels just awful about all that's happened. See, I brung this marble cake she made for you."

Joel glances at the saran-wrapped cake in its glass tray. "Mom's marble cake doesn't have those white flecks in it. She didn't make that."

Hugh brings the tray close to his face and studies the cake.

"Oh, yeah. That's right, too. Well, I don't know who the hell made the cake, but she wanted you to have it 'cuz she knows how much you like marble cake. She wants you to come over. Dallas and Shary are there with the baby — Minsy? Missy? I can't remember what they called her. Cute little thing. They all want to see you."

"Yeah, right. I'm sure Dallas is really pining to see me."

"The point is, your mom sure is sorry about all this nonsense and wants to see you for Christmas."

Joel looks away. Purses his lips. Looks down. Looks up. Looks behind himself. Looks beyond his father and the fraudulent marble cake.

"I am not a pincushion, you know. I'm not a loser. I was really, really, really hurt by Teresa's recent actions. Devastated, actually."

Hugh gets his face that says *the motor's running, wrap it up*, a face that Joel counts among his earliest memories.

"Is she prepared to apologize sincerely and extensively? Because if she's not prepared to —"

"Christ, Joel, she can't hardly hold her head up. I'm sure she'll say whatever you want her to say."

"I can't commit to anything without first checking with my life partner."

"What is that? You mean — Jeez. Ya, okay, but try and make it quick. The roads are bad."

Joel goes to the kitchen. Donald isn't there. He goes to their bedroom. Donald is sitting on the edge of the bed facing away from the door. Joel sits beside him.

"My mother is prepared to apologize profusely for everything. But I'll only go if you come with me."

Donald is crying. He holds an egg timer. "I'm sorry," he says, "I can't go. I have to visit my own mother."

Joel nods understandingly. "But your mother is no longer with us."

"I light a candle at her grave."

"Right. Of course. But we could do that tomorrow, couldn't we?"

"I always do it today. I'm sorry. Please don't ask me to visit with your family. I'm not up to it. I'm not — that kind of — gay — person. Yet. I'm sorry."

Joel is seized by Donald's plaintive, brimming eyes. Joel has fantasized about such wrenching exchanges with lovers; were his life simply a procession of one such exchange after another, he would want for nothing more. Donald is not handsome, nor charming, and his love is cautious, not cinematic in the least, and his flesh is dimpled and blinding-white save for the odd, old, silvery stretch mark ... Adult relationships involve the banishment of all fantasy, a willingness to work with what is offered. Joel knows this. He is gritty now, a realist; there's nothing filmic about his life now. He grabs Donald's hand and hoists their held hands in the air, just like Susan Sarandon and Geena Davis did at the end of *Thelma & Louise*.

He walks, resolute in imaginary high heels, back to his father at the front door.

"Unfortunately, I'm not able to leave the house at this time. Something has arisen with my partner that is very pressing. Please extend my indifference-mixed-with-resentment to all concerned."

Hugh shakes his head. "I give up on the whole lot of ya," he says. "This one has this stupid-ass hang-up, that one has another. I don't understand any of you. We never used to act so goddamn stupid when there was a family problem. When I had Bell's Palsy when you were ten, your mom stayed home from work and you cried and cried because you wanted to stay home, too."

"I remember that. I didn't think you'd remember that."

"Yeah, the three of us sat on the couch that first day and listened to records. I can't remember where Dallas was. And you taped my eye shut with masking tape 'cuz I couldn't blink it."

Joel sees his ten-year-old hand tamping down the tape on his father's face. "After I get everything sorted out with my life part — with Donald — I'll be able focus on family and my feelings about family."

"Aren't we lucky, then," says Hugh, walking away. "You be sure to keep me posted on your family feelings."

30

SHARY IS IN THE KITCHEN. Hugh's home. But only Hugh, it sounds like.

"Hi, Hugh. Your son got Swiss Chalet. I'm just putting it onto plates. I'm a bit barfy right now, but I might have some later. Can I fix you a drink?"

"Like what? I only drink 50."

"Oh. Can I open a 50 for you?"

"I'll do it. You don't know where the bottle opener is."

He cracks a 50. In the dining room Teresa and Dallas sit at the table in silence.

"Dallas got us Swiss Chalet, Hugh. Wasn't that nice of him?"

"It's the least I could do, I guess," Dallas says. "Now you're here, I've got something I want to say." He barks at Shary to come into the dining room. She enters with a plate of limp brown chicken. Dallas stands, and pulls a folded piece of paper from his front pants pocket. He tells Shary to sit. Shary says she has yet to put the fries on a plate and doesn't want them to get cold. Dallas says what he has to say is more important and to sit. Shary sits beside Teresa.

"I wrote this while I was waiting at Swiss Chalet," he says, unfolding the piece of paper. He clears his throat, exhales nervously.

"Hi, Shary. It's Dallas. I'm sorry I ran out of the house today. I am very stressed out. I'm sorry I told my dad about squirty-squirt. Anyway, I like you. When we met you said that you thought that you were ugly, but you're not, or at least I don't think so. You are very nice. You had a baby and it is mine. That is very interesting. It is nice living with you. I like it a lot when I come home and everything is clean. I like sleeping with you. I don't mean sexually, although that is also nice and interesting.

"When someone in your family is sick, it really makes you think about everything. You have been up my ass for a long time about getting married. I think we might as well. So why don't we. Get married, I mean. So do you want to? Get married? Love from Dallas."

Teresa smiles widely at this rare show of affection from Dallas and what must be the least romantic marriage proposal ever penned. He read the whole thing standing over Shary like a schoolmaster, and now he sits, foregoing even a hint of bended knee. Shary looks … conflicted, and … conflicted over being conflicted.

"Aw, Dallas," she says. "That is so sweet. You wrote that all at Swiss Chalet?"

"Yeah. Well, it was a big order, so I had to wait a while."

"Aw. And I know that you don't really like writing notes like that. So that was really sweet. Thank you."

When she doesn't continue, Dallas starts to squirm; he looks exasperatedly at his father, who shrugs and chugs from his bottle of 50.

"Yeah, *and*?" Dallas asks. "So what's it gonna be? I didn't write that just for the hell of it."

"Aw."

"Stop fuckin' saying 'aw'! Jeez."

Shary looks to Teresa, who fights to keep a neutral face.

"Can we maybe — talk about this more later, when we're back at home? There's so much going on right now. And the chips are definitely getting cold at this point."

Shary goes back in the kitchen for the fries. Dallas snorts, clucks, and throws up his hands. He is not used to not getting his way. He's not used to obstinacy, especially from someone well aware of his need for instant gratification.

When Shary returns with the fries, Teresa forces herself to exclaim over how good they smell, even though she can't smell them, and how yummy they're going to be, even though she's lost the sense of taste.

"I've asked you to marry me, Shary. You can at least have the respect to give me an answer, here in front of my mom and dad."

"Oh, gosh … Dallas. Okay. My answer is, I don't know. There is a lot to think about. I want to do what's best for Misty, and for me. And for you, naturally. We need to figure out what that is. What is best."

"So you're saying that marrying me might possibly be not the best thing for Misty and you?"

"That is not what I'm saying. Can I talk to you in the other room? Please?"

Teresa gestures at Dallas that he should follow Shary. More snorting, clucking, sighing. He slumps off with Shary to their bedroom. Teresa waits until she hears the door close, then rises to go eavesdrop.

"You. Sit," Hugh commands. "Give them their privacy, Teresa."

"I will, I just want to get the gist of what she's saying. I'll be back in a flash."

Teresa tiptoes to their door.

"I don't want to be married to someone who doesn't love me."

"Fuck. Did I not just say that I did in my note?"

"No. You said you 'like' me."

"And then I ended it with 'love from Dallas.' So you're full of shit."

"I don't know if I believe you. I'm twenty-two. I don't want to spend my life with someone who only *likes* me and only thinks that I'm *not ugly*. That's really not enough. I'm not strong like your mom. I can't get married and then ... supplement."

"What do you mean, *supplement*?"

"Like your mom. We had the nicest talk. She's so sweet. But I'm not going to marry you and then have affairs to feel fulfilled."

"She told you to do that?"

Silence. Then a hard thud — a hurled shoe? Teresa makes her way back to the dining room as fast as she can.

"Mom!" Dallas bellows.

"What did you do," Hugh asks a breathless Teresa back in her place at the table.

"Practically nothing," she says. "Shary was lamenting the way things are going with Dallas — you know how he can be like you, but worse — and I tried to reassure her —"

"And she really did; reassure me, that is," says Shary, followed by a crimson Dallas.

"Way to wreck my life, Mom. Way to wreck things with the woman I love."

"I was trying to help you, both of you. You don't want a wife who hates her life. She doesn't want a husband who hates her."

"You didn't tell her to — you didn't give her a *game plan*, did you?" asks Hugh with a wince.

"No, no. I just said supportive things. And I also encouraged her to, if need be, if it came to that, if she was really starving for special attention that her — Dallas — isn't giving her, that she might consider finding … Well, I told her about you and I, and how sometimes I've had the need to —"

"Oh, Christ. You didn't? Shit, they're not even married yet! They're not even engaged!"

Dallas makes a big show of finding and stepping into his shoes. "We have to leave. Get the baby ready. We have to leave *now*."

"Dallas, come on now," Teresa pleads. "Don't get all carried away. You know how I am. I'll try any angle to make things come together."

"No way. I was raised by an old whore, and now you're trying to make it so my baby is raised by a — new whore. No way. This is over. Shary, come on."

Shary doesn't move. "Dallas, you always get grumpy when you haven't eaten. Sit and eat."

"Put your fucking coat on and let's go."

"I'm eating," she says, helping herself to chicken and fries. "I get grumpy when I haven't eaten, too."

"What are you saying, Shary? Are you saying that you're a whore? You're going to take advice from a whore? You're a whore now?"

"That is not what I'm saying, Dallas. I'm saying that I'm starving and I'm going to eat."

Dallas, snorting and swearing, looks to his father for support. Not getting any, he looks to his whore mother. She extends a hand to him. He stomps off to the kitchen. He stomps back in.

"You're seriously gonna eat?" he asks Shary.

"Yes," Shary says with her mouth full.

He jolts one way then another, as though yanked about by angry ghosts. "Unbelievable," he says, and sits.

Shary portions out food for him. "See? We'll eat and get that out of the way. And then we can talk about who's this and who's that and everything. You know what? I think I prefer dark meat to white meat. I don't know why everyone is so crazy for white meat. This is really yummy, this bit of dark meat right here."

Teresa watches Shary gobble up her dear, dark meat. There's a step, she thinks: if you know what kind of meat you like, there is hope that you'll eventually find out what gives you an orgasm. Teresa eats a French fry, in full recall of how yummy a French fry can taste.

That night, after Shary relents and allows Dallas to drive her and the baby back to their place for further negotiation, and after Teresa has extracted a reluctant hug from Dallas and a promise to call the next day even if he's still angry with her and still thinks her a whoremonger, Teresa and a tipsy Hugh lie together on her double bed.

"Am I a whore? When you think of me, do you think of me as a whore?"

"Huh? Nah. You're good. We are doing good. But we're not the typical couple. Most men don't let their women run around."

"I don't need anyone to *let* me do anything."

"And I was just going to say that. I knew when I met you that you were something. And I had to have you, any way I could. I knew that I wasn't any — prince of the hill, or —"

"Prince of the hill?"

"Or you know what I mean. I knew that I was an average, y'know, an average person. So I had to let you do your thing. And that was hard, at first. Really hard. But then I decided that I wasn't going to get all up in knots over it. We've all got our quirks. I know a lot of people think I'm a sucker, or else dumb as a post, but I honest-to-God do not care one bit."

Teresa makes a book of her hands and covers her face. She mumbles something Hugh doesn't understand. He gently pries a hand from her face and asks her to repeat herself.

"I say," she says, "I hope I didn't disappoint you too much."

He wraps his body around hers. "You're great. Wouldn't change a thing," he says into her neck.

"I think I gave all of us asbestos poisoning when I was fixing up Joel's room in the attic."

"Hey? What? Nah. There's no asbestos in this house."

"But there used to be."

"Nah. I'm pretty sure when we bought it they said that everything was good and up to code."

"Hmm. I'm worried."

"I'm not."

Then they do what they rarely do: they cuddle tightly and say small things to each other, little confessions of no real importance.

Before she drifts off she asks if Joel liked the marble cake. Even though Joel carelessly slid it across a countertop, Hugh says yes, Joel liked it a lot, he was too proud to say so but his eyes lit right up and you could tell he couldn't wait to have a piece, that is for sure.

31

EDMUND DROPS BY THE HOUSE en route to suicide or the tubs. Beside a candle in the form of the Buddha he finds a rogue packet of crystal. He preps and smokes it. There's no zing, no blaze. Has he reached the absolute summit of PNP fun, after which there is only frazzled, sleepless tedium? He hopes not.

He checks his voice mail. A whispered message from Lila. *I know you've got your hands full, but I'm really hoping I might come over and stay for a bit. I overheard Marci talking to someone on the phone and she said something like "we'll do what needs to be done," and now I'm worried — I know this is cuckoo, but I'm wondering if she's using her film connections to maybe have me framed or possibly even "taken out," or something like that, because I lost the baby. That sounds so insane, now that I'm saying it. I'm just sick about all this. I don't know what to do. I love you; please call me.*

There is also a message from his mother, home again after a month in Greece with her best friend and housekeeper, a hobbled, eighty-year-old Filipino woman named Girlie.

Nothing from Binny. Things must be working out with the murderer. He feels happy for Binny, serenely mummified in a box on rollers under a bed somewhere.

He sits on the floor by the phone. The thing to do, of course, would be to close up shop and wait it out somewhere — Key West, maybe. He could find a nice rehab facility to wean off the crystal, a place with a huge pool, clay tennis courts, on-site deep tissue massage. That would be perfect. It's a good time to disassociate from life as he knows it, to turn austere and reflective, to nap. But then what? More of the same, minus party drugs. More of this silent house, as his friends grow meaner, sadder and more bewildered, losing babies, mooning over the dead, deking out of Tantric deliverance with the living. He locks up and heads to the village.

He passes the only bathhouse in the city he's never been to, the Cellar. He's been scared off by the horror stories: the ancient amputee, crawling up and down the dark halls, feeling for his teeth on the floor; the shit-caked man, beaming and beckoning from his room; even the very recently dead, done in by the lethal one-two of Viagra and poppers and not yet detected by the lone employee, a prickly old man who prefers to sit at the front desk, chain smoking and reading Judith Krantz novels.

Edmund stops, turns back. Maybe the hellishness of the Cellar will provide him with fresh perspective.

The front desk attendant warns Edmund before he checks in that there is only one other guy in the building. Edmund assures him that an almost-empty bathhouse will actually be the perfect environment for him; he can unwind, take a shower, sit in the hot tub. The attendant warns Edmund that there is no hot tub and, since yesterday, no hot water at all. This gives Edmund pause, but he quickly decides that bathing is not that important right now. The attendant gives Edmund a thin, tiny, white towel and the key to his little room.

Edmund doesn't bother disrobing. He flops onto the bleached sheet of his skinny bed. He craves a top-up; not a big hit, just a short puff. He can sense the edges of his exhaustion; he hears the muffled yelp of his middle-aged body, pushed past its limits and wanting only to lie motionless for days and days and days, bed sores be damned.

32

JOEL WONDERS, AS HE AND Donald peel the shells off their hard-boiled eggs, and Donald — once so enigmatic, such a challenge! — blathers on about girl singers from the thirties and forties, about Alice Faye's way with a lyric, Ruth Etting's verve and precision, and wasn't Vera Lynn the embodiment of spunk, if maybe Donald is not his predestined life partner after all. Ever since Joel chose Donald over his family at Christmas, Donald has come to life, gabby, giddy life, waking Joel at dawn with stiff kisses all over his face, full of plans for the day ahead, none of which account for Joel's objectives. It's as though, now that Donald has allowed himself to fall in love, he thinks that his own passions and tics are all that is needed to keep their affair afloat. Joel is thrilled for Donald, he really is, and he finds it a pleasure, in the main, to indulge Donald and observe his renewed vim. But when will Joel get the chance to play Liz Phair's *Exile in Guyville* and PJ Harvey's *To Bring You My Love* on Donald's stereo? When will Donald draw him out on subjects of interest to him?

And if Donald has no intention of ever investigating Joel as a person, well, that's a real concern. Because Joel may not be an artist, but that doesn't mean he wants to spend the rest of his life smiling and nodding and proofreading fan letters to Queen Elizabeth.

Then there's the button show. Joel has, these past months, immersed himself wholeheartedly in the button project: procuring the buttons, writing thank-you notes to high-profile button donors, polishing the buttons, writing crisp descriptions of each button for the display, grouping the buttons in elegant and unexpected ways. Until now Donald and Joel have been of one mind about the presentation of the button show; there would be no fanfare, no gaudy promotion. The celebrity buttons, be it Burton Cummings' button or the late, former governor general Jeanne Sauvé's button, would not be given any special treatment, but would be placed discreetly alongside the buttons of the common people. Now Donald has changed his tune. Ignoring the original title of the show — "Button Up" — which appeared on all the invitations, he now wants to call it "Buttons! Buttons! Buttons!" He wants to put a sandwich board on the sidewalk out front of the museum that screams "Buttons! Buttons! Buttons!" in magic marker. He wants to take an ad out in *The Miner and News* that says the same thing and also touts the famous buttons ("Come on out and see the button from Liona Boyd's cape!"). To top it all off, Donald has started wearing his hair in a braided bun.

"Why are you so afraid of joy?" is Donald's response when Joel asks if maybe the new approach to the button show is a little bit tacky. Joel reminds Donald that, historically, he has been the joyous, impassioned one in their relationship, not Donald. Donald doesn't want to hear it. This introverted man, once so committed to a "life of the mind," is too busy dancing on the spot in his filthy living room to Ladysmith Black Mambazo.

The night before the opening Joel and Donald work feverishly on a big banner to be hung in the entranceway: "Buttons! Buttons! Buttons!," this time in yellow felt.

"I've never felt this way about a display before," Donald says, glue gun in hand. "It's like I'm truly greeting and welcoming my community, where once I kept it at bay. When I did the First Nations costume show, I didn't send out invitations. This one, though ... I can't help but think that the energy of this show will prove infectious. The whole town will get caught up in button fever."

Joel looks up from the felt at Donald. Then he says the thing that he would not have said a week ago, the thing that other people might be saying but that he, as collaborator and lover, should never say: "They're only buttons, Donald."

Donald drops the glue gun.

"Only buttons. Well. Betrayal has a face. How could you say that to me, after all our work and worry?"

"I'm just saying, keep it in context, y'know? It's a beautiful presentation and I love it. But don't expect it to change the face of local culture."

"I don't have that expectation. You're upsetting me, Joel. I've made myself vulnerable to you and now it seems that you're using that against me as a weapon to hurt me."

"Donald, don't be crazy. I love you. You're my — very dear friend. It's important that you not lose your curatorial eye right now. This is still a work in progress. You may need to revise some things after the launch."

Donald looks away, puts a tremulous hand to his braided bun. "I need to walk away from this exchange. I don't feel safe. I don't know who you are."

Donald walks out of the lobby.

"Oh, c'mon, you *so, so* know who I am!" Joel calls out after him.

Joel returns to the felt. He snips away at a "B." He is twenty. He does not desire Donald, and at this moment the mere thought of him makes him swoon with dread. Years of silent screaming and Ruth Etting records yawn ahead of him. It's not the best premise for a marriage.

When he goes to gather Donald for the walk home, he's gone. At home he finds Donald standing by the buried piano, expectant, almost posed.

"I won't be destroyed in the name of love. Not again."

"That is so over the top, D. Really. I'm not going to destroy you."

"You can't say that with any certainty. I've been destroyed so many times."

"I thought the fisherman was your only lover."

"I haven't told you everything about myself. For good reason, I see now. I'm sorry. Don't leave me. I'm so happy. Please love me as the happy person I am."

"Yeah. No problem."

Donald's mouth falls open. "How can you be so declamatory? I'm not reassured. I've been reassuring about your insecurities — remember how I petted and praised your micro-penis when I first saw it? Why can't you extend the same tenderness to me?"

Joel is awash with feelings that are, more or less, new to him: he is annoyed at the sight and sound of this man; he is aghast that this man is turning to him for emotional sustenance, despite his own very recent professions to the contrary; he would not be entirely upset were this man to suddenly fall over, dead.

He lopes over to Donald. Pats him on the arm.

"Please don't pet me like a chow chow. Touch me with love."

SOMEONE IS HONKING their horn outside. Joel stills his hand on Donald's arm. Long honking, then lots of short honks. Joel worries that Donald will freak out again if he pulls away and goes to check on the honking.

"What if there's been an accident or something," Joel says.

"I'm sure it'll resolve predictably. Weave your arms through my body."

More honking.

"I don't know how to weave my arms through your body. Do you mean that figuratively?"

"I'm too weak to explain myself right now."

Lots of honking. Joel can't stand it. He bolts to the front door. It is his father's car. His father pops out as soon as he sees Joel.

"I been honking like a goddamn maniac! What the hell took you so long? Get in the goddamn car!"

"Dad, we've already had this conversation. My boyfriend is feeling fragile right now."

"I don't care if he's feeling a goddamn heart attack, I have had enough of this back and forth bullshit with you and your mother. Both of you acting so goddamn stupid. That's enough now. Get in the car."

"I'm sorry, I really, really can't."

Hugh stalks his way across the dead lawn. Joel has never seen him this livid.

"I am going to jerk you baldheaded," Hugh says, hot breath on Joel's face. "Don't think I won't, just because I haven't before. I'll knock your teeth out, see how your boyfriend likes ya then. Now get in the goddamn car!"

His father's fervour is mesmerizing. Wordlessly Joel grabs his coat from inside and follows Hugh to the car. As he buckles up he studies Hugh's face in profile and thinks: if only he'd displayed such parental passion when I was growing up! Who knows what sort of rapport we might've had? We could've been close. Closer than close.

33

WHY IS HE WRENCHING HER out of bed like this? Teresa was in a deep, lovely, dreamless, asbestosless, pain-free sleep. Why is he pulling her into the living room? What's the rush? He never rushes. Is there a fire?

Joel. Rigid on the couch, in the shirt and pants she bought for him last year. He looks rested. He's already more handsome than when she last saw him, with his slicked-back hair and sharp jaw set defiantly, adorably, to show her that he's still miffed. She wants to run over and cover his face with kisses, but she doesn't want to spook him. And also she can no longer run.

"You sit here," Hugh says, positioning her at the other end of the couch. "There, now," he says when she sits. "You two sit here and talk to each other and that'll be the end of it. I'm going to the legion."

"I'm not staying," Joel announces to his dad's back.

"You're staying, or you'll get a crack in the chops," Hugh says, not stopping, not turning back.

Teresa and Joel listen to Hugh drive away. Teresa watches Joel, who watches the carpet.

"Don't you look nice," Teresa says tentatively.

"I'm sorry, you do not get to have pleasantries with me. I am very angry with you. I've already buried you in my mind. Several times."

"I never buried you."

"That is so lame. Why would you bury me in your mind? I've done nothing wrong here. I'm the one who was wrenched from the family home. I came home to be with you and look after you, and you threw me out."

"I know that, I know." Teresa's face blazes. What a monster she is! An asbestos monster! She rocks in place. She knows she has to wait out his anger.

"I'll likely never be the same. I'm hardened now. I have no feelings. This whole experience has probably turned me into a psychopath."

She laughs, reaches, puts a palm to his cheek. "God, I've missed your bullshit! Everyone is always so … straightforward. Oh, Jolie, sweetie. Tell squishy mommy you forgive her."

He takes her hand and pulls it from his face, but doesn't let go. "I really don't know if I can forgive you," he says, seeing her hand, how thin, how still. "You were really mean. It's not like I'm a bad person. I don't steal things. I try not to hurt people. I'm sorry I'm not in the OPP. But that doesn't mean that I'm going to get murdered, or not try to do anything ever."

She pulls herself across the couch. Puts her head on his

shoulder. "Mom knows, squishy Jolie. Mom is an idiot an awful lot of the time. Mom thinks you're great. She just worries. She worries herself sick. I am not going to worry so much now. You're a nice person, everybody knows that. You just keep being nice, and you'll be all set."

"I really wanted to hang out with you when you're not feeling well."

"Oh, bunny, why not just stab me in the heart with a fireplace poker? Let's stop talking about all this before I cry myself into a stroke. Let's sit here and look at the Christmas tree."

They look at the Christmas tree.

"It's ugly. Did Dad do it?"

"Yeah. It's really no hell, is it? All the decorations are up in one little corner. And the branches are quite ratty, aren't they? Bless him. He's got his hands full."

"I haven't gotten you anything for Christmas. Sorry."

"You never do. Oh shit! I almost forgot again. I forgot to give Dallas his. Help me up."

He brings her to her feet. She pads into her bedroom. On the floor of her closet, under a blanket (still she hides the presents, as if there were kids in the house), wrapped months ago and dedicated accordingly on little white cards in her best cursive, are the many gifts she got Joel, Dallas and Hugh when she was in Winnipeg. The big thing she got Hugh is a fancy radio for his basement workshop. She got Joel two big things: an expensive parka from the Bay and that goddamn *Onobox*, that fucking Yoko Ono boxed set that he begged for that she had to special order at Bill's Sound Centre. The big thing she got Dallas, that she forgot to give to Dallas, is a camcorder, to document all the baby firsts (that way, she could make it out to both Dallas and Shary, without having to actually shop for Shary). She tries to think of a way to lift and carry everything to the living room. She can't.

"Jolie, come on in here," she calls, her voice froggy and thin. Once in her bedroom he sniffs the air.

"What?"

"Smells different in here. Not bad, though. Kind of like Orange Crush."

She pulls out a present, rips off the dedication card. "Here."

He pretends to be beyond big Christmas gifts, then tears at the wrapping, all giddy.

"A camcorder! Oh my God. Wow. Ooh, it's so fancy!"

"It was on sale. Will you use it?"

"Totally. I'm not sure how, yet, but … I can use it to tape — things."

"Oh, no. You were going to say 'sex.' Perish the — actually, yes, you should tape your sex. For evidence, in case you're assaulted or murdered. I'm sorry. That's something the old me would say."

She gives him the parka, which he pretends to like, and the Yoko Ono boxed set, which makes him scream and flail like a teen girl in the throes of Beatlemania. She laughs and watches him. How quiet this house would've been if he'd never come to be. What would she have done without him? Surely she would've arrived at things to do in the absence of this son, but any young ideas she may have once had are now distant and vague, harder to haul out than this pile of presents that makes Joel glow like Hugh's sad, little tree when it's all lit up.

34

THE DAY OF THE BUTTON show arrives. Joel's been back and forth these past days: sleeping at home, helping his father, sitting with his mother, then running to Donald's to mollify him. There, he professes his love over and over, assuring him that the button show is a masterpiece and not at all cornpone and tragic, confirming and re-confirming that Joel will be back with Donald just as soon as his mother dies. "When things iron out at home" is Joel's euphemism when he speaks with Donald, who alights on the phrase and starts using it himself: "So, *when things iron out at home,* you'll immediately let me know? I really do need you here with me as soon as *things iron out.*"

He is busy, spoken for at every turn, but not harried or frazzled; in fact, the ease in being with his family and tending to them quietly has given him new clarity when dealing with Donald. That creeping distaste for Donald's unsightly, frothing need has been replaced by a clean-cut sense of duty to the man, as his friend and employee. There will be time later to contend with their stilted romance.

He irons his father's dress pants. Hugh has been indefatigable, devastatingly gentle with Teresa, assertive and thoughtful with Joel. Has his father always been like this? Was it only Joel's pre-emptive scorn that made him perceive Hugh as a goony simp? In any case, he likes him these days. He likes ironing his pants.

Today they're going to use the wheelchair for the first time. Teresa suggested it: "There's no way in hell I can walk around the museum, with those wonky wood floors." She won't allow for his own, silent sadness in her company; she's busy pointing out how skinny her arms are, how swollen her feet, how laboured her breathing, how slurred her speech. He understands her need to narrate the process, keep it in check like that, but surely their closeness should mean that they both get to observe her dying from approximately the same side? Maybe not. That might be a naïve assumption. The night of Boxing Day she woke up screaming and he got to her before she woke Hugh. When he asked her what her bad dream was about, she said she didn't know. When he asked her if her bad dream was about death, she said she'd already said she didn't know what her dream was about, quit bugging her and go back to bed. *That* felt like a shared moment. Maybe not. Who can say what makes for a sacred moment of intimacy? Joel had thought he'd been having such moments left and right — his night of mutual truth-telling with Edmund. The time with Donald when the long-lost nudes were discovered. But now, standing here ironing, he understands that these instances were not sacred, were only examples of him passing time with strangers.

He helps Teresa pick out an outfit for the button show. It's a challenge. "I look like hell in everything," she says. She's not wrong.

"All that's left are my boobs. There's that to be said for lung. I've known some women who've gone from double D to concave after radical mastectomies. Granted, they're all still kicking, and I won't be. Give me that pink thing there, that smock thing. That'll do. Go get your dad."

"I can help you get dressed."

"Just go and get your dad, please."

He calls down to his father in the basement. Hugh comes up with a small, round, black straw hat with a rough clump of plastic red roses. "I found this in the ditch at the end of the lawn," he says, trying to hand it to Teresa. "I thought you might want it."

"Yeah, I just love wearing old lady hats fished from the ditch. Put it in a plastic bag and give it to my mother."

Hugh hands the hat to Joel, who picks it up with thumb and forefinger.

"Go get your mother's wig."

"I'm done with the wig, Hugh. My wig days are over."

"I think you look so sexy in it," Hugh says. "You look like Ann-Margret."

She laughs a hacking laugh. "Jolie will settle it. Do you like my wig? Do I look Ann-Margret or do I look like a dying clown?"

Ordinarily he'd automatically side with his mother's appraisal, but he sees his father look at his mother with — not desire so much as the solidarity of remembered desire, and opts to indulge him.

"If Dad likes you in the wig, why not wear it?" Teresa rolls her eyes and says nothing. Joel gets the wig. He's tried it on several times since he's been home; he must admit that it is a quality wig: the hair doesn't have that too-shiny sheen that most wigs have.

Joel insists on putting the wig on his mother. "You've been wearing it too high on your head, like a hat. If you really pull it on," he says, pulling it on her, "it looks much better."

"Oh, yeah," she says at her reflection. "It does look better. Thanks. How do you know about wigs?"

"There are lots of drag shows in Toronto. Some of the drag queens are really very beautiful. I don't know how they do it — seems like so much work."

"Well, if it's work, that counts you out, eh?" says Hugh, his voice less harsh than it has been around this topic.

"Are you saying you *want* me to be a drag queen?"

"Does it have dental coverage?"

"I — No, I don't think so."

"Well, dental is important. You can be going along fancy-free at ten dollars an hour, but if your teeth go haywire, it's game over."

Joel nods. It's true. Dental is important.

35

SHE CLUCKS HER TONGUE WHEN she sees the *Buttons! Buttons! Buttons!* sandwich board on the sidewalk. She can just imagine the kind of people that a ritzy museum opening would attract: people like Jocelyn Walsh, possibly with Digger in tow, but more likely her best friend, that accountant woman who got braces on her teeth at forty and teaches belly dancing, weekends at the rec centre. If they run into them she can bury her face in Hugh's parka or just sort of fall forward in her wheelchair and roll past.

Joel is the greeter today. He's changed clothes in the back: he now wears a dress shirt, pink and white vertical stripes, and grey slacks. Donald Tait must've bought him new clothes for the opening. Nothing wrong with that. She used to buy all of Hugh's clothes for him. But why didn't he just bring the new clothes home and dress up before they left the house? Were he and Donald Tait nude together in the back of the museum just now, doing things, then cleaning themselves up with the clothes Joel arrived in? Stop. She must stop. It's none of her business.

Last few weeks she's been going goofy like this; she gets caught on a detail — a word, an image, a tiny memory — and she loses the thread of conversation, forgets the person she's conversing with, forgets even, momentarily, where she is. It's likely the cancer, but how could a diseased brain offer up these long stretches of wayward thoughtfulness? You'd think a dying mind could only offer fog.

Hugh rolls her to Joel.

"This place looks fantastic," she says. "Job well done. I can't wait to look at all the buttons."

He kneels to hug her. He squeezes her, but doesn't hurt her. He smells like Joel should smell. Job well done. She remembers when they went to see *E.T.* and she had to carry him out of the theatre; he was bawling and babbling about nuclear war and how their house was probably going to burn down really soon. She held him like a baby in the front seat as Hugh drove home. He cried and cried. Crying can be so nice. She cries in his arms. Job well done. Hugh has stepped back to give them a moment, and to look at the rack of Kenora snow globes for sale.

"Can I push her for a while?" Joel asks his dad.

"Sure, yeah," he says. "I see ya got great big snow globes for sale, and then you also have little wee ones, too."

Joel takes her through the rooms of the museum.

"I quite like this little collection," Joel says, pointing at a panel. Already weepy, Teresa finds the mounted buttons unbearably moving; they're like pretty, miniature graves. Rita MacNeil's flower button, with its delicate, metal petals, could be a tombstone. Teresa herself has a button collection at home, in a wooden box in the basement — nothing nearly as impressive as these ones, of course, but she does remember once raking her hand through them in their box, blindly choosing one, bringing it close to her face to see which one it was, and to remember what garment it had fallen from.

"There's something really moving about these," Teresa says, patting at an eye. "You really get a sense of the human beings behind the buttons. Was that on purpose?"

"Was what on purpose?"

"The humanity behind the buttons."

"Oh. Umm. Yes, I'm sure it was. All Donald's brainchild."

"Well, you did a great job, in any case. Both of you. Really. I'm so proud."

Hugh finds them. "There you are. Christ, it's like a goddamn maze in here. I kept walking into closets. Thought I was going to have to call for help!"

"Hughie," Teresa beckons; she'd only ever called him "Hughie" in bed and once when he had Bell's Palsy. "Have you been looking at all the buttons? Aren't they wonderful?"

"Yeah. They're great, for what they are, like. Because they're buttons, right? I'm not missing something?"

"No," Joel assures him. "They are buttons."

"Yeah, but they're more than that, aren't they?" Teresa says. "They're like little people. And they're all saying 'hello.'" Now she's weepy again; who is she? Time was, you could slam a car door on her hand and she wouldn't whimper.

"Yes, I can certainly see that," Hugh says, patting her

shoulder. "I can for sure see that."

Donald Tait is dancing to the song he has blasting throughout the museum, "Rise Up! Rise Up!" by she-can't-remember-who. He sure looks happy; from what she knows of him, you could almost say, for a quiet man, he's delirious. As he bops past Joel catches his arm.

"Everybody really loves it," Joel says. "My mom especially."

Donald's delirium fades fast. "How nice. When you say, 'your mom *especially*' — have others expressed only a mild appreciation? Mr. Price, do you not like the exhibit as much as your wife?"

"Hey? No, I like it. It's good. Great effort."

"It's just a wonderful display, Mister Tait," Teresa says, trying not to cry again.

"Thank you! Aren't you lovely. You all are. I'm sorry if I'm hypersensitive to your response to the work — it's as though my very soul is at stake, with each and every viewing of each and every button. That sounds histrionic, but it's true. This is my defining work. And, of course, I absolutely could not have done it without your son."

Teresa can't seem to catch Donald's eye; he's madly glancing about. Please don't let him be on drugs.

"It's funny," she says, still trying for eye contact. "For some reason they remind me of graves. Chokes me up."

He gets that paranoid look again. "Graves? Are you being ironic? This is easily the most life-affirming show the museum has ever featured. There's a thumping heartbeat behind each and every one of these buttons."

Joel looks Teresa's way and rolls his eyes. She has missed these moments of … whatever you call it … conspiracy? She's relieved he can take this wound-up guy with a grain of salt.

"I certainly didn't mean anything negative," Teresa says. "Just the opposite, in fact."

"Thank you. I'm probably too close to the work. Ugh! How this ponytail annoys me!" he hisses, pulling the rubber band out of his hair. "Anyway, it's marvellous that you are able to graft your own experience of mortality onto the show. I get that. *I'll be your mirror*, as the song goes. One couldn't hope for more, as a curator. I love you all."

Donald does a Jackson 5 twirl and bops off. Joel winces at his parents. "I'm sorry," he whispers. "He's really not used to interacting with big groups of people."

"Did he just tell me he thinks it's nice I can see my dying self in his fucking button show?"

Hugh looks at his watch. "We want you to come over for supper," he says. "You and him."

Teresa forgot that she prodded Hugh to ask. She wishes Hugh could've sensed the awkwardness with Donald and not issued that invitation.

"That is so nice," Joel says, clearly touched by his dad's effort. "It's really okay, though. I know he's not really someone you'd want to — eat with."

"Just go and ask him so he can't say that we didn't offer," Teresa insists.

Joel nods and walks over to Donald. She watches her boy gently pull Donald away. She has never seen Joel interact with a lover before. He is assured, not skittish at all. He used to be so wispy when interacting with anyone other than her. He'll never be a politician, but it's nice to know he can speak his piece without going to pieces.

He returns to say that Donald has already made dinner plans, and wants Joel to join him as soon as possible.

Thank God he declined their invite; she hasn't the energy to make nice with a guy she already doesn't like. And she and Hugh need a moment alone with Joel, anyway: they have a very big favour to ask of Joel, the kind of favour that needs to be dropped delicately into otherwise light, pleasant conversation.

36

"HI-DEE-HO! IT'S THE Muffin Man!"

Edmund sees a small old man in a pale cashmere sweater poke his head into the dim room.

"I'm taking a break right now, thanks though," Edmund says.

"Oh! You! No, I'm not here for that! The Muffin Man doesn't go in for that kind of thing anymore."

He pushes the door open gently with a tray of fragrant muffins.

"I don't understand. There are no muffin men at the tubs," Edmund says blankly.

"Would you like a muffin? I've got chocolate chip, blueberry, and cranberry. The cranberry are my favourite. They're so zingy!"

"No, really, it's okay. I don't eat anymore. I don't suppose you have any tina?"

"May I come in?"

"Sure, yeah. Take a load off. Just make sure the muffins are far away from me."

The man places his tray at the foot of the bed and sits elegantly on the edge of the mattress. He wears little yellow shoes that appear, in the blue light, to be made out of wood.

"I drop by every now and then to see how everyone is doing. It's outreach."

"That's great. Who are you with?"

"Who am I with? I'm with you!"

"No, I mean, are you with PWA, or ACT, or the 519 …"

The Muffin Man smiles uncomprehendingly. "Holy yumpins, it's dark in here! Why not have a bathhouse that is bright and cheerful? What about you? Do you like it dark, Edmund?"

Edmund squeaks. "How — What is this? Did Lila send you?"

The Muffin Man glances lovingly at his tray of muffins. "Wouldn't that be a hoot, if Lila sent some little old man to come nab ya at the Cellar! No, no, Lila didn't send me. She's much too busy mourning the loss of her fetus and the end of her lesbian friendship."

"I'm obviously having a PNP-related psychotic episode," Edmund says. "But it will pass."

"The Muffin Man is the conduit for all the spirit voices you've been straining to hear for so long. Can *you* hear the voices of the AIDS dead as they haunt the halls here? Hundreds and hundreds of them. Memorable men, all of them wanting another chance to look sexy or make something pretty or say something smart. They walk the halls, and hover around you — there's one! And another! — and they resent your survival and your mediocrity, and try with all their spectral might to wreck your life at every turn."

"That's so mean."

"Oh! Who is that I hear?" The Muffin Man asks the air with delight and curiosity. "Could it be — it is! It's your precious Dean, come to visit in the form of a hand puppet."

The Muffin man's thumb and forefinger become a squawking yap. "Hi! I'm Dean!" says The Muffin Man's hand. "I was really great, and hot, and talented, and I sure did love Edmund! But then I died of AIDS. For a long time it looked like Edmund was gonna join me in the afterlife, but in the end, he lived. And I'm pissed. I was the one with passion and vision, and he's just a wastrel. It's not fair. I'm not serene. I don't wish Edmund well. I hate Edmund. I hate you, Edmund!"

He screams and swats at his head. He wants to run, but he forgets how to.

"Gosh," says The Muffin Man, "there sure is a lot of hate aimed at you from the AIDS dead. But there is help available."

"Fuck off, fuck off …"

The Muffin Man reaches for the muffin tray. "Have a muffin."

"Keep those fucking muffins away from me!"

"They're fresh from the oven. Try the cranberry one, it's so zingy!"

Edmund swats at the tray.

"Mind the muffins," says The Muffin Man sternly. "Either you eat a muffin or you face the wrath of the AIDS dead forever. And the wrath of Lila's dead baby. And the wrath of Binny, who has just been chopped up and canned, like rhubarb. Only a mouthful of muffin can promise you peace."

Some primitive shard of Edmund's brain knows to eat the muffin. He reaches for the tray. The Muffin Man and his muffins start to dissolve. Muffin mist, then nothing at all.

Edmund falls into the hallway. The man is gone. Edmund stumbles through the maze of rooms and corners until he finds the front desk. The desk guy is gone. Gone! There is a little bell on the desk to ring for service. He pounds the bell until the guy comes.

"For Christ's sake. Yeah?"

"I'm sorry. I just had an experience that was very distressing. I am really pretty sure of where I am coming from about this, but I would like — I just need to — Do you know The Muffin Man?"

The man slumps. "Come on, guy. I have been here for sixteen hours without a break, I don't have time to sing fuckin' children's songs with you."

"I'm sorry. I'm really sorry. I think I'm having a drug reaction."

"What's the drug?"

"Umm. Crixivan? And also maybe a little bit of crystal. And also I was forced against my will to smoke crack earlier."

The man sighs a tired sigh. "Wait here," he says, goes back where he came from. Is he calling the police? Should Edmund run away? Why can't he remember how to run?

The man returns with a plastic cup. "Have some of my apple juice. Go sit on that bench. Just breathe; try to count your breaths. I'll be relieved any minute, and I'll come sit with you."

Edmund sits on the bench. He tries to count his breaths. But there are so many of them.

The man sits beside him. "How you doing?"

"I — don't know."

"My friend, we are too old to be doing speed and getting crazy like this. I mean, no judgment — I been clean eleven years December 2nd. I been where you are, literally. I bet you stopped having fun a long time ago."

"Yes. I don't know. It's — I'm in transition. The AIDS dead hate me."

"What do you do for a living?"

"Oh. I'm — retired."

"Well, what did you do?"

"Oh. Nothing."

He laughs. "Well, no wonder you're climbing the walls! You're bored! You've got to do something, if you can."

"I have some major issues that are more pressing."

"I bet you don't. You get up, you make your bed, you go and mow the lawn for some old person. You'd be surprised how good you feel."

Edmund looks about anxiously; he doesn't want to hear about mowing old people's lawns.

"I know you're thinking 'I don't want to hear about that, I'm fucked up,'" the man says, terrifying Edmund.

"You know my thoughts? No, God, please no. Are you another incarnation of The Muffin Man?"

"My friend, I am not The Muffin Man, I promise you. I've just been where you are right now."

"Oh. But what about the AIDS dead?"

"Which AIDS dead?"

Edmund looks up and sees a string of old, white Christmas tree lights, strung above the front desk. The little lights are dimmed by dust but still lit, all of them

"All of them."

37

JOEL FINALLY TELLS HIS MOTHER, in the car, that her wig does, indeed, make her look like a dying clown. "Thank Christ!" she shrieks, whipping off the wig, opening her window and letting the wig get blown away. They both look back at the wig, in the middle of the road like a dead, red raccoon.

"Hey!" Hugh says, "that was a nice wig! Shary really liked that wig — you could've given it to her."

"Shary doesn't know what she likes, and anyway, I don't think I'll be seeing her again."

"Yeah, but I could've given it to her," Hugh says.

"What young girl would want a dead woman's cancer wig? Christ, Hughie, you have got some ass-backward ideas about what women want to wear on their head."

"I'm sort of sad I didn't get the chance to meet her and the baby."

"She's just a young girl with a baby, there's nothing to meet, really. She's nice, though. Hopefully she'll give Dal a real hard going-over before she agrees to marry him."

At home they eat Hugh's mushy spaghetti and watery meat sauce. Whenever Joel looks up from his plate, he finds Teresa staring at him with fawning eyes. It's too much, her undiluted love after a long day at the museum; their spats in the past were always resolved with a playful punch in the arm or, at the very most, a little note left at bedside: *I'm sorry I called you a dumb fucking slut. See you in the morning, Joel*; *I'm sorry I said you were "possibly too gay." You're not. There's no such thing as "too gay" except maybe for Liberace — do you remember Liberace? He's been dead for years. Love Mom xo.* Now she's sick and gawping at him. He asks his father if he has any new handiwork projects on the go; Hugh looks at him like he's never heard the word "handiwork" before.

"Nah. No time. I can't concentrate that good these days anyway."

"That was really nice, that button thing," Teresa says.

"I'm kind of sick of it now," Joel says.

Teresa moves herself on the couch, trying to find a comfortable position.

"And are you're going to — stick with him, then? With Donald Tait?"

"I don't know. Maybe not. I thought I really liked him, but the more I get to know him, the less I like him."

"Well, I'm sure he's got his qualities and all, but I didn't think he was very nice, and he's certainly not much to look at. You're such a good-looking kid, you should find someone cute your own age."

"I like older guys, though."

Teresa waves him off. "You don't know what you like. You don't want to get bogged down with some old-timer who's gonna drain you of all your pep."

"We'll see. How are you?"

"How do I look?"

He gives a sad smile.

"My doctor, have you met her? No, you haven't, I don't think — who is a woman, by the way, and she drives a half-ton so we know how her bread is buttered — last couple times I saw her she really rode me to talk more about being terminal, but what's there to talk about? I went a bit goofy over you and trying to — help you out. You're here now, though, so what is there to talk about? I'm not in denial. I told her, I said, 'I am not in denial, I think I'm doing damn good mentally, considering.' You know what she said I should do, as though she didn't even hear me? She said that when her aunt was dying she comforted herself by singing. Singing! Oh, yeah, next time I have break-through pain I'm gonna *sing it away*. Won't that be *cathartic*. Oh, she loves that word, my doctor. Cathartic, cathartic. If it's not cathartic, get the hell out of town. She's a good doctor, though. She's been good to me."

She drums her fingers slowly on the couch. Joel cries, tries to disguise it with a badly rendered sneeze. Teresa sighs.

"Jolie, it could be worse. It really could be worse. Remember my friend Janis from years and years ago?"

"Oh, yeah. With the black poodles. What happened to her again?"

"Flesh-eating disease."

A brown sedan zooms past on the right. Hugh pounds the horn. "Idiot! Oh, yeah, it's gonna make all the difference if you can speed through that yellow light. Dummy."

"Your father's a bit edgy because he has something to say to you."

She nods at his father. He grabs for his reading glasses on the dashboard, reaches for something in the pocket of his shirt. Is he going to profess his love and say all the sweet things Joel has always wanted him to say?

"Okay, so this is something that your mother and I both need you to do for us. You listening?"

"Go on, I'm totally listening."

"Okay. We need you to go to Winnipeg, by yourself, on the bus, and get us a book. It's called —" he says, putting on his reading glasses and opening the bit of folded paper. "It's called *This is the Final Exit*, and it's by a guy named Derek Humphry. I looked it up at the library."

"Nuh-no, Hugh, it's called *The Final Exit*, not *This is the Final Exit*."

"No, actually, it's called *Final Exit*. Really, Mom? You're gonna … When? How?"

"The 'when' is none of your beeswax, and the 'how' we don't know yet, which is why we need *The Final Exit* or *Final Exit* or whatever the hell it is. This is something that your dad and I have decided together. It's something your dad is going to help me with; we just need you to go get that book. We were going to take it out of the library, but that would look suspicious. And there's a copy of it at Scott Books downtown, but, of course, that's owned and operated by the biggest shit stain in the world, Jocelyn Walsh."

He's silent. He wants his mother to die with dignity and everything, but — when? Surely it's too soon? And what if they try it and bungle it, and she ends up worse off than she is? Although, he guesses, if they had proper instructions like *Final Exit*, they wouldn't bungle it.

"And I'll pay for the bus ride and incidentals and you can have a nice lunch at that place by the Bay while you're there," says Hugh.

38

HUGH DRIVES JOEL TO 488 Kirkpatrick, where Donald said he'd
been invited for dinner and drinks. Kirkpatrick is the town's
fancy street, with four- and five-bedroom houses, perfect
curbs, some modest attempts at topiary and even an in-ground
pool. The trailer park is a two-minute walk away, but while
Joel had plenty of trailer park friends in school, he didn't have
a single Kirkpatrick friend.

"So you get back to us soon about the Winnipeg thing," Hugh
says as Joel gets out of the car. "Don't dawdle over it."

The house looks like a yellow barn. The driveway is filled
with cars. He feels a clutch of dread as he approaches; only once
did he trick-or-treat on Kirkpatrick, and then only one house.
"Who are you?" said the lady who answered the door. "I'm a
genie," Joel answered. "No," the woman said, holding a mini
Kit Kat above his open goodie bag, "I said, '*Who* are you?'"

A vaguely familiar woman answers the door. She has braces
on her teeth and a clinky drink in her hand. "You're Donald's

helper-friend," she says. "I'm Michelle. Come on in!"

The house is filled with women sitting like mermaids on the furniture and floor. He doesn't see Donald, and then he does: he's leaning against the living room window, talking with a woman in a white angora dress. As he gets closer Joel sees that the woman is Jocelyn Walsh, mother of Joel's grade-school tormentor, bookstore owner, long loathed by his mother. Joel first sees her in profile; her neck wattle, which she always used to hide with turtlenecks even in summer, is gone. Hers is the first obvious plastic surgery Joel has seen in his hometown. It looks good, not grotesque at all. He can't wait to tell Teresa. He thinks of future gossip he won't share with his mother.

"Hi, Donald Tait and Jocelyn Walsh," Joel says with showy neutrality. Jocelyn turns slowly to Joel. She looks drunk.

"It's Joel," Jocelyn says with her underbite smile. "We were just talking about you. Don here says you really helped a lot with 'Buttons! Buttons! Buttons!' I think that show should be at the Royal Ontario Museum, I really do. It has elevated our town. See what can happen when you make an effort at something? Hopefully this will spur you on to other things."

"Yeah, hopefully. You look great. I like your new — look."

Jocelyn laughs. "My new look? What new look?" She puts a protective hand to her new neck. "Nothing has changed about my look in ages! I'm a rough-and-tumble girl that way; I couldn't care less about my appearance. Woo, someone is seeing things! Woo!"

Donald laughs uproariously at Jocelyn's display. Joel wants to punch his face in.

"Could I borrow Donald — sorry, *Don* — for a moment?"

"That depends. Are you going to have gay sex? Right here in Michelle's house? If so, can I watch? Woo, no, no. Just kidding! Not appropriate! Whoa! You guys are great. I'm going to go into the kitchen and see about my pasta salad."

Donald beams at her as she toddles off. He is also drunk.

"She's a total homophobe, you know. She's only being nice to you because she thinks you're a VIP now."

"You're so quick to ascribe dark motives to people. Everyone has been incredibly warm and supportive today."

"Well, I'm here, like you wanted me to be. Now what?"

"I'm having a wonderful time. I feel so … known, so … heard. One woman told me she considered me Kenora royalty, and then she did the cutest little curtsey."

What happened to the austere *I-lead-a-life-of-the-mind* Donald? The guy before Joel is just some deluded nitwit who wants to be popular. Joel's eyes alight and narrow upon Donald's left earlobe, gone crimson from rum and Coke.

"What I think would be really wonderful," Donald resumes, "is if you were to go stand at the other end of the room and talk with whoever's there, and that way people will see both of us holding our own conversationally and know that we're so confident in ourselves and our relationship that we can truly *own* a room from either end. It would be like the ultimate social coup, don't you think?"

"Not really. I don't really care about coups. And, to be honest, I didn't think you did, either."

"My personal growth today has been nothing short of seismic.

Total sea change. Terrifying, exhilarating. Please, I desperately need you to be here and be buoyant with me and gay in the old world sense of the word. Please? Pretty please?"

"I have a lot on my mind. I — I should go."

Again Donald does that whiplash shift from elation to theatrical despair, that quick change that Joel has seen one too many times in recent days.

"No, you can't go. You cannot. Your presence is crucial. Please don't go. If you go, I really cannot be responsible for my actions."

"I'm sorry."

"Fine! You're dead to me."

Joel turns to leave, braced suddenly by new knowledge: for all his desire and tentacled need for harrowing, sexy truths, he is not a drama queen. What a liberating realization!

He walks briskly down the driveway. Jocelyn Walsh runs out of the house calling his name. He turns back to meet her. She's visibly shaken.

"Donald has thrown himself on Michelle's living room floor. He's crying and he's saying weird things that none of us can understand. Please come and take him away. Michelle is so fussy — she can't have a big, crazy man sprawled out on the carpet like that. She's seconds away from calling the police."

He goes back inside with Jocelyn. Indeed, Donald is sprawled out on his back on Michelle's living room floor. Joel kneels beside him.

"For one brief, teeny weeny moment," Donald slurs, snot-nosed, "I thought I'd arrived at a state of grace. But that was just a mirage. Love is ... a butcher. That's okay, though, because I don't want to live. I don't. Your mother was right, the buttons are graves. Just kill me."

Joel grabs one side of Donald, Jocelyn the other. Slowly they pull him upright.

"So now I'm sitting up, so what. I still don't want to live."

"Let's maybe just go into the other room," Jocelyn suggests, "so you can have a little lie-down and not be in the way."

"Sure, just fold me up and tuck me away like last summer's lawn chair. As it should be."

"Shut. Up." Joel hisses as they haul him to his feet. Donald lets his head flop to the side like the dying Christ. In an empty bedroom, on a bed that looks like it has never been slept on, they let Donald drop. He moans for a moment, says something about being lost at sea, then drifts off. Joel and Jocelyn listen to him snore.

"Isn't he a handful," Jocelyn whispers. "Is he always like this?"

"I haven't seen him drunk before. But yeah, he can be a handful. He's not a bad person, though. Most gay people aren't, you know."

Jocelyn offers a look of bafflement. "Well, I know *that*. Oh, I so wish we could get past that awful misunderstanding from years ago. Can we *please* try to help each other get over that misunderstanding?"

"I have gotten over it."

Jocelyn's eyes brim with tears. Joel feels bad for his icy tone.

"Honestly, I'm really okay about that whole thing. My mother, on the other hand ..."

Jocelyn chummily tugs Joel into the hallway by his fore-finger. "That Teresa. At this point, I have to laugh. I wish we could just have a drink together and really hash things out. How is she doing, by the way? Has there been any progress?"

He's unaccustomed to such inquiries. Donald's attempts are always forced. He is a little undone. He's never spoken to Jocelyn Walsh, and she is warm, attentive.

"No. No progress. It's hard." He cries, puts a hand to his face. Jocelyn gently pries his hand away.

"I can just imagine. That's your mom, after all. I know how crazy about you she is. And I don't care how old you are, when you lose your mom ... You sweet boy."

She puts her arm around him. She's not a monster. She's just another protective mother.

"It's mostly just surreal now. She's even started talking about, like, her options. You know."

"Her — oh. You mean. Right. Oh, gee. It's just an impossible situation. Is there anything I can do? At all?"

"Just talking like this is really great. We don't really have a support network at all. Thanks for listening."

"Anytime. I mean that. Any time of the day or night. I'm a mom, too, you know. I'm first and foremost a mom, so when I see a kid in pain — any kid — I automatically reach out with all my heart."

They chat a bit longer. Finally, Jocelyn decides it's time to get Donald home, so they rouse him and push him through the house into the back seat of Jocelyn's car. And, once at Donald's, it's only when she has seen them both inside and Joel has reassured her that both he and Donald will be okay, that she, hesitantly, walks back to her car.

Joel watches Donald sleep for a while, listens to him snore and, periodically, fart. Donald doesn't need him now. He doesn't need Donald. Jocelyn Walsh's kindness has soothed and stabilized Joel, and he sets off on the long walk back to his parents' house.

HE SLEEPS DEEPLY, well into the late morning, when he's awoken by his mother, shouting. Dazed, numb-armed, he gets up to find his mother. Is this it? The pre-arranged moment of her death, that they refused to reveal to him?

No. She's at the kitchen table, in her spot.

"Look what that fucking bitch put in my mailbox!" she seethes, flapping the book in her hand. "That bitch sent me *Final Exit*! That is just fucking sick! And look what she wrote inside!"

He takes the book from her. On the empty first page, Jocelyn Walsh has written, in girlishly loopy handwriting: *Dear Teresa, I thought you might enjoy this, more than any murder mystery! Lots of love, Jocelyn.*

"Did you tell Jocelyn Walsh that I was looking for *Final Exit*?"

"No! Of course not. As if."

"Then she put this in my mailbox out of pure spite!"

He considers Jocelyn's act. While it was incredibly presumptuous of her to send his mother *Final Exit*, and with such a shockingly glib inscription, he's not convinced that she acted maliciously — or, at least, not only maliciously. It was actually quite intuitive of her, given how vague he was when they spoke.

"On the bright side, it saves me a trip to Winnipeg," he offers.

"She's fucked me. She has fucked me right up the ass. I can't go through with it now. I can't give her the satisfaction. I'll have to just go natural. Oh my God, wait — You don't think — What if your dad told her … in bed, like?"

He looks at his mother and laughs; the idea of Hugh, in bed with Jocelyn Walsh, sharing family secrets: that is some other family, some other set of lives. Even Teresa, despite her anger, has to chuckle at the thought of it.

39

HUGH SAYS THERE'S NO REASON why they can't go with their original plan, but Teresa won't hear of it. She already had misgivings about putting Joel through such an upset, and Jocelyn Walsh's prank settles it. She'll just have to go through the motions.

It's not so hard. She's in bed a lot now. Last night she was about to call for Hugh to bring her the heating pad when this swooping sense of déjà vu came over her and her right side tingled and she couldn't speak. A seizure of some sort. Her doctor had warned her about them. It passed. She didn't mention it to Hugh — what could he do if she did?

She doesn't care so much about anything, lately. It's not that she's depressed, or indifferent; it's more like she's narcotically calm, and is only roused by the secret, wordless utterances of her failing body. Even the Jocelyn Walsh episode: while it did get her goat, it didn't get her goat *good* like it would have even a month ago. But that's okay. Hugh and Joel are here all the time now. It's nice to have them close by all the time. Dallas sent a nice portrait-studio picture of him and Shary and the baby; in the photo he stands behind Shary in a chair. She has the baby in her lap. Everyone is smiling, but if you look close you can see that Shary is clearly leaning forward, to avoid Dallas's hands on her shoulders. Interesting. There was no mention of marriage in the letter enclosed.

She pulls the heating pad to her chest. She turns on her right side. Thank God for the heating pad. It's her and her heating pad, from here on out.

40

HE HAS FOUND HIS PLACE alongside his father in caring for his mother: Hugh tends to her intimate needs — cleaning and dressing her, helping her in the bathroom, portioning out her morning and evening pills. Joel keeps house. He can't cook, but he is always on the lookout for ready-made cuisine at the grocery store. After a few unbalanced loads — and another, colours and whites mixed, that stained everyone's underwear a faint purple — he is able to use the washer and dryer.

Mainly, he sits with her. As she grows less and less talkative, he talks more and more. He reads the newspaper to her, reports any gossip he's gleaned on his trips to the grocery store. Eventually, having run out of news, he curls up at the foot of her bed and free-associates on any topic that wafts through his head.

He won't settle romantically again, he tells her. He is finished with fucked-up older men. He'd consider dating someone his own age, but they would have to be extraordinary, singular, with a unique world view and some job security. He will not play the fool or subjugate himself simply because of his effeminacy, or somewhat flabby buttocks, or his blue-collar background, or his small-to-average-sized penis.

Every now and then he'll ask his mother if he's revealing too much, or if she's bored, but she always shakes her head and says to keep talking. She is soothed by his chatter.

He has never had much interest in drag, he tells her. And he's so, so grateful that he doesn't have to contend with the added headache of being transgendered, of hating the fact of one's own genitals. That said, he does think it's important that he at some point explore transgenderedness himself, even though he's not transgendered, because only through first-hand, journalistic experience can he be the best trans ally possible.

"Boring now," she whispers. "Tell Mom about how you used to want to be that girl from Fleetwood Mac, 'member that?"

"Oh my God," he says, rolling his eyes, "I am so over her. I was over her like six years ago."

"Come on, 'member when I walked in on you and you were having an imaginary fight, as the girl you like, with the other, nanny goat girl in Fleetwood Mac? Oh, you were so angry at her. You pretended to slap her."

"Mort-i-fy-ing. But yes, I did feel the need to champion Christine McVie. She was so talented and she just got shoved off to the side because she wasn't as conventionally pretty as Stevie. And she carried that rejection with her, and now she walks the highlands of Scotland all alone with her dog and her cigarettes, with no makeup on."

"What? I — can't feel my face. No, wait — yeah I can, sort of."

"Do you want me to get Dad?"

"No, it's fine. Keep talking."

"And in her solo concert video from '84, she looks terrified and she refuses to come out from behind her piano. She's like a beaten pet. It's so sad. And when she starts to sing her only solo top-ten hit, 'Got a Hold on Me,' she —"

"Okay, Jolie, that's enough. Mom's tired. You come back later."

Joel gets off the bed. This is how it's been, and he doesn't take it personally. She is so depleted that the mere presence of an upright, able-bodied person exhausts her. He goes to his room, sits before his video camera. He thought he'd have something to say, but now that he's recording, he realizes he doesn't have anything to say, only several languid poses he needs to strike for posterity.

His dad calls for him. He checks his clock radio. It's nearly nine pm. He's been playing in front of his video camera for over an hour.

Hugh is sitting with Teresa, who is asleep.

"She's gone, son."

"What?"

"She passed away."

"But when? I was just hanging out with her an hour ago." He kneels beside her and touches her face. Dead.

"It happened just now. In her sleep."

"How could you tell?"

"I could tell. I'm her husband. A husband knows when his

wife has died in her sleep."

Hugh strokes his wife's small, bald head. "There's nothing to tell. She was asleep, and then she — woke up a little, and I heard her say, 'Oh, hey, I'm having a heart attack, I guess, eh?' and then she fell asleep again and died."

His mother, the sum of his understanding of women and only friend, lies dead beside him. Hugh is haggard, slightly sweaty. They can talk about the particulars later.

Joel calls 911. He asks Hugh if he should call people now or tomorrow. Tomorrow, his father says. Joel feels a small spike of pleasure: his father has said his brother can wait until tomorrow.

The paramedics come. Two tall guys in their thirties. They treat his mother with great care, almost tenderness. Joel can't help but imagine himself being fondled by the paramedics. He feels guilt over this brief fantasy and goes and stands in the bathroom.

When they've gone, Hugh sits at his place at the kitchen table. Joel opens two bottles of beer and sits where his mother used to sit.

"What a woman," Hugh says, spent but dry-eyed. "How did I get such a woman? So smart, and tough. She never refused me, not once. In bed, like. She sure was nice."

Joel sips his beer and lets his father talk.

"Your mom gave you six thousand dollars. That's all she had in the world. So don't go saying nothing to Dallas, because she didn't give him nothing. Promise you won't say nothing to him."

"Of course I promise. Why would I bring that up with Dallas? We don't speak as it is."

"I don't know. Now, what are your plans again? Take it from the top."

"I am moving to Winnipeg, where I have already secured a bachelor apartment that doesn't have bugs. I am going to get a job, and I will not be picky about what kind of job. I am going to investigate all post-secondary education opportunities in Manitoba, and if a course catches my eye, I will submit it to you for your approval."

"Good."

"And what about you? Tell me your plans from the top."

Hugh chuckles. "Let's see. I'm gonna go to work, then I'm gonna come home. See how that goes."

Joel nods.

"You know, don't ever think I don't love you as much as your mom does," Hugh says, all slurry. "She's just more mouthy about it, that's all. It's hard for me sometimes to say what I feel."

Joel assures his father that he can feel his love. Joel suddenly knows what his future plans are; his father's grief has made everything clear.

"I know what I want to do with my life."

"Yeah? Good."

"I'm going to learn to sew on Mom's sewing machine. And I'm going to learn to crochet, and weave, and dry flowers, and garden, and can cucumbers."

"Oh, yeah. Well, there you go. But a canned cucumber is a pickle."

"Really? Oh. Anyway, these past weeks have settled it for me. Looking after the house with you, helping you, you know … I just want to keep helping you. Now that Mom is gone, I want to look after you and — this sounds weird but I mean it in the loosest sense — I'd like to try to be sort of like kind of a — replacement wife, like. Do you know what I mean?"

Hugh does this thing with his mouth and jaw that he does when he's taken aback: the jaw juts forward, the mouth draws sharply downward on one side.

"No, I do not know what you mean. You aren't my wife, you're my kid."

"I know, I'm just saying that I find homemaking gratifying and would like to function essentially as your —"

"Quit talking so goddamn stupid. Why do you have to say such stupid things? I had a wife; she's gone now. I don't need a replacement wife. And I sure as hell don't need my kid to — what? Propose to me?"

Joel is suitably mortified. "I just meant that I want to be of help to you."

"You want to be of help to me? You go get a job and a place to live that doesn't have bugs. That would help me. A lot. I'll be just fine on my own. All right?"

"Okay. Can I at least hold you for a moment?"

"What do you mean, 'hold' me? Could you *at least* 'hold' me? That sounds off. A father can hug his kid if he hasn't seen the kid for a while, that kind of thing. Otherwise … I'm just going to put this all up to you being upset about your mother."

Joel gets up from the table. His foolish notions will be his doom. Did he just make a pass at his father? When he was conceiving it all, it struck him as a very wholesome proposition: the dutiful son serving his father, like a Bible story. Joel burns with shame; is it his fate to forever think, and feel, and talk, as his father said, so goddamn stupid?

"I'm really sorry," he says, turning away. Hugh calls him back to the table.

"Now you listen, Joel Alan Price," Hugh says, struggling to stand. "There is not a goddamn thing wrong with you. Your mom was a good mom. She done a good job with you. Why do you want to get yourself all in knots and talk stupid and act like a punk, when you know full well you're just as plain as the rest of us? Eh? Why?"

"I don't know," says Joel, head hung. "I was just trying to —"

"Well, stop trying, and start doing. Do you even know your social insurance number by heart? Christ. Goofy! Come here now."

Hugh pulls Joel into a rough hug. Held by his good, calm father, Joel feels sorted and even soothed.

Then Hugh sways slightly, left and right, still holding Joel; it's probably just drunkenness, but the way Hugh's hand goes to the small of Joel's back as he sways would make this embrace look, to an outside observer, like a slow, mangled waltz.

Acknowledgements

I adore and revere these sage, helpful people: Marc Côté, Barry Jowett, Meryl Howsam, Bryan Jay Ibeas, Andrew Brobyn, Angel Guerra, Tannice Goddard, Barry Callaghan, Michael Callaghan, Gabriela Campos, Michael Rowe, Zoe Whittall, Gloria McIsaac, Shawn Syms, Scott Dagostino, Gord and Kim Sweeney, Pippi Johnson, Andrea Currie, Kaila Wilfert, Brandon Matheson, Patricia Matte, Debra Matte, Chris Letestu, Mikiki, David Beazely, Suzanne Bennett, James Huctwith, Lisa Foad, John Criscitello, Sky Gilbert, Benjamin Nemerofsky Ramsay, Julie DiCresce, Lila Cano, Kim Erskine, Brooke Rosenfeld, Kathy Speek, Ruby Rowan, Karmen Jacobson, and my beloved, Robert Matte.

The author gratefully acknowledges the support of Canada Council for the Arts and Ontario Arts Council.